HARD LINE

PAMELA CLARE

HARD LINE

PAMELA

USA TODAY BESTSELLING AUTHOR

CLARE

Hard Line
A Cobra Elite novel

Published by Pamela Clare, 2020

Cover Design by © Jaycee DeLorenzo/Sweet 'N Spicy Designs
Cover photo: prometeus

Copyright © 2020 by Pamela Clare

ISBN: 978-1-7352939-1-2

This book is dedicated to my father, Robert White, who loves science and has spent his life looking at the stars. When I was a kid, he and I used to stand outside together late at night and look at the Moon through a small telescope. For the sake of astronomy, he founded the Black Canyon Astronomical Society in Montrose, Colorado, with my mother's participation and support. For a time, he wrote a column for my newspaper called "Stargazer," which my staff affectionately referred to as "Stargeezer." The stars and planets have always been a part of our family life.

If I could, Dad, I'd name a galaxy after you.

ACKNLOWLEDGEMENTS

Thanks as always to Michelle White, Benjamin Alexander, Jackie Turner, Shell Ryan, and Pat Egan Fordyce for their support during the writing of this book.

Special thanks to my mother, Mary White, an RN and respiratory therapist, for her guidance with the medical scenes.

And a big thank you to my readers for their encouragement and for reading my stories. Thanks for exploring these imaginary worlds with me. You are the best.

GLOSSARY

SPT — South Pole Telescope

LO Arch — The Logistics Arch where supplies are stored

On Station — The act of being at the South Pole station

Going to Pole — Traveling to the South Pole

BICEP — Acronym for Background Imaging of Cosmic Extragalactic Polarization

IceCube — The IceCube Neutrino Observatory at the South Pole

Skiway — The runway at Amundsen-Scott Station

Cosmic Microwave Background — Relic radiation left over from the Big Bang

Skua — A kind of bird that scavenges whatever it can. Also, the nickname given to areas where South Pole residents trade and give away their belongings to others.

AUTHOR'S NOTE

This story is set in the unique environment of Antarctica, where few of us will ever go. Down there, they have some fun and unique slang. I've done my best to incorporate that into the story when possible without overwhelming my readers.

Also, the hero is Danish and, although he speaks English well, I have included some language errors for the sake of veracity. I speak Danish and lived in Denmark, so I'm familiar with the kind of pronunciation and syntax mistakes native Danish speakers make when speaking English. There are also Russian characters in the story. Their English isn't perfect, either. Those are not mistakes in the text; they are deliberate.

It's been a strange experience to write about the coldest place on earth while in the middle of a very hot summer. I will admit to being jealous of my characters at times. Can't it just be minus eighty for five seconds?

I hope you love Thor and Samantha as much as I do.

Pamela Clare
    August 19, 2020

1

April 6

T hor Ravn Isaksen put the ax back in his tool shed and locked it up, enough firewood stacked near the porch to get him through the next several days. It might be April, but in Colorado's high country, spring had yet to arrive.

He picked up an armful of firewood and carried it inside, where the fire had almost gone out. He had gas heat, of course, but he preferred the warmth of the woodstove. When the fire was burning hot again, he grabbed a beer from the fridge, stepped outside onto his deck, and sat on the bench he'd built from scrap lumber.

He drew in a breath, the air clean and fresh, no sound but the wind in the pines.

He'd bought this property just before the holidays, moving from a condo in Northglenn to this three-bedroom house in the mountains. His property abutted National Forest land, which made it seem far bigger than a mere fifteen acres. It also came with an endless view of the snow-capped peaks to the west. His nearest neighbors were black bears, cougars, elk, bobcats, and mule deer.

It was Thor's idea of paradise.

It wasn't that he didn't like people. He just preferred solitude.

He'd grown up an only child in the Danish countryside, surrounded by a dense birch forest, and had learned to be content in his own company at an early age. That skill had come in handy during his two years with Sirius Dogsled Patrol, the Danish special forces unit that guarded the unpopulated expanse of Northeastern Greenland. Some of the guys had struggled with the isolation and the cold, the darkness and the vastness of the landscape creeping inside them.

But for Thor, that had been salvation.

The hard part had been returning home. After Greenland, the world had seemed too loud, too rushed, too ... meaningless.

The only thing missing from his life was a partner. He had no interest in getting married. All the fuss and paperwork seemed like bullshit to him. Still, it would be nice to share his life—and his bed—with someone special. But he had yet to meet a woman who loved him enough to tolerate his profession.

As an operative with Cobra International Security, a private security company, he spent as much time out of the country as he did at home, leaving at a moment's notice. Women thought his job was sexy until the reality of broken dates, missed birthdays, and long absences sank in. Or maybe that wasn't it at all.

The last woman Thor had dated ended things one night after he'd failed to say anything about her expensive new shoes. He hadn't even noticed them. Amy had broken down on the phone, accusing him of being cold and uncaring. He hadn't known what to say. How could anyone care that much about something as frivolous as shoes?

Thor's time in Greenland had stripped him down, bared his strengths and weaknesses, testing him in ways he couldn't have imagined. It had helped him make peace with what he'd done in Afghanistan. It had showed him who he really was. He had no interest in small talk, and he didn't give a damn about shoes or possessions or fast cars or any of that stuff. They were *overfladisk*.

He searched for the English word.

Superficious? Superfictal? Superfiscal?

He wasn't sure.

Plus esse, quam simultatur.

Hellere at være, end at synes.

It was the motto of the *Jægerkorpset*—the elite Huntsman Corps—but it might as well be Thor's credo.

Rather to be than to seem.

Either he would meet a woman who meshed with his lifestyle, or he wouldn't. He'd already lived most of his adult life in the all-male world of spec-ops, serving first in the *Jægerkorpset* in Afghanistan before making the cut for Sirius. He had a lot of practice channeling his sexual energy into his work—and jacking off when he needed release. It wasn't as pleasurable as a night with a woman, but it was less complicated.

No emotional messiness. No one to disappoint.

He took another drink of his beer, let his mind go blank, and watched the sun dip below the horizon, its last rays turning the sky pink.

Buzz-buzz. Buzz-buzz.

His cell phone vibrated.

He drew it out of his pocket.

It was Derek Tower, his boss and one of the two owners of Cobra.

"Isaksen here."

"Get your cold-weather gear together and drive to HQ. We'll meet you there and head straight to the airport. We're flying to Christchurch, New Zealand, and from there, we catch an Air Guard flight to Antarctica."

Thor stood. "Did you say Antarctica?"

English wasn't his mother tongue. He must have misunderstood.

"We're going to Pole—Amundsen-Scott Station."

Hold dog kæft.

Shut the fuck up.

Thor had a hundred questions, but he knew Tower couldn't say much over the phone. "I understand."

The South Pole had been on Thor's wish list for years.

"It's Antarctic winter, and this operation is going to be extremely high-risk. Just getting to the job site is going to be the most dangerous thing we do this year. I'm asking only those of you who aren't attached—you, Jones, Segal. But if you want to opt out—"

"I'm in, sir."

Thor wouldn't miss this for anything.

～

Amundsen-Scott Station
South Pole

SAMANTHA PARK STARED at Dr. Decker, his words hitting her like a fist, driving the breath from her lungs. "She's ... *dead*?"

Decker nodded, jaw tight, lips pressed in a tight line.

"I'm sorry, Sam. We did everything we could, but it was too late."

Samantha shook her head. "No! No, no. This can't be happening."

Patty couldn't be dead. She was only thirty-two, healthy and active. She'd been fine yesterday.

Decker wrapped an arm around Samantha's shoulder and shepherded her into the infirmary. "Sit down. I don't want you fainting on me."

"I don't faint." She sat.

"I know you and Patty were close."

Samantha nodded, her throat tight, tears stinging her eyes. "We went to grad school together. We were ... uh ... housemates, too. This is our second year as winter-overs. She's my best friend."

Why was it so hard to think?

Shouts. Footfalls. Whispers.

Lance stuck his head inside, his brown hair disheveled as if he'd just gotten out of bed. "Sam? What's going on? Where's Patty?"

Sam looked up, shook her head, unable to say it.

Lance and Patty had been lovers for the past six weeks or so. Though most relationships on the ice were temporary and forgotten the moment people boarded the plane home, Patty had told Samantha last week that Lance might be different.

Decker gave him the awful news. "I'm sorry, Lance. Patty's dead."

"*What?*" Lance gaped at Decker, his face going pale. "She was fine last night."

"Sam found her in her bed this morning, unconscious and barely breathing. We intubated her, bagged her, got fluids going. She went into V-tach. We did chest compressions, defibrillated her, and pushed the meds—epinephrine, lidocaine, bicarb—but she bottomed out. Her heart stopped, and we couldn't bring her back."

"Keep trying!" Lance pushed past Decker.

Decker grabbed for him. "Lance, stop! You don't want to see this."

But Lance was quicker. He jerked aside the curtain that shielded Patty's body from their view—and froze. "Jesus."

Samantha gasped.

Patty lay there, unmoving and shirtless, her skin pallid, her eyes staring unseeing at the ceiling, a tube protruding from her mouth.

Kristi Chang, the station RN, stood beside her, tears streaming down her cheeks as she removed an IV from Patty's arm. "I'm sorry. We did everything we could."

Lance coughed as if choking back tears, took Patty's lifeless hand. "*Patty.*"

Samantha stood, took a step toward the bed. "If I had found her earlier... If I had gone to check on her the moment she was late for breakfast..."

Lance rubbed his thumb over the back of Patty's hand. "I should've been there."

Decker put a hand on Lance's shoulder, looked over at Samantha. "Don't do this to yourselves—either of you. This isn't your fault. She must have had some hidden condition, some undiagnosed pulmonary or cardiac problem. Until there's an autopsy, we won't know for sure what killed her."

Lance stroked Patty's cheek. "You're doing an autopsy?"

"Me?" Decker shook his head. "No. That won't happen until we get her body back to the US in November."

Lance wiped tears from his face. "That's seven months from now."

There were no flights in or out of the station during

austral winter. The risk of a plane's fuel freezing was too high.

Decker nodded. "We have no choice but to bag her body and keep it on ice."

"Oh, God." Samantha's heart constricted at the thought of Patty spending seven months, frozen solid, in a body bag in the subzero service arches below the station.

Steve Hardin, the winter site manager, walked in. "I heard that Patty... Oh, no! Son of a bitch! What the hell happened?"

But Samantha needed to get out of here.

She hurried past Steve and stepped into the hallway, where the others had begun to gather, worry on their faces.

Kazem Hamidi, a friend who worked with the BICEP2 telescope, was the first to speak. "Is Patty okay?"

Samantha pushed the words past the lump in her throat. "She's ... *dead*."

"I'm so sorry." Ryan McClain, one of the firefighters and an EMT, rested a hand on Samantha's shoulder. "How? Why?"

"I don't know."

"First, the satellite crash, and now this." Bai Zhang Wei, who studied neutrinos, raised his hands to his face in disbelief. "What is going on?"

"How can she be dead?" Charli Ortega, the coms manager, had tears in her eyes. "I didn't see this in the cards during her last Tarot reading."

Jason Huger, the breakfast cook, held up his smartphone. "How did she die?"

Shock and grief became rage.

Samantha knocked the phone out of his hand. "You're not putting this online, Jason. Patty didn't die to amuse your YouTube audience."

"Hey!" He bent down, reached for his phone.

But Ryan was faster. He picked it up, deleted the footage, and handed the phone back to Jason. "Show some respect, man, or I'll put your phone through the shredder."

"What happened?" Charli asked.

Samantha swallowed. "When Patty didn't show up this morning, I went to her room. She was unresponsive. I couldn't even tell she was breathing. Decker and Kristi tried to save her, but... I'm sorry. I can't."

Samantha turned and ran down the hallway toward her room, locking the door behind her. She sank onto her bed and sobbed.

COBRA'S private jet was somewhere over the Pacific, headed toward a refueling stop in Hawaii before Tower called Thor, Malik Jones, and Lev Segal into the conference room for a briefing.

"Sorry to keep you waiting and in the dark, but we're caught in a developing situation." He motioned toward the chairs. "Take a seat."

Thor sat, exchanged glances with Jones and Segal, the three of them eager to find out what was so important that the US government would risk sending them to Antarctica in the middle of austral winter.

Tower tapped at his pad, and a map of Antarctica appeared on the large monitor on the wall. "Eighteen hours ago, a new US military satellite with a state-of-the-art missile-control system crashed about three hundred fifty miles from Amundsen-Scott Station at the South Pole. It wasn't a mechanical failure. The satellite was hacked."

Thor gaped at him. "*Hacked?* Fuck."

"Holy shit."

"Who could do something like that?"

"We'll get to that in a moment." Tower tapped his pad, and a schematic of the satellite appeared on the screen. "Are any of you familiar with Golden Horde? No? I'm not surprised. It's the nickname given to a new guidance system that enables missiles to adjust course and coordinate with one another after launch. In the past, once a missile was in the air, it simply followed its trajectory until impact, like a cannonball. With Golden Horde, a sophisticated GPS and communication between missiles enable the weapons to act as independent swarms after launch, giving them the ability to respond to and overwhelm enemy air defenses—and making it possible for an operator to change their trajectory to new targets."

Jones grinned. "I like it."

Segal's gaze was on the screen. "That's game-changing technology."

Thor saw where this was going. "Someone wants to steal it."

Tower nodded. "That's the Pentagon's theory. Our job is to get to the crash site and retrieve sensitive components. But we've got serious obstacles to overcome if we're going to succeed. Isaksen, I'm placing you in command of operations on this one. You're the only one of us with experience in this kind of environment. I'm counting on you to help us prepare."

"Understood." Thor had anticipated this.

Tower fixed his gaze on Jones and Segal. "Will either of you have problems following orders from Isaksen?"

They had been with the company longer than Thor, and both had more straight-up combat experience.

"No, sir."

"Hell, no."

Tower went over the plan. "When a weather window opens, you'll fly to Amundsen-Scott Station on a specially equipped aircraft. It will be a rough flight. If the pilot is able to land, you'll have to disembark quickly. He has to keep the plane running during refueling, or the propellers and fuel will freeze."

"That's how it was in Greenland, too." Except then, Thor hadn't just offloaded himself and his gear, but also eleven dogs, the sled, and hundreds of kilos of supplies.

"If the weather holds, you'll take a Twin Otter with a ferry tank to the crash site, retrieve the package, re-board the plane, and head back to the station. Then it's just a matter of waiting for a window for your ride back. Due to altitude and consistently cold temperatures, weather at the Pole itself is fairly stable. But the continent overall has the harshest winds and coldest temps on the planet. Getting you safely there and back entails looking at the forecast along your entire flight path, not just local conditions."

That made sense to Thor.

"I'll remain in Christchurch, working as the go-between for our operation and the government of New Zealand. We'll check in via a laptop equipped with satellite VPN."

"Why retrieve the technology? Why can't we just blow it up?" Segal asked.

"Plastic explosives are unreliable in that kind of cold," Tower explained. "Also, by treaty, nations are required to remove all waste. Someone will have to fly out to the crash site in austral summer to remove the wreckage. If we blow it up, that would make their job close to impossible, wouldn't it?"

Tower and Thor spent the next few hours breaking

down each step of the operation, trouble-shooting the entire mission from beginning to end.

"What happens if we get hit by a storm while we're out there?" Jones asked.

Thor didn't mince words. "We freeze to death."

Tower's lips pressed into a frown. "You'll take survival gear—enough to hold out several days on the ice, if necessary."

Thor glanced at his smartphone. "It's minus fifty-seven Celcius there right now—minus eighty-two with the wind chill. Antarctic storms can bring katabatic winds that are equivalent to a Category Four hurricane. But, sure, let's take a tent and maybe some hot cocoa with marshmallows, too."

Segal snorted. "Smartass."

Jones looked worried. "How about a snow cave or sheltering on the plane?"

Thor shook his head. "It's not snow. It's ice. You don't dig. You drill. The plane's fuel will quickly turn to unusable slush, and then we freeze."

Segal looked at satellite photos of the crash site. "How do we know the components we need to remove are accessible? What if they're buried in the ice?"

Tower answered. "The Pentagon has a scientist at the station who will handle that part of the operation, someone who has experience with space tech. It's our job to get that person to the site and keep them safe."

"Are we expecting polar bears?" Segal asked.

"There is no life inland in Antarctica." Tower pointed toward a black dot on the map. "But Vostok Station—the year-round Russian base—is four-hundred fifty miles from the crash site. The Russians have kindly offered to help our salvage efforts, but Washington has declined."

"Intelligence believes the Russians are behind the hack?" Segal asked.

"It's all speculation at this point. It could be the Russians. It could be the Chinese. Both have bases within striking distance of the crash site, though Kunlun, the Chinese station, isn't staffed during the winter."

"If it's the Russians, the team at Vostok might have known about it ahead of time." Thor was just stating the obvious. "In the time it takes us to get to Antarctica, they could easily beat us to the crash site. Also, this area of the continent—Dome A—has the coldest temperatures ever recorded on earth."

He'd been researching Antarctica since they took off from Denver.

The four of them sat in silence, the full scope of this operation hitting home.

"You should know that the NSF—the National Science Foundation—has fought the Pentagon every step of the way on this," Tower said. "By treaty, no nation is allowed to have a military presence in Antarctica unless the military serves a scientific purpose. That's why they're sending us. You're security, nothing more. You'll go in armed with revolvers and bolt-action Enfield rifles—"

"Bolt-action rifles?" Jones stared at Tower as if he'd lost his mind.

Thor laid it out for him. "Your M4 would freeze up in the cold. We carried Enfields in Sirius. It was the only rifle we trusted against polar bears."

Jones looked unimpressed. "Huh."

Tower picked up where he'd left off. "Your weapons come out only at the crash site and only if needed. I'm told you can expect a less than cordial welcome from the staff on station."

Segal's expression went sour. "Nice."

It didn't bother Thor. Who cared what the researchers thought of them so long as they got the job done?

Tower met each man's gaze in turn. "I'm not exaggerating when I say this might be the most dangerous mission in Cobra's history. You cannot let this technology fall into hostile hands."

2

April 9

When Steve called Samantha into his office, she thought it had to do with Patty's death. Instead, it was about the crashed satellite.

"A security team is on its way here from Christchurch. They'll be flown out to the crash site to retrieve sensitive military technology and take it back to the US."

"That's crazy. What if they crash—or land in a crevasse? They're risking their lives, and for what? Technology?"

"It gets crazier." Steve drew a breath and exhaled, as if he didn't know how to tell her what he had to say next. "The NSF wants you to go with them to remove the components."

What the hell?

She gaped at him. "Go with them? I'm an astronomer. I have work to do here. I don't know anything about military systems. They need to send an expert, one of their own people. I'm not going out there. Are you bonkers?"

This was her second year as a winter-over. She knew how dangerous it was to fly in austral winter. It had happened only a few times in Antarctic history in response to medical emergencies. Besides, Samantha got enough of the cold every day on her fifteen-minute walk to and from the Dark Sector Lab and SPT—the South Pole Telescope. She wasn't leaving the station and going out on the ice.

Hell, no.

"Look, I know you're going through a hard time right now, but out of the fifty people down here, the NSF and the Pentagon believe you have the skill to do this. They requested Patty, actually, but... They're not going to risk sending anyone else."

"Are you saying I have no choice?"

"Of course, you have a choice, but you have to understand what's at stake here. There's a top-secret system on that satellite that could mean the deaths of millions of innocent people if it fell into the wrong hands. Patty would have done it."

"Don't try to manipulate me, Steve. The satellite is sitting in the middle of the continent in winter. It's not like ISIS is going to sneak in and steal it."

"No, but someone else might."

"Who? The Russians? The Chinese? Their stations are staffed by scientists just like us. We don't do world politics or Cold War bullshit down here."

Researchers from around the globe came to Antarctica to work together for the sake of science. There were no international tensions here, no military presence. There was barely any law enforcement—just the Special Deputy US Marshal who worked as the station manager at McMurdo.

"Don't be naïve. You heard what Vasily said last time we saw him. 'All the science is a pretext for maintaining a presence here so we can stake a claim.'"

"Vasily was drunk."

Everyone had been drunk that night, one of the few times that astronomers from different countries could gather at McMurdo for a drink.

"In vino veritas." Steve crossed his arms over his chest, sat on the edge of his desk, his brow furrowed as if he weren't sure what to say next. "What I'm going to tell you is classified, which means you cannot repeat this. Understood?"

"I know what 'classified' means." Did he think she was stupid?

"The satellite didn't crash due to a malfunction. It was hacked."

"*What?*"

"The Pentagon was able to do a partial trace on the hacker before the satellite crashed—no idea how they managed that—but they say the hack came from some-where south of the Antarctic circle."

The breath left Samantha's lungs. "Are they sure?"

"I trust the Pentagon to know their stuff."

"Holy shit." Samantha sank into Steve's chair, mind racing.

If the hack had, indeed, come from down here, then someone wasn't the scientist they claimed to be. They were using science to hide a hostile agenda.

Steve walked to the map of Antarctica on his wall and pointed. "The satellite came down here—that's roughly halfway between our location and Vostok Station."

"You think the Russians hacked it?" Samantha wanted to laugh.

"I'm pretty sure the Pentagon does."

Samantha didn't care about politics. She'd spent her adult life studying the Cosmic Microwave Background, learning what it had to say about distant galaxy clusters. She preferred the wonder and excitement of scientific exploration to the cynicism of politics. One elevated humanity, while the other seemed always to drag it down.

And if someone gets their hands on this technology and people die?

How would she live with herself then?

"You'll get hazard pay, of course. I'm sure the Foundation would consider itself in your debt. Imagine the benefits—"

"Stop!" She stood. "I don't care about money. I need to think about this."

Steve nodded. "You've got six hours. That's when the Cobra security team arrives. I've got schematics of the satellite for you to study—when you make up your mind, of course. We'll put together the tools you'll need."

"Great." She turned toward the door.

Steve wouldn't let it go. "I know that the idea of flying now is scary. I'd be afraid, too. But if I had your skillset, I'd do it for the sake of my country. They've already found pilots willing to take the risk."

First Patty's death, and now this.

Samantha would have to be crazy to say yes.

She stopped, turned. "Send me the schematics. If I die out there on the ice, I will haunt you and this station."

Steve opened his mouth to speak, relief on his face.

She held up her hand to stop him. "*Don't* thank me."

THOR WATCHED out the window of the specially outfitted C-130 Hercules Globemaster, a broad expanse of ice barely visible in the darkness of Antarctic night. The long flight had been turbulent so far.

Jones grinned. "Segal's going to puke."

Segal did look a little green. "Shut up."

Tossed about by air currents, the plane bounced and shimmied, once dropping so quickly that Thor's stomach seemed to get left behind. It wasn't until they neared their destination that the turbulence finally died down.

Across from him, Segal, looking recovered, held up his neoprene mask, which had a built-in ventilator to warm the air. "Is this really necessary?"

These guys had no clue.

Thor glanced at his phone. "It's minus sixty-eight Celcius out there right now. If your trachea freezes shut, you die. If you breathe freezing air for too long, you damage your lungs or die."

Thor made eye contact with Jones and Segal. "Respect the cold as if it were an enemy trying to kill you, because it is. We'll be at almost ten thousand feet elevation, but we're coming from Colorado so the altitude won't hit us as hard as it does most new arrivals. This is one of the driest places on earth with humidity at only one or two percent. Stay hydrated. When the plane lands, a ground crew will deal with the freight. Just grab your gear and be ready to move."

In addition to the clothes and equipment they needed to complete their mission, they'd brought crates of fresh fruit and vegetables—a luxury down here—as well as parts needed for an urgent machine repair.

The pilot spoke into their earpieces. "You can see the lights of the station below on your left. We're landing now. Stay buckled."

Thor felt the pilot slow the plane's velocity and glanced out the window to see the station. Amundsen-Scott looked like a moon base, an outpost in the middle of inhospitable territory, its windows little rectangles of light.

Skis hit the snow. The plane slowed, turned around, and taxied back toward the station before coming to a stop.

Thor and the others unbuckled and got to their feet, putting on their gloves, masks, and hats. "The first blast of air is going to be a shock to the lungs. The cold will make any exposed skin burn."

Thor opened the door, lowered the stairs, the cold rushing in. "Let's move!"

He was the first one out, his lips curving into a smile at the sight of the wide-open ice-scape that surrounded them, a stiff breeze hitting him in the face, making the skin around his eyes tingle and burn.

Jones gasped. "Holy shit!"

Segal coughed, a reaction to the cold. "The Viking wasn't kidding."

The ground crew was already unloading the pallets and refueling the plane. Then four men walked by, carrying something between them.

A body bag.

Thor watched over his shoulder as they carried it on board, buckled it into a row of seats, then stood around it for a moment in silence.

What had happened? An accident, perhaps?

People who worked in Antarctica were given thorough medical exams before coming down to ensure that no one had underlying medical conditions.

"Let's get the hell indoors." Segal hurried by, his boots squeaking on the ice, Jones behind him.

But Thor hung back, the skin around his eyes already numb. This C-130 had rockets that fired to help it take off at altitude, where the air was otherwise too thin for a plane of its size. He didn't want to miss that.

The ground crew finished unloading the pallets, and the

fuelies disconnected the hose, shouting to one another over the thrum of the propellers. Then the doors closed, and the plane taxied toward the skiway, accelerating until it skimmed over the ice. Then the rockets fired, blazing orange in the darkness, the extra boost of speed giving the plane the lift it needed to get airborne.

"Godspeed." Thor watched the C-130 disappear into the starlit sky, then turned toward the station, catching up with the others.

Amundsen-Scott Station was a long building with thick, steel posts that elevated it off the ice. The ground crew drove by with the pallets, while Thor followed Segal and Jones up a sheltered stairway to the first floor. They passed through two sets of thick steel doors and found themselves at the end of a long hallway, where a handful of people milled around, more out of curiosity than to welcome them.

Thor removed his mask, goggles, hat, and gloves. The others did the same.

"Damn, look at these guys." A kid filmed them with his smartphone. "We're screwed. They're going to take all the women."

"No one comes to Antarctica for the women, Jason." A man whose dark hair and beard were shot through with gray confiscated the kid's phone, deleted the footage, and slipped the device into his pocket. "I told you to stop filming people without consent."

"What about my phone?"

The man ignored him, faced Thor, and held out a hand. "I'm Steve Hardin, winter site manager here at Amundsen-Scott. Welcome to the South Pole. I'll show you to your berths and give you a tour of the station."

SAMANTHA WILLED herself to concentrate as she did the last calibrations to set up the SPT for the next thirty-six hours of surveys. She'd had trouble focusing all day, her mind numb, her motions wooden. But she couldn't afford to make a mistake. If she caused an instrument to malfunction, it could halt research until November when the first plane of the summer season arrived. As she was unlikely to get another grant to return here, that would be catastrophic.

She'd never lost anyone close to her apart from a grandfather she didn't remember. The whole thing seemed unreal. Some part of her kept expecting Patty to walk through the door in her red parka, a smile on her face, to tell Samantha this was just a bad dream. But that wasn't going to happen.

Patty was dead.

Last night, Samantha had written an email to George and Karen, Patty's parents, offering her condolences. But nothing she'd written had felt adequate. Nothing could express the fullness of her grief. It had been one of the hardest things she'd ever done.

Tears blurred her vision, forcing her to stop. "Damn it."

She wiped the tears away, fought for control of her emotions. She couldn't do this. She couldn't fall apart. She had to do her work plus Patty's now. They'd fought so hard to get this research grant. It had meant everything to both of them.

Pull it together.

She drew a few deep breaths, then got on with her adjustments and set the telescope to scan. It would make ten or eleven scans of a particular area of space before she repeated this process. The observations were transmitted to the SPT computers, which automatically saved and processed the data.

Her radio squawked.

"Sam, Sam, this is Steve."

She reached for it. "Hey, Steve. Samantha here."

"We're set for the memorial service at eighteen-hundred hours in the lounge."

"Thank you."

Steve had asked her to say a few words because she had known Patty best. But Samantha was a card-carrying introvert, the thought putting a knot of dread in her stomach. She didn't like public speaking, especially when she was upset. How was she supposed to talk about Patty without crying?

Samantha cleaned up and dressed for the walk back to the station. If this were a typical day, she would have kept working, but she needed time to think about what she was going to say. She put on all of her layers—snow pants, fleece, parka, bunny boots, two pairs of gloves, mask, hat, goggles, hood. She turned out the lights, left the telescope to work, and stepped out into the darkness and freezing cold.

Flags marked the path back to the station, which came in handy when high winds caused whiteout conditions. But the wind wasn't bad tonight, the green light of the Aurora Australis dancing overhead, the Milky Way arching across the sky.

Samantha stopped, watched, willing herself to speak past the lump in her throat. "It's beautiful today, Patty. I'm so sorry you're not here to see it."

Maybe Patty *could* see it. Maybe she saw it more clearly now than Samantha did. Maybe all of their questions about the universe were answered for her.

It would be nice to think so.

It was then Samantha noticed a man standing on the path about thirty feet ahead of her, his gaze focused upward.

At first, she thought it must be Steve, but this man was taller than Steve and wore a white parka. NSF-issued parkas were bright red.

Then it hit her.

He must be one of the private security guys. She'd heard the plane arrive.

It was too cold for her to stand here, waiting for him to go indoors first, so she started walking again, irritated with him for interrupting what had felt like a private moment.

You're irritated because of what he represents.

The crashed satellite. The mission to recover the military components.

She'd never understood other women's fascination with military men. Sure, they were physically fit, and some were good-looking. But too often they had more testosterone than brains, reminding her of the JROTC boys on the football team who had bullied her in high school. Besides, this security team was encroaching on a space reserved for science. She didn't like that at all.

She might have passed him without saying a word if ignoring him wouldn't have been obvious. They were two of a little more than fifty people down here.

He turned his face toward her, mask and goggles concealing his features. "Hello."

"Hi." She had to ask. "Are you lost?"

He *was* tall, towering almost a foot above her.

He chuckled, looked up at the sky, speaking with an accent she couldn't quite place. "I was just watching the aurora."

Her gaze followed his. "It's not always as bright as it is tonight."

"Yes, I'm sure."

"Enjoy the view, but don't stay out too long." She walked by. "The cold sneaks up on people."

He fell in beside her. "It's not too bad right now."

Behind her goggles, Samantha rolled her eyes. "Yeah. It's not too bad."

He was trying to act tough. Typical male behavior. It was minus fifty-five Celsius without the wind chill. Skin could freeze within minutes.

"What are those lights?" He pointed. "That's not part of the station, is it?"

"That's what we call Summer Camp. It used to be an overflow space before they built the new station. Most of the buildings have been dismantled or are used for storage. But two of them are still in use, one as a climbing gym and the other as a café or nightclub when people are stir crazy and just need to get out of the station."

"A climbing gym? I might have to check that out."

They walked the rest of the distance in silence, the man letting her walk up the stairs first. She opened the first door, holding it for him.

"Thanks." He returned the favor at the second door.

"Thank you." Inside now, she pulled off her goggles and mask, turned to ask him his name—and stared.

Whoa.

He was ... *very* attractive. Square jaw with reddish stubble. Full lips. An elegant, straight nose. High cheekbones. Tanned skin flushed from the cold. Blue eyes with dark lashes. Short blond hair.

He said his name, pulled off a glove, held out his hand.

She took it, shook, his hand so much bigger than hers, his fingers warm. "I'm Dr. Samantha Park. I didn't quite catch your name."

He gave her a lopsided grin. "Thor Isaksen. Just call me Thor."

Named for a Nordic god. Well, he probably had an ego to match.

"I have to go. We're having a memorial service for my best friend." She managed to make the words sound casual.

His brow furrowed. "I'm sorry to hear that. Was he or she the person whose body they loaded onto the plane today?"

She stared. "You saw them load her onto the plane?"

He nodded. "Unless it was someone else."

Patty wouldn't have to stay on ice all winter after all. She was going home to her family. That should have come as *good* news.

Then why did Samantha suddenly feel so bereft?

Tears filled her eyes. "Excuse me. I need to get ready."

She hurried down the hall toward the AI berthing area and her room, leaving Thor behind her.

3

Thor made his way with Jones and Segal to the BI Lounge, his thoughts on Dr. Park, the woman he'd met earlier. She had walked out of the building with the big telescopes, so she was probably an astronomer. She couldn't be much older than thirty, her face youthful and pretty, her skin clear. Her long pale blond hair had been tied in a knot and was held in place by a pencil. She'd been crying, her blue eyes rimmed with red. She hadn't known they'd sent her friend's body away, and he felt bad to have been the one to tell her.

Thor knew how much it hurt to lose a friend.

"Anyone else feel like we're on the Moon?" Jones asked.

Segal glanced around them. "Or a space station?"

"I know what you mean," Thor said.

He had to respect the people who'd designed and built this place. It was a sophisticated facility, intended to support science despite the harshest climate on earth. It had a hydroponic greenhouse, a science lab, offices, a large gym, a weight room, a sauna, a medical facility, a post office that was open in the summer, a machine shop, and a metal-working shop. There were also massive unheated storage facilities that they called service arches. To reach the arches, one had to go down an icy, unheated, four-story stairwell they called the Beer Can because of its cylindrical shape and metal walls.

They hit a bottleneck outside the Bi Lounge, people moving through the door in silence, the mood somber. The lounge was a good place to *hygge*—get cozy—filled as it was with overstuffed sofas and chairs. There was a pool table close to the door, a large television on one wall, a dartboard, and a small kitchen in the back.

During their tour, Hardin had told them the lounge could serve as a life raft in dire emergencies. It had its own communications and computer center and its own power plant. It also had thick doors that sealed tight.

Thor went to stand in the back with Jones and Segal, leaving the seats for the others. They'd come to the service only because Hardin wanted to introduce them. They were the new kids in town, and Hardin wanted to do whatever he could to dispel any rumors and lessen tensions about their presence here.

Thor spotted Dr. Park sitting close to the front, her eyes puffy from crying, the pencil still in her hair. Hardin knelt beside her, his hand on her shoulder, the two of them speaking quietly together. Then Hardin got to his feet, an image of a smiling woman with short dark hair appearing on the TV screen.

"As you all know, we lost Patty three days ago. I thought it would be good to come together to remember her. We'll create a shrine for her in the ice tunnels, so think about what should go there. But before we start, I wanted to introduce the three newbies standing in the back. The satellite crash is a secret, which, naturally, means we've all been talking about it. They're here to retrieve some sensitive components, and then they'll fly back to the States."

"Yeah, good luck with that," someone muttered.

"They're flying out to the crash site *now*? That's crazy."

Hardin pointed to the nearest person. "Why don't we introduce ourselves—just your name and what you do here."

"Kazem Hamidi. I'm an astrophysicist at the BICEP lab."

"Nick Pappas, astrophysicist, IceCube."

"Bai Zhang Wei, astrophysicist, IceCube."

Dr. Park went next. "Samantha Park, astrophysicist, South Pole Telescope."

"Kristi Chang, station RN."

"Greg Martin, astrophysicist, BICEP."

Thor did his best to catch their names and retain them, but being introduced to almost fifty people at once was a bit much.

Afterward, Hardin met Thor's gaze. "Mr. Isaksen, did you want to say anything?"

Thor stepped forward. "I'm Thor Isaksen. This is Lev Segal and Malik Jones. We're grateful for your hospitality. We'll do our job as quickly as possible and stay out of everyone's way."

"Are you military?" blurted Jason, the kid who'd tried to film them earlier.

Thor shook his head. "No, absolutely not. We work for a security company."

It was the truth. None of them were with the military —not now.

"They're mercs—mercenaries," said a man whose name Thor couldn't recall. He wore an Oakland Raiders sweatshirt —and a disapproving frown on his face.

Thor ignored him, handing the floor back to Hardin.

"Thor and his team brought in freshies—apples, oranges, bananas, grapes, salad fixings, tomatoes, and—wait for it—avocados. They'll be available in the galley tomorrow morning."

That made people cheer.

Hardin gave them a moment to settle down. "I guess I'll start. I met Patty last February, the start of her first winter here. She was one of those faces I was always happy to see— kind and cheerful, even when winter-over syndrome kicked in. That's more than I can say for some of you."

Quiet laughter.

Hardin chuckled, too. "Patty participated fully in life on station. She was supportive of others and a good team player, always willing to pitch in, no matter what the job. She was a member of the Three Hundred Club. She also put together an entry for last year's Antarctic Film Festival— Werewolves in the Dark Sector."

That brought laughter, cheers, and applause.

"I could go on, but Sam knew Patty better than anyone. I've asked her to say a few words." Hardin stepped aside.

Dr. Park stood, her gaze meeting Thor's for a moment as she moved to the front of the room. He could tell she was nervous. "Patty and I met in grad school at Berkeley—two women working on PhDs in astrophysics. We became housemates. We were an odd couple. She was the extrovert. I was the introvert. I probably wouldn't have done anything but study and work on my dissertation if not for her. She was always telling me to lighten up. I helped her with fluid dynamics, and she taught me about living."

Charli, the coms manager, and Kristi, the RN, choked back tears.

Thor listened as Dr. Park talked about her long friend- ship with Patty, sharing funny anecdotes. He laughed along with the others. Still, it was strange to be an outsider during such an intimate expression of communal grief.

"Patty got me out of the house. She made me laugh. She made life brighter for the people around her. She and I have been friends and research partners for so long that I'm not sure how to do this without her. I can't ... I can't believe she's gone." Dr. Park was fighting tears now, too. "She loved her work. She loved the vastness and the mystery of space. I'd like to think she's closer to understanding those mysteries now, wherever she is. I can't believe I'll never see her again. I miss you, Patty."

Dr. Park's expression crumpled as tears overcame her at last, her pain tugging at Thor. The man in the Oakland Raiders sweatshirt stood and hugged her, his expression twisted by grief, tears on his face.

Thor seized the moment to make a quiet exit, threading his way across the lounge and out into the hallway, the others behind him.

"Too bad," Jones said. "Patty sounds like a nice woman."

Thor was sorry, too.

"Let's get some supper, check our gear, and catch up on sleep." Thor led them down the stairs and toward the galley. "We meet in the small conference room at oh-eight-hundred with the scientist who will be flying to the crash site with us. If this weather holds, we should be wheels up before noon."

SAMANTHA HAULED herself out of bed early the next morning, emotionally drained from the memorial service. She took her allotted two-minute shower, grabbed breakfast in the galley, then dressed warmly and made the trek to the Dark Sector to check the SPT, waving to Kazem, who stood outside the BICEP2 control room smoking a cigarette.

The telescope was operating perfectly, the observations it had sent back since last night intriguing. She didn't have time now to study them in any depth.

Patty would never see them.

Dragging, whether from grief or dread, Samantha made her way through the frigid cold back to the station for her meeting with the security team. She found them already in the conference room, sitting around the table with cups of coffee. She poured herself a cup, stirred in creamer, then joined them.

Thor was in the middle of a conference call. Despite the situation, she couldn't help but notice once again how attractive he was, his razor stubble and navy-blue cable-knit sweater giving him a rugged look.

He would never be interested in you.

Samantha had no illusions about her attractiveness to men. She had straight hair that wouldn't curl, a plain face, and breasts that barely filled a B cup. Worse, she had a doctorate in astrophysics.

We intimidate men, Samantha. Most of them want to be smarter than their girlfriends. That will never happen with us—unless one of us dates the ghost of Albert Einstein or Stephen Hawking.

That had been Patty's theory.

Who cares anyway?

They were about to leave on a mission that would probably get them all killed. Why was Samantha wasting time wondering what Thor might think of her?

"What about activity at Vostok?" he asked.

A man's voice answered. "Strong winds have kept them pinned down for the past few days—a stroke of luck. The

Pentagon has directed us to take a hard line against *anyone* who attempts to steal these components. Is that understood?"

"Yes, sir."

The Russians *were* in on this? That wasn't just a crazy theory?

So much for her starry-eyed notions about international scientific cooperation.

No more vodka for you, Vasily, you bastard.

Thor was looking at a satellite image of the continent. "Thanks for the update. We'll check in again shortly before we fly out."

And then the butterflies hit, dancing in Samantha's stomach.

She couldn't believe she had agreed to do this.

"Dr. Park, it's good to see you again. I didn't realize you were the expert assigned to this mission. Thanks for joining us."

"Please just call me Samantha. Titles seem pointless down here."

He acknowledged her with a nod. "You've studied the schematics?"

"I haven't had a lot of time, but, yes, I have looked at them." She'd been surprised at how similar some of the components were to the SPT's positioning system.

"You'll have more time to study them on the flight." Thor turned his laptop so the others could see the satellite image. "There is a Condition One storm moving toward McMurdo Station, as well as a storm moving inland from the east that will pass over the crash site before veering north. We've got a twenty-hour window to get to the site and back to the station so that our pilot can fly safely back to McMurdo."

Samantha held up her hand to stop him. This was all

moving too fast. "I'm sorry, but I have to ask. Have any of you done anything like this before? Have you worked in Antarctica? Because, frankly, this mission is suicidal. You have no idea what they're asking you to do, what they're asking *me* to do. Also, I can't remember your names, except for Thor's."

Thor's brow furrowed. "You're right. We should tell you a bit about ourselves."

A good-looking Black man with a goatee reached out, shook her hand, his brown eyes warm. "I'm Malik Jones. I served with the US Army Rangers for ten years. I've never been to Antarctica before—or the Arctic for that matter. But I have served on many rescue operations around the world."

The one with thick dark hair and hazel eyes spoke next. "Lev Segal, formerly with the Israeli Defense Forces. I've never worked in this environment, but Isaksen has."

Samantha met Thor's gaze. "Lance was right. You *are* mercenaries."

"Private security." Thor took a sip of his coffee. "I served with Denmark's Huntsman Corps before joining Sirius Dogsled Patrol. I spent two years patrolling Northeastern Greenland with a team of sled dogs during Arctic winter. We patrolled for up to four months at a time, traveling on sea ice, going overland, living in the open, sleeping in tents in temperatures that sometimes fell below minus fifty Celsius."

She stared at him, her exchange with him yesterday evening coming back to her.

Are you lost?

I was just watching the aurora.

Enjoy the view, but don't stay out too long. The cold sneaks up on people.

It's not too bad right now.

He hadn't been trying to act tough. He was accustomed to the cold.

He went on. "The biggest difference between the Arctic and the Antarctic is the humidity. Greenland is humid. We sometimes got a meter and a half of snow in twenty-four hours. Here, it's very dry, and we're at a much higher elevation. The wind is worse, and the temperatures are more extreme. This is your second winter here, right?"

She nodded, still taking in what he'd told her.

A meter and a half of snow in a single day? Wow.

"Please feel free to speak up if you believe we're missing something. You have more experience here than we do."

Samantha appreciated his willingness to listen to her, but he was the expert. "I've spent my time here inside the safety of this station, apart from my daily walks to and from the Dark Sector lab. When it's really cold, Patty and I..."

Her words trailed off, pain lancing through her when she realized what she'd said.

"We're sorry about your friend." Thor's gaze was warm with sympathy. "It's hard to lose someone."

Samantha's throat went tight, his compassion taking her by surprise. "Thanks."

Thor gave her a moment, then he went over the plan in detail. They would fly in a Twin Otter with a ferry tank to the crash site. While the pilot kept the plane running, Thor, Malik, and Lev would assist her in removing the components in any way they could and locking them in a special steel lockbox. Then they would board the plane with the package and fly back to the station.

"We won't have a lot of time once we get there—not even a half-hour. We don't want our fuel to freeze."

The butterflies in Samantha's stomach went into a

frenzy. "That's not enough time. If I were removing those components in a lab, I'd give myself an hour."

What the hell did they expect from her—miracles?

Thor's gaze met hers. "We'll be right there, doing whatever we can to help. Also, your body mass is lower than ours, so you'll lose heat faster. You need to layer up more than usual and be alert for signs of hypothermia."

"When do we leave?"

"Our plane left McMurdo two hours ago. It should be here by ten. That gives you an hour to get ready."

Samantha had to say it. "You said you welcomed my advice. Here it is. Your guns and muscles and military experience won't save us if things go wrong out there. Wait until spring to retrieve these components when it's safer to fly."

Thor stood, closed his laptop. "I wish we could."

THOR WAITED with Jones and Segal near Destination Alpha —the station's main entrance—for Samantha, his mind focused on the task ahead of them. Not only would they need everything to go right, they would need a bit of luck, too.

Thor had flown in a prop plane over Greenland. He knew what they were facing.

"The flight will be rough." He spoke quietly, doing his best not to be overheard. "You two got your motion sickness patches?"

Jones chuckled. "I'm not the one who gets sick."

"Fuck you." Segal glared at him.

Thor had his in place, and he'd made sure Samantha got one, too.

He spotted her walking down the long hallway in her

red NSF parka, a bag of gear, food, and extra clothing slung over her shoulder. She had almost reached them when the man who'd accused them of being mercenaries ran up behind her.

"Did you know they sent Patty's body back to the States?" He looked enraged.

"I found out after she was already gone."

The man raised his voice, his face going red. "Why didn't anyone tell me?"

Samantha touched a hand to his arm. "I'm sorry, Lance. No one told me, either."

"Sorry to be so angry, but I never got to say goodbye."

"None of us did. I need to go." Samantha walked on, leaving Lance behind.

Then Lance spotted Thor and seemed to put two and two together. He grabbed Samantha's arm, turned her to face him. "You're not going with them, are you?"

"Yes. The NSF asked me to do this."

"That's crazy. Do you know how dangerous this is?"

"I don't have a choice, Lance."

"Bullshit!" Lance turned his anger on Thor, Jones, and Segal, stomping over to them. "If you soldier boys want to risk your lives over a satellite, fine. But you're not taking Samantha on that plane. She's a scientist, not a tool of the military."

Thor ignored him, met Samantha's gaze. "Are you ready?"

But Lance didn't back down. He strode up to Thor, pointed a finger in Thor's face. He was a good six inches shorter than Thor, but, oh, he was angry. "You are *not* taking her out on that plane. You have no idea what it's like out there."

"Is that so?" Thor understood the man's rage but didn't like his attitude.

Samantha stepped between them. "He knows, Lance. He's got a lot more experience surviving in these conditions than you or I."

"What do you mean by that?"

But Hardin must have heard the shouting. He came down the stairs from the administrative offices. "Back off, Lance. Sam is in good hands."

Lance got in his face. "Why did you send Patty's body back without letting me say goodbye?"

"What the hell are you talking about?" Hardin looked genuinely surprised. "I didn't authorize that. Are you sure?"

From outside the station came the sound of a small plane landing.

"Let's move out." Thor shouldered his gear.

"Samantha, stop! Nothing on that satellite is worth your life!"

"We'll bring her back." Thor and the others put on their masks, goggles, hats, and gloves, grabbed the duffle bags, and left the shelter of the station.

It was sixty-eight below, cold enough to suck the breath from Thor's lungs even with the mask. They walked quickly over the ice to the waiting Twin Otter, its propellers still running as a team of fuelies worked fast to get it in the air again.

Samantha fell in beside Thor. "I'm sorry about Lance. He's upset about Patty's death. We all are."

"You don't need to apologize for him. He doesn't bother me. We were told not to expect a warm welcome."

"Son of a bitch," Jones muttered from behind his mask. "This cold is unreal."

Thor chuckled. "It's colder where we're going."

The pilot, who'd been watching for them, opened the door. "Let's move, people! As soon as we've refueled, we take off."

Thor let the others go first, and then helped the pilot retract the stairs and lock the door. He and the others took off their gloves and masks and stowed their gear. All but two sets of seats had been removed to make room for the ferry tank, which would fuel the plane when its main fuel tanks ran out.

"The plane isn't pressurized. I'll activate the oxygen system when we pass twelve thousand feet." The pilot checked to make sure they had stowed their gear properly. "We'll be flying into a stiff headwind, so the flight out will take close to three hours. It should be faster on the way back."

The pilot made his way to the cockpit, calling back to them over his shoulder. "Strap in. This will be a rough ride."

They buckled their safety belts, Samantha in the window seat, Thor in the aisle seat where he could stretch his legs. Then the plane began to move.

Samantha's face was pale, her hands clenched around her gloves.

Thor couldn't blame her for being afraid. She was a scientist and didn't have their training. She wasn't accustomed to danger. She'd been asked to risk her life to solve a problem not of her making, and she had agreed.

He tried to reassure her but assumed that she was too smart to fall for platitudes or bullshit. "We'll have a steep climb when we first take off, and the flight will be rough. I know this isn't what you wanted, Samantha, but I admire your courage for agreeing to be part of this mission."

"I regret it already."

4

Samantha drew a breath, tried to calm her nerves as the plane accelerated down the skiway. She needed to be logical about this. Freaking out wouldn't add a single moment to her life. The NSF and US government had sent people they believed were up to this task. She had to trust that they knew what they were doing. If she—

The plane lifted off, its nose pointing sharply skyward.

She gasped, grabbed Thor's hand.

Warm fingers closed over hers, a strange awareness tingling through her. "Are you afraid of flying?"

Embarrassed and a little alarmed, she drew her hand away. "Only in the middle of austral winter."

Get a grip!

None of the Cobra guys seemed nervous. From the impassive expressions on their faces, she could only assume that taking extreme risks was routine for them.

You can worry when they start to worry.

Unexpectedly, that thought helped to calm her.

She reached inside the inner pocket of her parka and drew out the schematics for the satellite, studying them to keep herself busy. It wasn't the schematics that got her mind off her worries, however, but the fact that Thor was sitting beside her. She was oddly mindful of his presence. His long legs stretched into the aisle. His shoulders were so broad that they encroached on her space—not that she minded. His scent was pleasingly male. She even imagined she could feel his body heat.

You're being ridiculous.

Sure, it had been a long time since she'd been with a man, but macho tough guys weren't her type—even if she did find him attractive.

Focus.

She willed her gaze to meet the page. How she approached removing the components depended entirely on how the satellite had landed. For all she knew, the parts she needed to remove were too high off the ice for her to reach. Or perhaps they were buried in the ice as a result of impact.

While the plane jerked and bobbed through turbulence, she pored over the satellite's design. The GPS and tracking components were surprisingly similar to the SPT's GPS. Of course, there was always that chance that the crash had mangled the module, making the parts harder to remove. She could only wait and see.

The pilot's voice came over the PA system. "We'll be passing twelve thousand feet in a few minutes. I'm activating the cabin oxygen system."

A mask dropped out of the overhead compartment just in front of Samantha. She did what flight attendants taught passengers to do, pulling the tubing down, slipping the strap over her head, and positioning the mask over her mouth and nose.

She studied the schematics for a few more minutes,

memorizing the internal connections, then slipped them back into her coat pocket.

"So, it's a piece of cake?" Thor's words were muffled by his oxygen mask.

"I could do it with my eyes closed." She looked up to find Thor watching her, and her pulse skipped.

He didn't look away but seemed to study her, his gaze warm. "What made you want to become an astro... astrophys ... astrophysicist. That's hard to say."

"How do you say it in Danish?"

"*Astrofysiker*."

"I don't know. That seems harder to me."

"Danish isn't easy to pronounce."

She answered his question. "My mother was a high school science teacher, and my father teaches biology at UC-Berkeley. They bought me a small telescope for my tenth birthday, and I fell in love with the stars."

She told him how she'd taken that telescope out every night the sky was clear, her father standing beside her as she made observations. "It was all silly stuff—lunar craters that looked like faces or new constellations that I invented. My father was so patient, standing there with me each night, helping me become proficient with the telescope."

"He must be proud of you."

She nodded, feeling strangely light-headed, her fingers tingling. She'd never flown in an unpressurized aircraft before and hadn't known to expect this. If the others could deal with it, so could she. "My brother is a propulsion engineer for NASA. We're a family of geeks, I guess. How about you? How did you end up in Greenland?"

"I've always loved the outdoors. My father was a forester, and I worked for him during the summer when I was a teenager. My mother taught English in the primary school. I went to the *gymnasium*—that's our high school—in the math and science line, and then studied mechanical engineering in Copenhagen for two years. I needed to do something more physical, so I left the university and joined the Danish Army."

She listened, his accent soft and charming, as he told her about his time in the Huntsman Corps, the Danish Army's special forces unit. But his words seemed to slow down, her thoughts unraveling.

Black spots.

They danced before her eyes.

It was hard to listen, so hard to stay awake.

"Samantha?" Thor's face swam before hers. He looked angry. "She's hypoxic."

He pulled her mask off her head and replaced it with his own, holding it over her nose and mouth, reclining her seatback. "Just breathe, Samantha, deep and even."

Someone shouted to the pilot that her O2 wasn't working.

The reply was lost to her as her eyes drifted shut, her mind hovering on the brink of unconsciousness.

∼

"*NEJ, FOR HELVEDE.*" *No, damn it!* "She's losing consciousness."

Why hadn't he noticed she was in trouble sooner?

The pilot's voice came over the PA once more. "I brought six tanks—enough to get us all there and back, plus two spares."

Jones removed his mask, unbuckled his safety belt. "I'll go check the tanks."

He started toward the back of the plane, where the O2

tanks hooked into the system, his steps unsteady thanks to almost nonstop turbulence.

Segal stood, too. "I'll help."

Thor focused on Samantha. They needed her mind to be clear when they landed. Without her, this mission would fail.

Seconds ticked by, and still, she didn't open her eyes.

Was his oxygen also not working?

No, her color was starting to come back now, her breathing steady. Then her eyes fluttered open, confusion on her pretty face.

"What...?"

"You became hypoxic. How do you feel?"

"Headache. A little dizzy."

He realized he was hovering over her, only inches away from her face—close enough to kiss her. Some part of him liked that idea—the same part of him that had liked it when she'd grabbed his hand.

Hva' fanden? What the fuck?

He sat back, irritated with himself. "You should have said something."

"I'm sorry. I thought it was just ... low air pressure. I didn't know."

She's never done this before, remember?

She looked up at him, clearly worried. "What about you? You need oxygen, too."

"I'll be fine for a little while. Jones and Segal are trying to fix the problem."

If they couldn't find the cause, they would have to share O2.

"What were we talking about? You were telling me something."

"You asked about my time with the Huntsman Corps in Afghanistan."

"Yes. Right. I remember. Did you see combat?"

"Our job was to go after high-value al Qaeda and Taliban targets, which meant we got into a lot of firefights."

"That sounds scary." She seemed more alert now.

"Fear comes from not knowing. Training offsets fear. If you know how to react and have confidence in yourself and your comrades, there's less room for fear."

Of course, terrible things still happened. They'd lost men on his last deployment, good soldiers blown apart by an IED. But Samantha didn't need to hear about that—or how far he'd gone to avenge his friends.

"I can't imagine having people shooting at me."

"I can't imagine working with a giant telescope. I'd be afraid I'd break it."

She looked at him as if he were crazy. "If you know what to do, it's not scary."

"Exactly." He couldn't help but grin.

She'd made his point for him.

Her eyes crinkled, her smile hidden behind her mask. "I see what you did there."

Jones and Segal made their way back to the front.

"It was a bad regulator. We found a spare." Segal sat, buckled in, put on his mask.

Jones did the same. "It should be working now."

Thor took Samantha's mask for himself, letting her keep his. "If you feel tingling, dizziness, confusion—anything at all—tell me right away. You're essential personnel on this mission. We need you to be clear-headed."

"Right." She raised her seatback upright once more. "Thanks—to all of you."

Jones turned, looked back at her, a smile on his face.

"That's why we're here. Our only job is to get you safely in and out."

"Is that what private security companies do—keep people safe?"

That wasn't the whole story, but close enough.

"We're not hired to fight, if that's what you're wondering." He saw on her face that's exactly what she'd wanted to know. "If the person we're protecting is attacked, we fight back. Most of the time, we act as a security team for traveling CEOs and government officials, though we helped in a hostage rescue recently."

"I'm sorry I called you mercenaries. Do people ever shoot at you?"

"Oh, hell, yes." Jones chuckled. "I took a round to the chest in Mazar-e-Sharif."

Segal cracked open a bottle of water. "A lot of Cobra boys got hit on that one."

That operation had happened shortly before Thor joined the company. But this conversation wasn't helping Samantha. "There won't be any bullets flying when we land. The cold is the only real threat to us on this operation."

While Thor answered Samantha's questions about the selection process for Sirius, Jones and Segal drifted into a discussion about the movie *The Thing* and the possibility of finding space aliens or dinosaurs frozen in the Antarctic ice.

Samantha stared at Thor. "Only *six* guys make the cut each year?"

"That's only if they can find six guys who qualify." Thor would forever be grateful that he'd made it. He wasn't sure where he'd be otherwise. Two years on the ice had helped him put Afghanistan behind him. It had saved him. "The year I joined, only five men made it. The last was cut at the end after losing his temper."

"That's really strict."

"When you're out on the ice for four months at a time with one other person and a team of sled dogs, you can't afford to be emotional. They only take people who can keep their heads in a crisis."

"You must be very level-headed."

He was—most of the time.

Jones pivoted in his seat. "This dude is ice cold. You're talking to the great-great-grandson of a god. He's a direct descendant of Odin, you know. That's what the official Danish genealogical records say. I've seen the PDF."

"Odin? The Norse god?" Samantha looked up at Thor.

"Yes. Obviously, it's not true."

"Ask him about the time he denned with a mama polar bear, because that's real."

Thor laughed at the shock in Samantha's eyes. "He's exaggerating. I—"

The pilot's voice cut him off. "I just got a report that a plane lifted off from Vostok a short time ago. Radar shows them heading for the crash site. They're farther out than we are, but you're going to have company."

SAMANTHA EXHALED as the plane came to a stop, her hands still gripping the arms of her seat, her knuckles white. It had been a rough landing, but at least they hadn't tumbled into a crevasse. "Good grief!"

Wind buffeted the small aircraft, its propellers still running.

She stood, put on her hat, hood, snow goggles, mask, gloves, and headlamp, the satellite schematics tucked inside her parka. "What about the other plane?"

Thor rested a reassuring hand on her shoulder, his gaze meeting hers. "Let us worry about the plane. You focus on the satellite."

The men moved quickly, pulling out rifles and putting on masks, headlamps, goggles, and gloves.

"Rifles over your shoulders. Pistols holstered." Thor took a rifle and the steel lockbox out of his gear bag. "We'll set up the tent on her windward side to create a windbreak and offer some shelter."

Lev grabbed a large duffel bag. "I've got the tools. Jones, grab the tent."

Thor turned and shouted to the pilot. "How much time can you give us?"

"It's minus eighty with a wind chill of minus one-ten. No more than twenty minutes, if that."

Samantha's stomach knotted.

Twenty minutes. What they were asking of her seemed impossible, and yet she had no choice but to get the job done. If any of the plane's systems froze, they would die. If they got caught in the storm, they would die. If she didn't retrieve the components, lots of other people might die.

You can do this.

If she could access the components, that is.

"I'll go first and make sure the ice is stable." Thor opened the door, letting in a gust of frigid air. He walked a path to the satellite and back, then returned for her and helped her down the stairs.

She pulled her hat down over exposed skin that burned, turned on her headlamp, and looked out on devastation.

The satellite's various antennae and solar arrays were strewn across the snow in a thousand shattered pieces, the main body lying there like a battered corpse. The clean-up crew had a big job to do next summer.

She lowered her head against the wind and walked over to the mangled remains of the satellite. It was badly damaged, looking nothing like the images she'd memorized. She tried to orient herself, their headlamps the only source of light. "That must be where the thirty gigahertz antenna connected. This held a solar array. That must have been where the dual subreflectors attached to the module."

Thor walked beside her. "Where do you want to set up?"

She pointed. "Over there."

Thor motioned to the others. "Let's get that tent set up!"

The men struggled to complete their task in the wind, while Samantha opened the tool bag, the wind chill already penetrating her layers. A blow torch would have made this easier, but they were unreliable in this cold. She took out a hammer and chisel, which she used to punch through the aluminum alloy paneling until she'd made a big enough opening for a close-quarter hacksaw.

"Like this," she heard Thor say.

He seemed to be in his element here, more so than the others.

"I think you've done this before," Malik said.

"A thousand times. Tighten that down. There. We're good."

The tent *did* make a difference, sheltering her from the worst of the wind.

Thor told Malik and Lev to shelter inside. "Do what you can to stay warm, so you're good to go when that plane arrives."

She kept sawing, the blade slicing through metal. But she needed to go faster. She couldn't spend ten of their twenty minutes just getting into the module. Unfortunately, aluminum was one metal that gained strength in extreme cold.

The saw blade snapped, unable to take it.

"Damn." She bent down, rummaged through the tools for a replacement blade.

"What can I do?"

"The blade broke. I need a new one."

"All you're doing is cutting open this paneling, right?"

"Yes."

Thor gave her something—hand warmers. "Get inside the tent. Activate those if you need them. We'll handle this part of it. We're good at wrecking shit. Come on, boys, let's rip this open."

She stepped inside the tent as Malik and Lev stepped out, her breath turning to ice crystals that danced in the light of her headlamp. Through a crack in the tent flap, she saw the men using the hammer and chisel to punch out a large opening in the panel.

A few minutes later, Thor ducked his head inside the tent. "You're on."

She stepped out and peered into the module, adjusting her headlamp. The GPS unit was there behind wires and internal supports. She reached into the bag for the wire-cutters and a battery-operated drill. But in these heavy gloves, her fingers weren't nimble enough to do the job. "I have to take off my gloves."

Thor stood beside her. "Activate those hand warmers. You'll be able to work for only a minute or two at a time."

She shook the hand warmers to start the chemical reaction, slipped them inside the pocket of her parka, and pulled off her gloves.

The air was so frigid it felt like plunging her hands into hot steam.

She bit back a gasp at the pain and did her best to focus, only too aware that the clock was ticking.

"Slow is smooth, and smooth is fast." Thor's voice was calming.

She cut through one set of wires and searched for the screws that held the GPS unit to the supports, her fingers already growing stiff.

Thor took the drill. "Take a rest. Tell me what to do."

She shoved her hands into her pockets, the hand warmers almost unbearably hot. "See that metal box just beneath that electrical node? That's what we came for—that and the unit just beside it."

He looked inside, studied the situation. "Got it."

He positioned the drill, the small device whirring as he removed the first bolt. Then Thor looked up at the dark sky. "Here they come."

Samantha heard it, too—the sound of an approaching airplane.

5

Thor shoved his hands into his pockets to warm them and watched the plane circle overhead. "Segal, you speak Russian, right?"

"Enough to get by. Come on, Jones. We're the welcoming committee."

Thor didn't need to tell them what to do. He'd worked with them for three years in many different situations. He trusted them not to allow anyone to come near Samantha or the satellite.

Samantha struggled to position the drill for the next bolt. "This battery isn't going to last long in the cold."

"Worry about that when it happens."

"What if they point guns at you or start shooting?"

"They're not going to open fire. They can't be that stupid. They'd be proving their guilt. Besides, we have bigger problems right now. The wind is picking up. Just focus."

The front edge of that storm system was moving closer.

Samantha removed a bolt and stuck her hands inside her pockets again. "One of the bolts is hidden beneath a twisted strut. We're going to have to cut through."

"I see it." Thor replaced the blade of the saw and began cutting through the strut as the plane landed and came to a stop. He focused on the job and left the intruders to Jones and Segal. The sooner they had these components in their hands, the sooner this would be over. "That's one done."

But his exposed fingers couldn't take more.

It was Samantha's turn again.

From some distance behind them came a man's voice in heavily accented English. "We are from Vostok Station and have come to help."

Samantha shook her head. "Right."

"Don't worry about them. Just focus on that GPS unit."

Segal chuckled. "The six of you flew out here in dangerous conditions from four hundred miles away to help —and you're carrying weapons."

That was Segal's way of warning Thor that they were outnumbered—and that the Russians were armed.

"You have rifles, too, I see. You are military, yes?"

"We're not military, no. The rifles are just to protect us from polar bears."

"There are no polar bears in Antarctica."

"We were misinformed."

Segal was lying. The Russians were lying. Everyone knew it.

That was international relations in a nutshell.

Meanwhile, Samantha had stopped sawing, her hands in her pockets again. "This is taking too long."

"We're almost there." Thor glanced at his watch. "We've got eight minutes."

"Who is in that tent?" the Russian asked. "We are happy to help if you are having trouble. You must get back into the air soon, yes?"

"Thanks, but we'll manage." Segal sounded like he was

enjoying this. "There's a storm headed this way. You might want to worry about your own safety."

"What are you saying?" The Russian sounded truly surprised.

"Didn't you know? We're going to be racing to get back ahead of it."

Thor took over once again, cutting through the strut in a second place and removing it from the module. He tried to pull the GPS unit out, but it was attached to something on the other side. "It's still bolted in somewhere, and my hands are too big to get back there. When you can feel your fingers again, see what you can do."

Samantha drew her hands out of her pockets, reached inside the module. "It's bolted into something. There's no way the saw will fit in here. Maybe I can shatter the casing and retrieve what's inside. They didn't tell us to bring this back in one piece."

"I like the way you think."

She retrieved the hammer and chisel and gave the alloy casing that surrounded the GPS unit a few hard blows. "I'm in."

She dropped the tools and fought to free the component's internal workings. When she drew her hand out again, Thor's headlamp caught it.

Blood frozen on her palm.

He took her hand. "You cut yourself."

She stared at her palm. "I didn't feel it."

"Get your hands in your pockets, and step back into the tent. I've got this."

He reached inside and ripped out chips, circuitry, and some kind of processor, dropping them in a steel lockbox. "Is that everything?"

He stepped back, slid his hands into his pockets, his fingers completely numb.

Samantha looked. "I think that's it."

She unzipped her parka, drew out the schematics, and stepped back into the tent and out of the wind to study them. "Yes, we've got it."

"I'm going to escort you back to the plane and get you and the components safely onboard again." Thor put on his gloves, locked the steel box, and shouldered the bag of tools. "If they're going to make a move to steal this, they'll do it now. Once you're out of the cold, we'll break the tent down and join you."

"I understand." She put the hand warmers in her gloves and slipped her hands inside them. "Be careful."

"We will." Thor stepped around the side of the tent, cold wind hitting him hard.

There, not twenty feet away, stood six men with headlamps, their path blocked by Segal and Jones.

SAMANTHA FOCUSED on taking one step after the other, relieved she'd done what she'd been sent to do. Now that she wasn't distracted by the job, the cold had become unbearable, the shelter of the plane seeming so far away. But it wasn't over yet.

There were still the six Russians behind her—double the number of Cobra men. If she, Thor, and the others got safely aboard the plane, they still needed to take off and make it back to the station so the pilot could get back to McMurdo alive.

Too cold now to be afraid, she took one step after another.

Thor tucked an arm through hers, steadying her, helping her to go faster. "Keep moving. You're almost there."

As they neared the plane, the pilot opened the door and lowered the stairs. "I was about to come after you. We need to go—*now*. That storm is moving in faster than we thought it would."

"We'll get the tent and be right back." Thor helped Samantha up the steps, setting the bag of tools and the steel lockbox near her feet.

Then the stairs came in, and the pilot shut and locked the door.

Warmth.

The suddenness of the temperature shift left her feeling disoriented.

"I'll grab you a heated blanket." The pilot disappeared toward the front.

"Thank you." She peeled off her gloves with stiff fingers, took off her goggles and mask to find her eyelashes covered with frost.

Shivering, she walked with wooden steps to her seat, took the blanket from the pilot, and wrapped it around her parka, tucking it beneath her chin, the warmth heavenly.

Outside her window, Thor, Malik, and Lev faced off with the Russian team. The six men finally turned and trudged back to their plane. While Malik kept watch, Lev helped Thor take down the tent. Then the three men ran toward the plane.

The pilot opened the door again, lowered the stairs. "Let's go!"

The men climbed aboard one at a time, stowed their gear, and stripped off their masks, their eyelashes and Malik's beard white with frost.

The pilot raised the stairs, went to close the door. "We've got company!"

In a heartbeat, Thor and the others had their rifles in hand.

Samantha's adrenaline spiked.

A Russian, still masked, walked up to the door, hands raised, speaking in panicked English. "Our plane—its fuel line is frozen! Please, take us back with you."

Thor, Malik, and Lev shared a glance, their expressions hard.

"It could be a ploy, a way to grab the package," Jones said.

Segal spoke to the man in Russian, then turned to Thor. "This guy is scared shitless. I think he's telling the truth."

Thor seemed to consider this.

Samantha had to say it. "If he's telling the truth and we leave them, they'll die, and the world would rightly blame us."

There was no one else to come along and rescue them out here.

Thor turned to the pilot. "Can the plane carry seven more?"

Seven? Of course. The six men, plus their pilot.

"Fuck." The pilot let out a gust of breath. "We don't have enough oxygen for everyone. You'll have to share. The extra weight means we'll use more fuel and take longer to get back—*if* we get back. Can you control them?"

Thor seemed unruffled and in command of the situation, his confidence reassuring. "No problems there."

"Then get them on board. We needed to leave five minutes ago. Our propellers and fuel line might freeze, and then we're all dead. I'm going to get us moving."

"Take this and lock the cockpit door behind you." Thor

handed him the lockbox with the components. "Segal, tell our new friends we're taking their weapons. They've got thirty seconds to get aboard."

Lev shouted something to the Russian, who motioned to the others.

Samantha watched, pulse racing, as desperate men scrambled across the ice, running toward their only chance at survival.

But what if they were lying? What if they had concealed weapons and hijacked the plane? What if they killed them all and simply took the plane?

One by one, the men climbed on board, handed their rifles to Malik and Lev. When the last one had made it, Thor pulled up the stairs and secured the door. Samantha noticed that he still had his pistol, as did Malik and Lev.

They weren't taking any chances.

He shouted to the pilot. "Let's go!"

Lev and Jones stowed the rifles. Then Segal spoke to the Russians, who sat on the floor alongside the ferry tank with no safety belts. From Lev's gestures, Samantha could tell he was explaining that they would have to share oxygen. The Russians nodded and began taking off their goggles and masks. And there among them was Vasily.

He saw her, surprise on his face. "Sam?"

But then the plane was moving.

Thor took something from the overhead compartment —a first aid kit—and sat beside Samantha. The frost from his eyelashes had melted, dripping down his face like tears. "You know him?"

She held out her palm, which was now bleeding freely and had stained the blanket. "I met him at McMurdo when we first arrived. A group of us researchers got together. There may have been drinking."

He opened the kit, cleaned the wound, his fingers cold, his brow furrowing when the sting of the antiseptic made her gasp. "Sorry."

"It's not your fault." She watched him work. "You're not what I was expecting."

"Oh, how so?"

"You're kind. No swagger or chest-thumping or sexist jokes."

He chuckled. "You were expecting a shitting jerk, then. You don't have a very high opinion of military guys, do you?"

She suppressed a smile at his syntax error. English speakers didn't use the word *shitting* quite like that. "I guess not."

He bandaged the cut and put the kit under the seat in front of him just as the little plane lifted off, shaking in the wind.

THOR PASSED the O2 mask to Samantha, their heads close together so as not to waste oxygen. As soon as they'd gotten airborne, Jones had gone to the back to reconfigure the oxygen system, giving the seven Russians four tanks to share, while he, Segal, Samantha, and Thor split two between the four of them.

It wasn't ideal, but they'd had no other choice.

Thor could never have abandoned anyone in those temperatures. Rarely had his time on the ice of Greenland involved wind chill that extreme. When it had, he and his teammate, Bengt, had staked the dogs, put up their tent, and crawled into the same sleeping bag for warmth.

The dogs with their thick coats could survive it.

People couldn't—not for long.

Samantha handed the mask back, her fingers accidentally brushing his, the contact human and warm. He knew she was afraid, but she was handling it well. For someone who hadn't wanted to be a part of this mission, she'd done a great job.

If the flight out had been turbulent, the return trip demonstrated exactly why people didn't fly in Antarctica in the winter. Twice, the plane had suddenly lost altitude, seeming to free fall before the pilot was able to gain lift again. The man deserved a medal as far as Thor was concerned. In a lesser pilot's hands, they'd already be dead.

So far, their Russian guests hadn't tried to pull anything. Then again, without safety belts, they had to hold on to the straps that secured the ferry tank or risk broken bones. None had spoken a word since takeoff.

The plane shook and bounced like a plaything.

Samantha handed the mask back to Thor, her gaze meeting his. She was so close he could smell the sweet floral scent of her shampoo.

"You should drink. You're probably dehydrated." He nudged the seat in front of him with his knee. "That goes for you guys, too."

Jones elbowed Segal. "The Viking says to drink."

"Water—or does he have something stronger?"

Samantha reached for the bottle of water she'd tucked into the seatback pocket, opened it, drank deeply. "Where do you live when you're not saving people?"

Thor gave the mask back to Samantha. "In the mountains about an hour and a half west of Denver. I bought a house up there—"

The plane dropped again, losing altitude all at once.

Samantha gasped, grabbed Thor's hand, their guests

grunting and shouting in alarm as inertia flung them against the overhead compartment.

But just as quickly as it began, it was over, the plane still aloft.

Thor could have released her hand then, but he didn't, instead holding fast. "It won't be too much longer."

"You must think I'm a big baby."

He grinned, shook his head. "Being brave doesn't mean you're not afraid. You did great out there. The NSF sent us the right person for the job."

Reluctantly, he released her hand.

What's with you, man?

"I couldn't have done it without your help."

"I only did what you told me to do."

A few minutes later, the pilot announced that they were now below twelve thousand feet and that he was shutting off the oxygen system. "We're past the worst of the turbulence. Conditions near the Pole are calm."

She breathed a deep sigh of relief when at long last, the aircraft's skis touched the ice. "Oh, thank goodness! I can't believe we made it."

Thor couldn't help but smile. "Of course, we did."

The Russians cheered.

Thor unbuckled his safety belt and stood. "You two watch over our guests. I'll get Dr. Park and the package back to the station. We need to clear the aircraft quickly so the pilot can get back to McMurdo."

Segal got to his feet, explained the situation to the Russians.

Thor watched as they disembarked, waiting for the pilot, who appeared carrying the box with the components. "Fantastic flying, man."

The pilot shook Thor's hand. "Happy to do my part."

By the time Thor and Samantha had reached the stairs to Destination Alpha, the pilot was in the air once more, racing the storm to McMurdo.

Samantha opened the door. "I can't believe it's over."

But it wasn't over for Thor, Jones, and Segal. They'd retrieved the package, but now they were stuck at the station with researchers who didn't want them around—and seven potential hostiles.

6

Samantha had never been happier to see the inside of the station than she was at this moment. Exhausted and drained, she took off her goggles, mask, hat, and gloves, eager for a cup of hot coffee. She turned to Thor, Malik, and Lev. "If you're hungry, there's food in the galley. They'll start serving supper at six. And thank you—all of you."

Thor met her gaze, his lips curving in a slight smile. "You did the hard work, so we should be the ones thanking you."

Steve came down the stairs, made eye contact with her, relief on his face. "Glad to see you back. Mission accomplished?"

Samantha and Thor answered at the same time. "Yes."

Steve glanced around at the unfamiliar faces. "Who are these guys?"

Vasily and his friends milled about, looking lost and bedraggled.

"Just some Russians we picked up at the crash site." Thor pointed. "Vasily there speaks English. Segal speaks Russian. He can help you out."

"Just great." Steve looked about as excited by this as

Samantha had expected him to be. "Let's get them settled. We can grab toiletries and other basics for them off the Skua table. Do they have a leader?"

None of this was Samantha's problem. She left Steve to deal with it and headed down the hallway toward the AI wing, uncomfortably warm now in these heavy layers.

Thor caught up with her. "Hey, I had something to go over with you, but I don't want to risk anyone hearing."

That was mysterious—and interesting. "Okay."

She wouldn't forget how he'd helped her today. He'd recognized her hypoxia, giving her his oxygen, holding her hand. He'd even bandaged her cut.

He followed her to her room, people casting him curious glances as they passed. "What do the scientists here have against guys like us?"

He didn't seem bothered by the situation, just curious.

"Too many researchers have had their work appropriated by the military. They discover something or create something new, only to see it used for violence."

"Like Einstein's research and the nuclear bomb."

They started down the stairs to the lower level.

"Yes, exactly. Some are happy to sell their work to the Department of Defense or private contractors, but many aren't." It wasn't a problem for Samantha because her work had no military applications—not yet anyway. "Sometimes, professors don't have a choice. The university owns the research and sells it to military contractors."

"I get it." He leaned against the wall, arms crossed over his chest, while she fumbled in the pockets of her snow pants for her room key.

"There's also the growing militarization of Antarctica, with governments like China, Russia, and the US playing fast and loose with treaty regulations." She found her keys, unlocked her door, opened it. "Many of us see any armed presence here—and that includes you Cobra guys—as undermining regulations that have maintained Antarctica as a science preserve for decades."

If this offended him, he didn't show it.

"We won't be here for long. May I come in?"

"Yes."

He followed her into her room and shut the door. "What about you? Is that why you thought we'd be assholes?"

"I didn't put it that way." She'd take her words back if she could. "I knew some football players in high school and boys from NJROTC, too, and they—"

"What's NJROTC?"

"Naval Junior Reserve Officer Training Corps—a pre-military program for high-schoolers. They had big egos. They bullied kids like me, smart kids."

"Bullied you?"

Did he not know the word?

"They called me names, hit me, made fun of me, told me I was ugly."

Thor frowned, his blue eyes looking into hers, his expression serious. "I'm sorry to hear that. That's not the kind of men we are."

"I see that now. Is that what you wanted to discuss?"

"No, but thanks for your honesty. Be careful around the Russian team members, okay? We don't know anything about them. We don't know if they were lying or telling the truth, but they know you were at the crash site. They know you retrieved something from that wreckage. If I were you, I wouldn't let them into my room or go anywhere in the station alone, especially not the service arches or ice tunnels."

"Okay." *Well, darn.*

Could she admit to herself that she'd hoped he'd come here to kiss her?

As if.

A man like him could have any woman he wanted.

She took off her parka, touched at least that he'd thought about her safety. Then again, that was his job. "You really think they're behind this?"

He arched an eyebrow. "Do you believe they flew out to the crash site with weapons in the middle of austral winter just to lend us a hand?"

It wasn't impossible, but it *was* highly implausible. "No."

"If they're here to get a second chance at the package, they could try to get it through you. I'm serious, Samantha. Don't take risks. We'll be leaving when the weather allows. You should be safe once we're gone. I'll put together a more specific security plan for you this afternoon."

A security plan?

"What about the ... *package*?" She used their term for the Golden Horde components. "We don't have much security here—no surveillance, no keycard entry systems. Most doors aren't even locked. There might be a safe in Steve's office."

His lips curved in a grin that made her pulse quicken. "We'll keep it secure. Don't worry about that."

She waited for him to explain, but he didn't. "Right."

He reached for the doorknob. "Do you want to join me for supper?"

Warmth rushed into her cheeks.

What the hell was wrong with her? Was she so sexually deprived that attention from a good-looking man made her blush and messed with her head?

You're smarter than that.

"I'm going to get some coffee and then check on the telescope. I've missed an entire day of work." Yes, she was turning him down cold—until the moment she didn't. "But, yeah, I'll meet you there. Six?"

What had she just done?

"Sounds good. Thanks again. You might have saved millions of lives today." He opened the door, turned back. "You should get a medic to look at that cut."

Then he was gone, leaving Samantha to stare at the closed door.

THOR MET in private with Tower, Jones, and Segal for a quick debriefing, sharing in detail all that had happened so far.

Tower stared at him from the computer screen. "The Russian team is *there*? At Amundsen-Scott?"

Segal leaned in so Tower could see him. "I believe they were telling the truth, sir. We didn't have the time to run over to their plane to see whether it was functional. They were terrified—and willing to turn over their rifles. If they were telling the truth and we had left them to die, we'd be on the world's shit list right now."

"Understood." Tower's face was fixed in a frown. "Is the package intact?"

"No. The only way to remove it in the time available was to gut the unit."

Tower nodded. "What's your plan for keeping the contents secure?"

Thor had put some thought into this. "I gave the site manager my locked carry-on bag full of Legos and scrap metal from recycling to store in his office safe."

Segal and Jones chuckled, shook their heads.

"*Legos?*"

"They had some at the station shop. Legos are Danish, you know."

Tower ignored that last bit. "So, the carry-on is a decoy."

"Yes." Thor ignored Segal and Jones, who found the Lego thing funny. "I had to revise our original plan to take the Russian presence here into account. Our rooms, Dr. Park's room, and Hardin's office seem like the places they'll try to search first."

"Where is the package?"

"It's locked in the steel case, which is hidden in the ceiling of one of the empty berths across the corridor from ours. Segal used his lockpicking skills to gain entry. No one has any reason to enter, and no one knows the package is there apart from us. We installed motion-activated cameras there, as well as in our rooms. If anyone breaks in, the three of us will be notified on our phones and get an image of the intruder. Hardin placed the Russians in a different berthing area."

"What about Dr. Park's safety?"

"I've cautioned her against being alone with any members of the Russian party. She spends most of her time at the Dark Sector Lab, a kilometer away from the station. Her research partner died suddenly a few days before we arrived, so she's alone out there whenever she's working. I think one of us should be with her."

"Agreed. If our Russian friends are there to snatch this technology, she could be a target. That's true for all of you."

"We're all carrying concealed just in case, and we've got our two-way radios. I'll make sure Dr. Park gets a radio as well."

Knowing how easily they malfunctioned in extreme cold, he'd packed spares.

"Good work today. We'll get you home as soon as the weather allows."

The meeting was over, so Thor packed up the laptop and cord.

Jones stood, stretched. "I'm hungry."

"You're always hungry." Segal got to his feet, too. "I have a new appreciation for you tonight, Isaksen. I've never been that cold. It's *painful*. Sleeping in a tent in that weather? Hell, no."

They made their way back to their rooms so that Thor could stash the laptop and then walked upstairs to the galley, where people were lining up cafeteria-style for the evening meal. Most ignored them. Others shot them cold looks. Some of the women—and there weren't many— looked them up and down.

Yeah, that happened sometimes.

The scents of fried chicken and pizza made Thor's mouth water, reminding him that he hadn't eaten since breakfast. He glanced around for Samantha, saw she was ahead of them in line.

"Damn, that smells good." Jones grabbed a tray and started filling it.

"You'd think he hasn't eaten in a week," Segal joked. "Leave something for the people who work here, man."

Thor got the chicken, mashed potatoes, and salad, then saw Vasily get up from his table and head straight for Samantha, who now sat alone, waiting for them to join her. Forgetting to grab a fork or anything to drink, he carried his tray toward her.

Vasily veered off.

Thor sat beside Samantha, saw the bandage on her hand. "You saw the medic."

She spread a paper napkin on her lap. "Yes. Kristi, the station nurse, said you make a good field dressing."

"I've had some practice."

"I bet. Did you—"

"It's happening." Jason, the kid who liked to film people, walked up to the table, an apple in hand. "I knew you'd take the women. When do you leave again?"

Irritation flashed over Samantha's face. "Jason, you're out of line."

"They've been here a day, and you're already all over them. Just saying." Jason shifted his attention to Thor. "Antarctica is a sausage fest, and you guys make it worse."

Thor hadn't heard that phrase before. "Sausage fest?"

Jason laughed. "Lots of dicks. You know. *Sausage*. More men than women. It was hard enough getting laid before you guys showed up."

Samantha glared at him. "Most of us are here to do research. Not every interaction between men and women is sexual, Jason."

Jason snickered. "Especially not with *you*. The other guys say you never hook up with anyone. If a woman can't get laid in Antarctica—"

Thor shot to his feet, glared down at the kid, enraged, Samantha's words about being bullied still with him. "Apologize—*now*."

A hush came over the galley, heads turning their way.

Jones stood, too. "You need to watch your mouth, son."

Segal got to his feet, as well, a piece of buttered bread in his hand, his mouth full, his gaze fixed on the kid.

Jason looked from Thor to the others, took a couple of steps backward. "Sorry."

Then he hurried away with his apple.

Thor sat once more, taken aback at his reaction. He met Samantha's gaze. "You shouldn't have to put up with that."

She looked away, her cheeks flushed. "Jason's just an idiot."

Had Thor embarrassed her by making a scene?

"He's pouring water out of his ears."

"He's ... what?" She looked completely confused.

"You don't say that in English?"

"Not unless someone has literal water in their ears."

"It means that what he's saying isn't true. It's nonsense."

"Ah."

But Jones watched Thor, a grin on his face. "Did you see that, Segal? Damn! The Viking finally lost his cool."

It was then Thor realized he needed a fork and a beverage.

SAMANTHA WAITED outside the coatroom by the main entrance for Thor, who insisted that he or one of the other Cobra guys accompany her to and from the Dark Sector Lab. She needed to catch up on work and check the telescope. But what she really wanted to do was hide.

If a woman can't get laid in Antarctica—

Samantha cringed to think that Thor had heard those words. True, he'd confronted Jason and had seemed genuinely angry on her behalf. She was grateful for that. But he had witnessed it, as had everyone else in the galley.

It had been mortifying.

Sometimes, Samantha didn't understand the world. Only about fifty people in any given year got to spend austral winter here. It was an honor, and it came with a lot of work and responsibility. Who had time to think about getting laid?

You only say that because men don't pay attention to you.

She ignored that inner voice—or tried to.

She'd had two boyfriends—one in college and one in graduate school. The college boyfriend, Scott, had broken up with her a few weeks into their relationship by telling her he'd never really found her attractive. Nathan, her boyfriend in grad school, had turned everything into a competition—grades, research, relationships with professors. He'd broken up with her when she'd gotten a prestigious post-doc position at the University of Chicago, insisting that she'd only gotten the job because she was a woman and not because she'd earned it.

After that, Samantha decided she had better things to do than date.

She'd come here to work, to do ground-breaking research about relic light in the universe, not to meet men. She shouldn't care what that idiot Jason said or what anyone else thought about her. Even so, Jason's words had hurt.

She spotted Thor down the hallway. It wasn't hard with his white parka. He was also a lot taller than most men, and he walked with the kind of grace that came from being physically active.

He saw her, drew his hat over his head, his mask in his gloved hands. "I just heard that the pilot made it back to McMurdo."

"I'm so relieved to hear that. Ready?"

They put on their masks, pulled up their hoods, and walked out into the cold, making their way down the stairs to the ice. A faint aurora danced around the edge of the sky, a small breeze fluttering the flags that marked the path to the Dark Sector.

"I brought something I'd like you to carry with you until we leave." He drew a small two-way radio out of his pocket. "This way, you can reach me, Jones, and Segal, no matter where you are, day or night."

She took the device from him. "But I already have a radio."

"Yes, I know, but we're not on that frequency. I want you to be able to reach us in case of an emergency."

She slipped the radio into her pocket. "You truly believe I'm in danger?"

"I can't say for certain, but I want to be prepared. That's the most important part of any security operation—identifying potential risks and finding ways to mitigate them before anything happens."

That seemed logical.

"I feel very protected, so thank you."

"You're welcome."

For a short time, they walked without speaking, their boots squeaking on the ice, Thor's long stride making her work to keep up.

"What is the Three Hundred Club?" he asked out of the blue.

"It's about putting your body through three hundred degrees of temperature shift." Samantha had never seen the appeal of that. "First, you sit in a two-hundred-degree sauna and get hot. Then you leave the station naked except for boots, walk around the South Pole marker, and then head back into the sauna to warm up."

He chuckled. "That sounds fun."

"Why did you ask?"

"Some people are talking about doing it tomorrow night. I guess it's supposed to get below minus one hundred. We Cobra guys were invited to join in. Have you done it?"

"No way." Samantha laughed. "Patty did. My ancestors are Finnish—Park comes from Parkkonen—so I love the sauna. But streaking in the cold just sounds to me like a great way to get frostbite in sensitive places."

The idea of being naked in front of the entire staff didn't appeal to her either.

Thor chuckled. "If you're hot from the sauna, it takes a while to feel the cold."

"You're going to do it?"

"Yes."

She'd thought he was too focused on his job to do something so silly. But some part of her—the part that planned on watching—was excited about this.

Are you seriously going to gawk at his naked body?

Yes. Yes, she was.

They reached the stairs that led up to the SPT control room. She gave him a tour, explaining in basic terms the kind of research she did. "We're looking at relic light— light from shortly after the Big Bang—by scanning space for a certain kind of electromagnetic energy. My work focuses mostly on galaxy clusters."

He asked smart questions and understood more than she had expected, proof that he'd studied the sciences.

"Can we go up to the roof?"

He wanted to go outside again?

"Of course." She led the way.

He stared up at the sky, clearly in no hurry to get back indoors. "I've never seen so many stars. Even in Greenland, the stars were never this bright."

"The cold freezes the water vapor out of the air, and the atmosphere here is stable. That's why it's so clear. That's one reason we do so much astronomical research here."

He pointed with a gloved hand. "The Southern Cross. Musca over there. Tucana."

She was surprised—and impressed. "Where did you learn your southern constellations?"

"When I left Sirius, I found I couldn't go back to my old life. I traveled a lot. I spent some time backpacking in the Himalayas, Australia, and New Zealand. I met a Maori man who taught me how his people saw the sky. I tried to learn more."

He hadn't been able to go back to his old life.

What did that mean?

"I'd love to hear more, but I'm freezing my butt off."

He chuckled, the sound almost enough to warm her. "Let's get you back inside."

She stayed just long enough to check the readouts, but exhaustion from the day's ordeal caught up with her. Thor walked with her back to her room at the station, where she thanked him and wished him a good night. Then she brushed her teeth and crawled into bed. The last image in her mind as she drifted off was of Thor staring up at the stars.

7

T hor sat in the sauna's heat with Jones, Vasily, Hardin, and Kristi, the station nurse, all of them naked apart from their towels, their boots waiting outside the door. The warmth felt incredible after the day's frigid cold, loosening stiff muscles, releasing endorphins, making Thor sweat.

He had spent the day with Samantha at the Dark Sector lab, reading journal articles about the SPT and watching as she recycled the refrigerators that kept the telescope's detectors cold enough to maintain the necessary sensitivity. The technology fascinated him. But now it was time for something completely different, something more up his alley—pitting himself against the elements.

Segal had volunteered to stay indoors to keep a watch on the package. "Go freeze your balls off if you want. I've had enough cold on this mission."

A small crowd was waiting outside the sauna for them to exit, drop their towels, put on their boots, and head outside to the Pole marker and back.

Vasily scratched his hairy chest. "We Russians have a

long history of the *banya*—what you call *sauna*. It keeps men healthy and strong."

"Not just men," Kristi replied.

Thor hadn't missed the way she'd been looking at Jones.

"You Americans have so many women here. In winter, we have no women."

"How very evolved of you." Jones met Kristi's gaze.

Nå, for helvede.

Well, damn.

The attraction was mutual.

Thor hoped Jones had the sense not to get distracted. They hadn't come here to get laid. Their mission was to bring the Golden Horde technology back to the US and keep Samantha—Dr. Park—safe in the meantime.

Speaking of distracted...

Thor was fascinated by Samantha's explanation of how she used differences in the Cosmic Microwave Background to map distant galaxy clusters. He didn't fully understand the science, but he got the basic principles. Samantha had come alive while talking about her work, her pretty face lighting up, her reserve falling away.

"Am I boring you?" she'd asked.

"Not at all." He admired both her expertise and her passion.

As far as Thor was concerned, intelligence was fucking sexy.

"Hey, Viking." Jones elbowed Thor, bringing him back to the present. "Kristi asked where you got that big scar on your thigh."

"I fell on my own knife while on the sea ice in North-eastern Greenland as part of Sirius Dogsled Patrol." It had been a stupid accident, a tumble on his skis that had cost them hours of travel and put him at risk for infection. "I had to suture it myself."

Kristi studied it. "It looks like you did a good job. What are those scars on your wrists and forearms?"

"Dog bites." It had been a hazard of the job. "When one of the females on the sled team goes into heat, the males fight each other. I had to break it up."

"Ouch!"

"I have heard of this Sirius," Vasily said. "You are Danish then, yes?"

Thor met the man's gaze. "Yes."

Someone knocked on the door. "It's time!"

Thor stood, anticipating the thrill of stepping into the cold.

"Remember, men, cover your genitals with your hands once we get outside," Hardin said. "A dick can get frostbite pretty quickly at a hundred and two below. Kristi, you'll want to cover your, uh, chest. Also, don't run. The cold air will do a number on your lungs if you do."

Hardin pushed open the sauna door, and they walked out one by one.

Thor stepped into his boots, dropped his towel, and moved toward the door.

"Check out the sizeSituation too hot. We are being watched. Deal is off. There will be no further contact.

her moaned. "What about the six-packs?"

"How long are they staying?" asked yet another.

Giggles.

Had they never seen an adult male body before?

Nudity just wasn't a big deal in Thor's culture. People went nude on Danish beaches and in public parks all the time—senior citizens, pregnant women, little kids.

Samantha stood alone near the door, bundled into her

parka. Her gaze jerked from Thor's cock to his face, a rosy flush in her cheeks. "Be careful out there."

Thor couldn't help but smile, amused. "Thanks."

He followed Hardin outside, cupped himself with his hands, and hurried down the stairs to the ice, Jones and Kristi behind him. Steam rose off his body, the cold making his skin tingle. Cheering people in parkas and masks motioned them forward with flashlights, creating a guided path through the dark to their goal several hundred feet away—the ceremonial South Pole.

"This feels fantastic!" Kristi shook her head. "My hair already has icicles in it."

Thor kept a brisk pace, boots squeaking, his breath turning to ice crystals.

"I'm starting to feel the cold," Jones said. "How about you, Viking?"

"It's ..." he searched for the English word for *forfriskende*... "refreshing."

Jones laughed. "Would you listen to him?"

"What does your tattoo symbolize?" Kristi asked from behind him.

It took Thor a moment to realize she was speaking to him.

"It's just a raven. That's my middle name. *Ravn*."

Thor smiled up at the sky, the aurora blazing around them, the Milky Way stretching into the distance overhead. He wanted to absorb it all—the stunning beauty of the sky, the scent of the ice, the clean air, the sharp tingle of cold against his skin.

There ahead, stood someone waving a flashlight, the flags that surrounded their goal barely moving in the breeze. As they drew closer, Thor saw the marker—what looked like a barbershop pole with a silver ball on top.

The ceremonial South Pole.

Kristi cheered as they circled it and started back toward the station. "This is crazy. I've got frost on my pubes."

They walked faster on the way back, the heat from the sauna largely dissipated, the cold growing uncomfortable. Back to the station, up the stairs, and inside again.

They were welcomed back like heroes with cheers and applause.

Samantha stood just inside the door, worry on her face. She walked over to Thor, spoke quietly so no one would overhear. "It's Vasily. When you all left, he got dressed again and went downstairs toward your berthing area with the other Russians."

Thor grabbed his towel. "Stay here."

SAMANTHA TOOK OFF HER PARKA, draped it over her arm, waiting for Thor and Malik to step out of the men's changing room. She ought to have followed Vasily or at least asked him what he was doing. Instead, she'd stood there, watching him walk away in his towel.

Vasily isn't going to steal the components.

What would he do with them? It's not like he could run out the back door and thumb a ride to Moscow. He was likely stuck here until November, just like the rest of them. The most he could do was hide the package somewhere in the station and hope no one found it.

Thor emerged, wearing jeans and that navy-blue cable-knit sweater, towel in hand, radio clipped to his waistband. "I'll get you back to your room."

"What about Vasily?"

"I know exactly where he is." Thor held up his radio.

"Oh."

The two of them walked toward the second-floor AI berthing area, the image of him naked burned into her mind. She'd known he would be hot, but...

Damn.

He was a Nordic god come to life. Broad pecs. Muscular arms. A six-pack. Obliques. A huge, beautiful, uncircumcised dick. And then there was the rear view. A raven tattoo on his upper back, the tips of the bird's outstretched wings reaching his shoulders. The tight globes of his perfect ass.

The sight of him had put flutters in her belly, made her ache.

Forget it. He's not interested, and you have work to do.

She waited till they were out of earshot of the others. "Is everything okay?"

"Our Russian friends were outside our rooms having a friendly chat with Segal. It seems they got lost on their way to their berthing area."

"You don't believe that." She could tell from the tone of his voice.

"Do you?"

"No." It wasn't a big building. Different parts of the station had different color tiles on the walls making it hard to mistake one area for another. "You think they tried to steal the, uh, package?"

"I think they took advantage of the distraction to do some recon."

"Recon?"

"Reconnaissance." He explained. "Before anyone tries to take it, they have to figure out where it is and what obstacles stand in their way."

"Oh. Right." She clearly didn't think like a military guy. "I almost followed them, but I knew you'd be back soon."

"You did the right thing, waiting to tell me. I don't want you putting yourself in harm's way. You've done enough already."

Why his words left her feeling flustered, she couldn't say.

She changed the subject. "You did it. You're now a member of the world's most exclusive and insane club. How was it?"

He grinned. "It was good—inwigorating."

He'd gotten the *V* mixed up with a *W*.

"I think you mean 'invigorating.' With a *V* sound."

"Really?" Thor held the door for her as they moved from the hallway to the berthing area. "Invigorating."

"Patty said the same thing."

"And you've never thought to try it?"

A part of her had wanted to, but *no way* was she going to run around nude in front of everyone. "I guess I'm a little more self-conscious than the rest of you."

They reached the door to her room and stopped.

"That's too bad. It really is fun."

"If I had a body like Kristi's, maybe..." The words were out before Samantha could stop them.

Oh, God.

She had just bared her insecurities to him, which was a thousand times worse than being naked. She would have disappeared inside her room to wallow in humiliation, but he made no move to leave.

His gaze moved over her, a faint smile on those lips. "Kristi is pretty, but so are you. Trust me. From where I stand, Kristi doesn't have anything on you."

Samantha's cheeks grew warm. She stood there for a moment, staring up at him, her brain going blank, some part of her wishing he would kiss her.

Your key.

She fished it out of her pocket. "It's late."

"I hope I didn't make you uncomfortable just now."

She looked away. "No, I did that to myself."

He tucked a finger beneath her chin, lifted her gaze to his. "You've had a rough week, Samantha. Go easy on yourself."

There was no judgment in his eyes, only concern.

Some of her embarrassment melted away. "Thanks."

"What time should I meet you tomorrow?"

"I usually get breakfast at around seven. I try to get to the lab by eight."

"I'll meet you in the galley. And don't forget your radio. It won't do you a bit of good if you don't keep it with you at all times."

"Got it." She unlocked her door. "Goodnight, Thor—and thanks."

He gave her a smile that made her breath catch—and walked away.

She flicked on her light, locked her door behind her, and flopped onto her bed.

Good God.

How could she be so stupid?

She had a full-blown crush on Thor Isaksen.

THOR GOT into bed and closed his eyes, images of Samantha running through his mind. Samantha in tears at her friend's memorial service. Samantha looking terrified on the flight back from the crash site. Samantha concentrating as she did calibrations on the SPT. Samantha's face alight with passion when she talked about galaxy clusters. Samantha blushing like a teenage girl when he'd caught her checking out his cock.

She was a mass of contradictions. A razor-sharp mind and confident when it came to her field of study. Reserved and insecure when it came to her sense of herself as a woman. Was that the result of being bullied as a kid? Did she truly believe she wasn't attractive? That's not exactly what she'd said, to be sure, but she had implied it.

If I had a body like Kristi's, maybe...

Thor had been serious when he'd said Kristi had nothing on her. He'd seen Kristi, and she was sexy—sweet face, dark hair, light brown skin, round ass, full breasts with dark nipples. But he didn't need to see Samantha naked to know he'd find her sexy, too. Despite her layers and winter clothes, he could tell she was willowy like a dancer. Her breasts were small, and he loved the sweetness of small, delicate breasts.

Heat rushed to his groin.

Stop thinking about her breasts.

He needed to focus on his job, not Samantha. Tower had trusted him enough to place him in command of this operation, and he didn't want to fail.

He willed himself to think of something else.

Russerne. The Russians.

He'd left Samantha and walked back to his room to find them gone.

Segal had given him a quick update. "I heard them out here wondering which room was yours. When I confronted them and asked them why they'd backed out of ice streaking and what they were doing here, they said they'd changed their minds and had gotten lost on their way to their rooms. It's bullshit, of course."

"Of course." But Thor would rather see them here,

outside his room, than outside Samantha's. He was armed and trained for combat. She wasn't.

There was one other thing that struck him. Vasily knew about Sirius. Thor had never met anyone outside of Denmark or Greenland who knew what it was. That meant Vasily must have some military experience.

Or perhaps he was old KGB.

Thor would check in with Tower, bring him up to date.

He had just begun to drift off, a dream about the Antarctic sky and running naked coalescing in his mind, when the alarm on his phone went off.

He sat bolt upright, grabbed it, and was on his feet when he saw.

On his screen was a black-and-white image of a naked Jones undressing Kristi.

Thor reached for his radio. "Jones, this is Isaksen. Turn off your fucking camera."

He heard Kristi giggle through the wall, watched Jones on his screen as he walked over, dick swinging, and switched off the device.

The image on Thor's phone went black.

Hold dog kæft!

Fuck.

But that was just the beginning. A few minutes later, the soundtrack began.

"Oh, God, yes! Ahhhh!" Kristi's moans went on until Thor was tempted to pound on the wall or knock on the door. "Ahhhh! Fuck me! Oh, like that! Yes!"

Listening to the two of them fuck didn't do anything to cool his blood, his cock rock hard now. But no way was he going to get off to the sound of Jones getting it on.

Her cry was quickly followed by Jones groaning.

Great. They'd come. Now maybe Thor—and Segal, who

could surely hear this, too—could get some sleep. He would have to talk to Jones in the morning. It was one thing to get laid during downtime on the job. It was another to keep the rest of them awake while doing it.

Thor closed his eyes again. But thoughts of Samantha wouldn't leave him—and neither would his hard-on.

He took himself in hand and let himself imagine that they were alone in the Dark Sector Lab, peeling off each other's layers. He pulled the pencil out of her hair, let the blond strands fall around her shoulders. Then he bared and kissed those sweet, small breasts until she writhed and moaned.

He finished undressing her, kissing his way over her belly, caressing the flare of her hips, grasping the curves of her ass, tasting her. Then she undressed him, took his cock in hand until he ached for her. He sat in her chair, helped her straddle him, and buried himself inside her, letting her ride him until her head fell back and she cried out.

He sucked in a breath as he came, climax washing through him in a rush. But the sensual heat of his fantasy was all too quickly replaced by cold reality.

He cleaned the cum off his hand and belly with a tissue, closed his eyes, and fell asleep at last, his dreams full of Samantha.

8

Thor got up early and hit the gym to burn off fatigue and sexual frustration, going for a run on the treadmill and lifting weights. Then he took a quick shower and met with Tower from his room, bringing him up to date.

"They said they were lost, but I don't buy it."

"Neither do I. They were checking things out—the location of your rooms, how you'd respond, any potential security."

"Vasily, the one who speaks English, knew what Sirius was. When he overheard me mention it, he knew I was Danish. If we looked into his background, I'm sure we'd find ties to Russian intelligence, maybe the KGB."

"I already got the names of the Russian guests from Hardin, and we're running them by our contacts at the CIA and DHS. We'll let you know if anything pops." Tower reached toward his keyboard, shared his screen. "In the meantime, care to explain this?"

There was a photograph of Thor, naked, just before he'd stepped outside, Jones right behind him, dicks hanging out for the world to see. It was part of a blog post. "South Pole Adventures," by Jason Huger.

Den forbandet idiot. That fucking idiot.

Thor would deal with him later.

"Jones and I joined the Three Hundred Club last night, sir."

"That's what it says in the caption. What the fuck is that?"

Thor explained, making it clear that Segal had stayed by their rooms. "It doesn't hurt the mission to do what we can to fit in here and partake in their culture."

"No, I suppose it doesn't. And you're both okay—no frostbitten dicks?"

"We're good, sir. Any idea when you'll be flying us out?"

"It looks like we'll get a break in the weather in eight days, but that's still far enough out that the meteorologists are just guessing."

"Understood." Thor signed off and met Segal and Jones in the hallway, he and Segal sharing a glance.

Yeah, Jones had kept Segal awake, too.

Jones took one look at them and knew they were pissed. "Things got a little noisy last night. I hope we didn't keep you awake."

"You did—along with everyone else in this berthing area." Thor didn't hide his irritation. "No one cares if you get laid on your downtime, but be discreet, man. We're not welcome here, and last night did nothing to improve that."

Jones got a cocky grin on his face. "Can I help it if she enjoyed herself? Nurses, man. They know anatomy."

Segal glared at him. "Next time, tell her to keep it quiet. It's not like she can't control herself."

"Maybe I just blew her mind."

Segal snorted. "Do you think she carries on like that

when she gets herself off? Nah, man. When a woman makes that much noise, it's theater."

"Maybe that's how it is with you, but no woman has to act when she's with me."

"*Fuck.*" Thor swore under his breath. "Enough. Let's get breakfast."

The two ribbed one another—quietly—as they walked to the galley, where he found Samantha sitting with Kristi, who wore blue scrubs for her shift. Their heads were close together, Kristi speaking excitedly about something.

Thor had a pretty good idea what that might be.

Their conversation ended the moment Kristi saw them. Her face lit up in a smile, and she motioned to Jones to sit beside her.

"No embarrassing her," Jones whispered.

Thor shot him a look. "I wouldn't do that."

"No, but *he* might." Jones pointed to Segal, who rolled his eyes.

The three of them filled their trays—scrambled eggs, breakfast potatoes, toast, bacon, coffee—and joined the women.

Samantha's hair was down for the first time since Thor had met her, her pale blond strands hanging to the middle of her back. Thor shouldn't have noticed or cared—but he did. He wanted to touch it, to run his fingers through it.

She looked up but didn't quite meet his gaze. "Good morning."

"Good morning." He sat, sipped his coffee. "Did you sleep well?"

She nodded. "You?"

Thor met Jones' gaze. "Well enough."

Just then, Jason walked by, wearing his kitchen uniform, phone in his hand.

In one move, Thor stood and grabbed it from him. "Hardin told you to quit taking photos of people without consent. I'll give this to him when I see him later. We'll see what he has to say about your latest blog post."

The kid's face turned a furious shade of red. "Give it back!"

Then Lance, who was sitting at a nearby table, got to his feet. "Jason, it's your own damned fault. Hardin warned you. Don't you have more eggs to scramble?"

Jason glared at Lance and walked away. "Fucker."

Lance stepped forward, held out a hand. "I haven't introduced myself yet. Lance Barclay. I'm the winter IT guy. Sorry for how I acted when you first got here. I've been pretty torn up by Patty's death."

Thor shook his hand. "No worries. I understand."

"What was that about?" Samantha's gaze followed Jason back to the kitchen.

"He posted nude photos from last night." Thor didn't mind being seen naked, but he worked in global security. He didn't need his face all over the Internet.

"Nude photos?" Kristi pulled out her phone to look. "Hey, that's me! He posted naked photos of me! Jason, you ass! You need to take this post down—now! Shit. I need to go. See you later, Sam. You, too, Malik."

Jones watched her walk away, making Segal roll his eyes once more.

With Kristi gone, Thor went through the plan for the day. Segal, as the only Russian speaker, would get to know their new friends. Thor would accompany Samantha to the Dark Sector Lab this morning, while Jones joined her in the afternoon. This arrangement wasn't just about Samantha's security. It was about mission priorities. Thor needed to get some distance where Samantha was concerned, and Jones needed something to do besides Kristi.

It was time for all of them to focus on their jobs.

SAMANTHA HAD MADE a mental checklist of what she would say this morning. She needed to set things straight with Thor, restore her sense of dignity, and convince herself that she did *not* have a crush on him. But so far, she hadn't said anything, trudging in silence toward the Dark Sector Lab, Thor beside her.

It didn't help that Kristi had shared explicit details of her night with Malik—or that Thor was so damned good-looking. He'd walked into the galley, and her thoughts had scattered, attraction hitting her like a jolt of caffeine. She'd been able to see the outline of his pecs through his dark blue Henley, for God's sake!

Okay, maybe that had been her imagination. But who could blame her? The memory of his naked body was fixed in her mind.

Just start with the apology.

She drew in a breath. "I want to apologize. I've been struggling to cope with everything that happened this past week and have been out of sorts. I'm not usually as unprofessional as I was last night."

"You don't owe me an apology. Who said you were unprofessional?"

"Uh... Well, after what I said ...I've said a lot of stupid things since you arrived."

"Like I said, you've been through a rough time. Cut yourself some slack."

"Thanks for understanding." Next on her checklist was

mentioning her extra workload without Patty and her need to focus and not talk to him while in the lab.

She led the way up the stairs, unlocked the door, flicked on the lights, and began to remove her layers. "There's not a lot of things to do here, I'm afraid, especially now that Patty's gone. I should have suggested you bring a book so you won't be bored."

"You do what you need to do." He hung his parka by the door, tucked his mask in its pocket. "I don't need to be entertained. If there's one thing I'm good at, it's keeping myself occupied."

Okay, well, that had been easy.

"There are chairs in the break room, and you know your way around, so make yourself comfortable." She took off her parka and walked to her computer to check the detector readouts.

Everything was working fine—except for the light above the desk. Patty had called it their alien autopsy light. They had planned to replace the bulb, but they'd never gotten around to it. It wasn't something Samantha could do alone because the bulb was six feet long.

Maybe Thor could help.

She found him in the breakroom, making coffee. "Oh. Thank you."

"You're welcome." He handed her a mug, grinning as he read the words on the side. "'Astronomers do it in the dark.'"

Grief hit Samantha in the chest, an ambush of pain.

Samantha accepted it, poured in creamer, and stirred, her throat going tight. "This was Patty's favorite mug."

Thor watched her, his blue eyes warm with concern. "I'm sorry. I know what it's like to lose a friend."

Samantha took a sip, swallowed hard, willed herself not to fall apart, not to cry. "Did you lose friends in combat?"

He nodded. "Three guys I served with in Afghanistan, three good friends, were killed during my last deployment. We were tracking down a high-value target through an area with lots of opium poppy fields, and we hit an IED."

"I'm so sorry."

Thor's gaze dropped to his coffee, his brow furrowed, his jaw tight. "I was blown clear. I had some shrapnel wounds but nothing serious. But three of my friends were killed. Mads and Felix died instantly. Lars died while I held his hand. I lied to him. I smiled and told him everything would be okay."

Samantha's throat went tight again. "You tried to comfort him."

"Yeah." Regret clouded Thor's face. "There was nothing else I could do. Lars was ripped up. He was..."

"I'm sorry." Could she possibly be more thoughtless? "I shouldn't have asked. It's really none of my business. I don't mean to dredge up dark memories."

"It's okay." Thor smiled, a sad smile. "You didn't dredge up anything. That memory, the grief—it's always with me. But I've had time to make peace with it. You haven't."

Tears blurred her vision. "How do you make peace with it? I don't know why she died. I didn't get to say goodbye. She was okay one minute and then..."

Thor reached out, brushed a tear from Samantha's cheek. "Eventually, you quit asking all of those questions, the ones with no answers. Why them? Why not me? Could I have saved him? You accept that it hurts, that they're gone, and you keep going."

Samantha sniffed, nodded, grief a knot behind her breastbone. "Can you... Can you help me change a lightbulb?"

THOR CARRIED his dinner tray to the small conference room, where he, Segal, and Jones could speak without being overheard. He took a seat, the scent of spaghetti and meatballs making his mouth water. "Where's Dr. Park? I didn't see her in the galley."

"She took a tray to her room." Jones had taken over her security detail after lunch and had escorted her back to the station at the end of her shift. "She's pretty down about her friend's death. She wants to pack up the woman's things so they can be shipped back to her family in November."

Thor knew from experience how tough that was. When Lars, Felix, and Mads had been killed, he'd cleared out their lockers and gotten their personal belongings ready to send back to Denmark. It was one of the hardest things he'd ever done.

He dug into his spaghetti. "Segal, how did it go with your new friends today?"

"Their names are Vasily, Vlad, Dmitri, Oleg, Pavel, Iosef, and Maksim. I beat Vasily at pool and darts, and Oleg beat me at chess." Segal leaned in, a grin on his face. "Get this— chess is banned at the Russian bases down here. Some guy got so angry after losing a game that he put an ice pick through the winner's chest. It wasn't the first time that a sore loser stabbed someone over a chess game."

Jones winced. "An ice pick?"

Thor wasn't surprised. "I met with Hardin today about Jason and that damned blog post. Hardin told me the Russian scientists are heavy drinkers. You know what else he told me?"

Segal and Jones looked up from their plates.

"He says he got several complaints that one of us got

lucky last night and kept the entire berthing area awake. He made it clear that it can't happen again."

Jones shifted in his seat. "Yeah, man. I get it. Sorry."

Segal jabbed a meatball with more force than was necessary. "If it happens tonight, I'm knocking on your door, brother."

Thor waited until he'd finished chewing to ask his next question. "What else did Vasily have to say? I hope you talked about more than chess."

Segal pointed at Thor with his fork. "He asked a lot of questions about you. He asked about Cobra and Dr. Park, too."

"He was interrogating you?" Jones laughed. "Weren't you supposed to be interrogating him?"

"You'd be surprised what people give away when they think they control the conversation." Segal wiped his mouth on his napkin. "Vasily is dying to know what we took from the wreckage and why it was so important that we risked our lives for it. He's not stupid enough to ask directly, of course, but that was the subtext."

Jones looked confused by this. "Doesn't he know already? Isn't that why he was out there? If they had no clue what was on that satellite, why would they hack the satellite and bring it down? Why would they risk *their* lives to come after it? That makes no sense at all. Nah, man. He's playing you."

"Or maybe they truly *don't* know." Thor was just thinking aloud now. "Maybe they were tasked with retrieving it but weren't told what it was."

"That sounds like the Kremlin we all know and love," Segal joked.

"You know who else asked a lot of questions about you, Viking?" Jones chuckled. "Dr. Park wanted to know if you were single, whether you had kids, where you lived between missions, what it's like to work with you. She's got a thing for you."

Thor tried to ignore the part of him that liked this news. "You're imagining things. She's just going through a hard time right now."

"Hard time or not, she likes you."

Segal changed the subject. "Any word from Tower about when we fly out?"

Thor shared what Tower had told him. "Make yourselves at home because we could be here for a while. Worst-case scenario, we won't be leaving till November."

Segal narrowed his eyes. "You like that idea, don't you?"

Jones took another bite of spaghetti. "There *is* something beautiful about it. I've never seen a sky so full of stars."

They finished eating and carried their trays back to the dish pit.

"I'll catch up with you both later." Thor started toward the hallway.

"Where are you going?" Segal called after him.

"I want to check on Dr. Park and see how she's doing."

9

Samantha stood in the center of Patty's room, tears filling her eyes. "How am I supposed to do this? How am I supposed to say goodbye to you?"

Patty had strung fairy lights around the room to brighten things up, her walls covered with images from space. The Horsehead Nebula. The Whirlpool Galaxy. The Milky Way. The Milky Way photo had a pin poked into it in the Earth's approximate location with a tag that read, "You are here."

Academic journals. A laptop. Cell phone and computer chargers. An unopened bottle of Tylenol Patty had just bought from the store to help with cramps. Lip balm. An empty bottle of wine beside the bed—perhaps Patty's last bottle of wine.

Artifacts of a life.

"You should still be here, Patty." Samantha drew in a breath, exhaled.

She'd brought a couple of empty cardboard boxes up from the LO Arch—the Logistics Arch. Most of this would go home to Patty's family, but some would go to the shrine in the ice tunnels, while the rest ended up on the Skua table, where people swapped and scavenged gear. Patty would want that.

Samantha started on the drawers, tucking Patty's panties and bras into a box and setting her boots, socks, and long underwear aside for Skua, along with the rest of her cold-weather gear. Next, she packed the contents of Patty's small desk—pens, sticky notes, earbuds, lip balm.

There, in one of the drawers, she found it.

Patty's journal.

Samantha ran her fingers over the leather cover with its engraving of the Copernican model of the solar system. Patty had kept a journal for as long as Samantha had known her, taking time every night to write in it before going to bed. During grad school, she sometimes read what she'd written to Samantha—limericks about annoying professors, thoughts about her work, accounts of the fun they'd had together. Patty had filled at least twenty journals, all of them placed neatly on her bookshelves in the apartment in Chicago.

Samantha sank to the floor, hugged the journal, unable to hold back her tears, a gaping hole in her chest.

"Samantha?"

Samantha gasped, found Thor standing in the doorway. She got to her feet, set the journal aside, wiped her tears away. "Sorry, I—"

"Hey, Come here." He drew Samantha into his arms, held her. "It's okay to cry. Patty was a good friend. Losing her hurts."

Samantha relaxed into his embrace, some part of her desperate for the comfort he offered, his words bringing a fresh rush of tears. And for a time, they stood there, Samantha weeping, her cheek against his chest.

She drew back. "I got your shirt wet."

He glanced down. "That's the closest it's come to being washed in a while."

She laughed, reached for a tissue, wiped her eyes. "We do have a laundry room, you know. You get to do one load a week while you're here."

"I just came to see whether I could help."

"You already have." She glanced around them. "You could take down the fairy lights. You can probably reach them without standing on a chair."

"On it." He reached up and carefully removed the strands.

"I think I'll put them with the rest of the Skua stuff."

"Skua? Aren't those birds?" The confusion on his face made her smile.

"We have a Skua table. People give stuff away, swap things, and leave things for the next people who arrive. We call it the Skua table because real, live skuas are such scavengers."

Thor nodded as if he understood, his lips curving in a smile. "That's clever. But you should keep the lights. You said she made your life brighter. These lights could be a symbol of that. I could put them up for you."

Samantha stopped where she stood, touched to her core that he'd heard her, that he'd understood. "I ... I hadn't thought of that. Thank you. I like that idea."

He set the lights aside and began taking down the photos. "What do you want to do with these pictures?"

"We should put one of them in her shrine and send the others to her family."

A knock at the door.

Lance stuck his head in, his gaze shifting from Samantha to Thor. "You ask *him* to help but not me?"

She opened her mouth to answer, but Thor cut her off. "She didn't ask. I came to check on her and volunteered."

Lance walked in. "What are you doing with Patty's stuff?"

"Most of it is going home to her family. They're the rightful owners now. I'll put some of it out on the Skua table. Do you want to pick something for her shrine?"

"Where's her journal?" Lance glanced toward the desk. "I want that."

Samantha reached for it, held it against her chest. "That belongs to her family."

Lance tried to take it from Samantha. "I want to read what she wrote about me."

"You can't do that." Samantha turned her body away from him, kept the journal beyond his reach. "Her private thoughts are her business, not yours. The fact that she's gone doesn't change that."

"Oh, come on!" Lance reached for it again. "She didn't keep anything from me."

"But she didn't let you read her journal, did she?" She saw the flare of irritation on his face and knew she was right.

"What gives you the right to act as her executor?"

Thor came up behind Samantha, his presence making Lance take a step back. "Samantha was Patty's best friend. She's known her longer than anyone else here. *That* gives her the right."

"Patty and I were lovers. That has to count for something, even here on station. I feel like I'm being erased from her life." Lance grabbed a small silver ring off Patty's shelf— the ring with the horseshoe that she'd worn on her pinky finger. "I'm taking this."

Thor blocked Lance's attempt to leave. "Samantha?"

"That's okay. He can have it."

Thor stepped aside, watched him go. "Is he always an asshole?"

"No. Just since Patty died."

~

THOR WATCHED as Samantha carefully arranged Patty's belongings on the Skua table alongside other items people had given away—electric razors, gloves, socks, hats, earbuds, unopened toiletries.

Samantha stepped away from the table. "Now, she can still be a part of life down here, even if the people who end up with her things never knew her."

"That's a good way to think of it."

Vasily and four of his friends walked by, probably on their way to the Bi Lounge, Vasily's gaze fixing on Samantha.

He stopped. "Good to see you, Sam. I am sorry about Patty. Who would think that one so young would die?"

Samantha crossed her arms over her chest—a protective posture. "Thank you, Vasily."

"You must join me sometime for a drink in her memory." He held up the bottle of vodka in his left hand.

"I would like that." Samantha watched them walk away. "I would never have imagined that he'd be involved in something like this. Vasily, a spy? We had so much fun with him and the others on station at McMurdo."

"Most spies don't seem like spies."

Samantha looked up at him. "Have you met real spies?"

"Yes—a few." Holly Andris and Gabriela Marquez, both Cobra employees, had once worked for the Central Intelligence Agency. Elizabeth Shields had been an Agency counterterrorism analyst. "If you met them, you would have no idea that they'd once worked for the CIA."

"Wow." Samantha gaped at him. "You've led a more interesting life than I have."

That made Thor laugh. "I don't know about that. Mapping distant galaxies, working at the South Pole—that seems pretty interesting to me."

They walked back to Patty's room, where two taped and labeled boxes waited to be moved into storage.

"I had planned to put these down in the LO Arch, but what if someone finds them? I don't want Lance taking Patty's journal."

Thor wouldn't put it past Lance to steal it. He'd already tried to grab it from Samantha's arms twice. But Thor knew how to handle this. "I can keep them secure. I'm good at that, you know."

Flirter du med hende? Are you flirting with her?

Maybe he was.

This afternoon when he'd held her, he'd meant only to comfort her. She was grieving, and she was more or less alone with fifty people she didn't know well, people who, from what Thor could see, weren't going out of their way to show her sympathy.

But then she'd rested her cheek against his chest, relaxing into him. Damn, it had felt good. She was soft in the right places and smelled sweet, her hair like silk beneath his hands. He hadn't wanted it to end.

You're an idiot, man.

Samantha was vulnerable. She was grieving. The last thing she needed was to get physical with a guy who'd be leaving as soon as Tower could land a plane.

She's interested in you, too, and you know it.

Yes, but he didn't have to act on that.

She smiled, light chasing away the grief in her eyes. "Security is your thing."

PAMELA CLARE

"Exactly. We can take her belongings back to the States when we fly out and make sure her family gets them."

"You would do that?" She seemed surprised.

"Of course."

"That means so much to me. I'm sure her parents will appreciate it, too."

They carried the boxes to Thor's room, the motion-detector camera setting off the alarm on his phone. Thor set the boxes on his bed and canceled the alarm. Jones and Segal would see it was him and not come running.

"You've got video surveillance in here?" She stared up at the camera.

"Don't share that fact with anyone, okay?"

"Right."

Later, when Jones or Segal was there to watch his back, Thor would lock the boxes in the other room with the case of components. Lance wouldn't find them there.

"What do you say we go put up the fairy lights in your room?" Thor was grasping now, trying to find reasons to stay near her.

"I'd like that."

They went back upstairs to Samantha's room, where Thor, under her direction, hung the lights along the ceiling line, fixing them in place with push pins. He had to climb onto her bed on his knees to reach that part of the wall.

He jumped to the floor. "Okay. Light them up."

Samantha plugged them into the outlet behind her desk then hurried over to the door to switch off the lights. "I love it."

The little LED lights weren't bright, but they cast a cheery glow over the room, their light playing over the features of Samantha's face.

Oh, he was tempted to kiss her, so tempted.

You're out of your mind.

He hadn't come here for that.

She looked into his eyes. "Thanks, Thor. Facing this would have been so much harder without your help. And thanks for keeping her things safe."

"You're welcome." Because he couldn't stop himself, he kissed her on the cheek.

But at the last second, she turned her head, threw her arms around his neck, and kissed him right on the mouth.

Hell, yes.

It was a tentative kiss, little more than a peck on the lips. But then Thor took control, drawing her hard against him, attraction flaring into desire as he got a feel for her. The heat of her body against his. The timid touch of her tongue. Her sigh when his tongue returned the caress and his mouth claimed hers at last.

God, she was sweet.

Thor hadn't planned this. He had no idea where it was going, but he didn't care. Kissing her was—

"Isaksen, this is Jones."

For helvede. Damn it.

Thor broke the kiss, looked into Samantha's eyes. "We're not finished."

"Isaksen, you copy?"

He yanked his radio off his waistband. "Isaksen here."

"Hardin wants to see you right away—both you and Dr. Park."

SAMANTHA WALKED beside Thor down to the office wing, her lips still tingling, excitement shivering through her. She'd done it. She'd surprised them both. She'd kissed him. She wasn't usually that brave with men.

He hadn't pushed her away. Instead, he'd kissed her back.

It had been as amazing as she'd hoped it would be, the kind of kiss she'd fantasized about but never experienced. He hadn't rushed her, instead taking his time, his body hard against hers, his arms strong around her.

Now, he walked beside her, awareness stretching between them even though they weren't touching, his words echoing through her mind.

We're not finished.

God, she hoped not. She wasn't sure why Steve wanted to see them, but she hoped she and Thor would pick up where they'd left off afterward.

Someone was practicing in the music room, chords of electric guitar drifting down the hallway. Up ahead, Ryan and a couple of his firefighter buddies left the B1 Lounge, probably heading to bed. It was getting late.

She followed Thor into Steve's office, found Steve sitting in his office chair, arms crossed over his chest, his expression dark. He didn't acknowledge them at first but sat, staring at nothing. He looked distressed.

When he said nothing, Samantha said his name. "Steve? Are you okay?"

"You wanted to see us?" Thor asked.

He looked more upset than Samantha had ever seen him, his jaw tight. "I just heard from Katherine Reyna. She's the Special Deputy US Marshal on station at McMurdo. She had some news you'll want to hear."

Samantha's thoughts jumped to the pilot who'd flown them to the crash site, but he'd made it safely back to McMurdo. It couldn't be that. The Russians, then?

"Patty's body made it back to the US. Her family met her at the airport."

Samantha's heart hurt for them. "I can't imagine how hard that was."

"Yeah, well, it gets harder."

Her stomach knotted.

What the hell did that mean?

Steve continued. "Her family didn't want to wait for the coroner's office and paid for an independent autopsy. The results came back a few hours ago. Patty didn't die of natural causes. The medical examiner ruled it a homicide. Methanol poisoning."

"She was ... She was *murdered*?" The blood seemed to drain from Samantha's head, her knees going weak, the room tilting on its axis.

Strong arms caught her. "Hardin, get up. Move!"

Thor settled her in Steve's chair, knelt beside her. "Put your head between your knees. Just breathe, Samantha."

He stroked her hair, his face close to hers. "In. Out. That's good."

Steve began to speak again, but Thor stopped him.

"Whatever you need to say can wait until she's had a chance to recover."

"Should we take her to medical?"

Samantha shook her head, slowly sat upright. "No. I'm okay."

But she wasn't. Not really. Someone had killed Patty. Someone had poisoned her, stolen her life. Her death hadn't been a random tragedy. It had been a deliberate act.

Thor stood, a hand resting reassuringly on her shoulder.

"W-who could have done this? Who would want to hurt Patty?"

Steve shook his head. "I don't know. But Reyna wants

you to investigate, Isaksen. She can't make it here to do it herself, so she wants you to be her eyes and ears. She wants to deputize you and your men."

Thor doubted Cobra would consent to that. "We're not detectives."

"You guys are the closest thing to law enforcement we have on station."

But Samantha's mind raced, her thoughts scattered. "Methanol poisoning? Methanol has two carbon atoms. Ethanol has one. If I'd gotten to her sooner... If we'd known what it was..."

She lowered her head to her knees again, breathed, her body trembling.

Thor's hand moved up and down her spine. "Is there anything else Dr. Park should know? I'd like to get her back to her room so she can rest."

"The NSF is asking that we put certain rules in place here on station, but that's something for us to discuss. I don't think Sam needs to be a part of it."

Thor knelt beside her again. "When you're up for it, Samantha, I'm going to walk you back to your room, okay?"

She nodded, sat up again, her hands gripping the arms of the chair. "I'm sorry."

"Stop apologizing," Thor said. "You haven't done anything."

She slowly got to her feet, cleared her throat. "Thanks, Steve. I'm sorry you had to be the bearer of bad news."

Steve ran his hands through his hair, weariness lining his face. "I've never had to share news like that before. We'll have a staff meeting tomorrow morning at nine. Isaksen, let's talk after you get her settled."

Samantha seemed to be trapped in a nightmare as they left Steve's office and moved down the corridor to the main hallway and back toward her room. Thor stayed beside her, his hand resting in the middle of her back. People shot her curious glances, but she barely noticed.

They reached her door. She fumbled in the pocket of her jeans for her keys then struggled to get the key into the lock.

"Let me." Thor took over, opened the door for her, and followed her inside, the fairy lights still on. "Why don't you lie down?"

She kicked off her shoes, climbed into bed, and sank back onto her pillow. "You aren't leaving, are you?"

"No." He called to Malik and Lev on his radio. "Meet me at Samantha's room. Segal, bring a surveillance kit. Jones, bring Kristi."

Someone here—someone they all trusted—had killed Patty.

It was almost too much to absorb.

But the next thought sent ice through her blood.

What if they killed again?

10

Thor stayed with Samantha while Kristi took her vitals and asked her a few questions, Jones and Segal standing outside her door. His priority was getting Samantha settled for the night and making sure she was safe.

"I'm fine. Really, I am. I'm just upset about Patty. I packed her things."

"Your blood pressure is still a bit low. Have you ever fainted before?"

"I didn't faint. I just…"

"Uh-huh." Kristi clearly wasn't buying that.

Thor had told Samantha not to give Kristi the whole story—not yet. He wanted to check in with Tower and the Deputy US Marshal at McMurdo and meet with Hardin before letting the news out. Until then, all anyone needed to know was that Samantha was upset after packing up Patty's things and that she'd had a dizzy spell.

"I think you're exhausted and grieving and have had a tough day, but if you have any other symptoms—headache, chest pain, difficulty breathing—I want you to buzz Decker or me right away." Kristi reached into the medical bag she'd brought and pulled out a blister pack of pills. "Here are a few Xanax. Take one at bedtime. They might make you dizzy, so don't take them during the day, okay?"

Samantha nodded. "Thanks."

Kristi turned to Thor. "Are you staying with her for a while?"

"Yeah."

"Call me if you need anything—or send Malik."

Thor waited until Kristi was gone. "I'd like your permission to set up surveillance in your room—the same kind of surveillance you saw in mine. It's a motion-activated camera, so if anyone enters while it's on, it will alert you—and us."

"You think the killer will come for me?"

She looked so shattered at that moment that Thor wanted to hold her. Instead, he took her hand. "I'm not saying that anyone's after you. I just want to keep you safe."

She nodded. "Okay. Thanks. Sure. Just tell me how it works."

There wasn't room for Jones and Segal in the room with him, so he took the surveillance kit from Segal and set it up. "I think I'll put the camera here. That way, you can have it on at night without setting it off every time you roll over. I want you to feel safe so that you can sleep."

"Someone killed Patty. I just can't believe it."

"It's a lot to take in." He couldn't blame her for being overwhelmed by it all. "We'll do our best for her—I promise."

He showed Samantha how to arm the camera and deactivate it, and then he synced it with her phone and theirs. "Remember not to tell anyone about this—not Kristi, not Lance, not even Hardin."

"Okay." She sat there, smartphone in hand, as if she

didn't know what to do next.

"Why don't I step outside so you can put on your pajamas? You go brush your teeth and do whatever else you need to do before bedtime. I'll get water for you, and you can take that Xanax. How does that sound?"

She got to her feet, looked up at him, a sad smile playing on her lips. "Somehow, I don't think this is part of your job description."

"Keeping you safe is absolutely part of my job, but the rest of it..." He reached out, ran a knuckle over the silky curve of her cheek. "I hate to see you hurting."

He left her to change, joining Jones and Segal in the hallway. "She's getting ready for bed. As soon as we get her settled, we need to talk."

"And then you'll tell us what the *hell* is going on?" Jones asked.

Segal answered for him. "That's the idea."

Looking exhausted, Samantha stepped out of her room wearing a white cotton tank top and pink pajama bottoms with red hearts on them, slippers on her feet, a small bag of toiletries in her hand. "Hey."

"Dr. Park."

"Ma'am."

It was the first time Thor had seen her wearing something other than bulky sweaters. He'd been right—she was willowy, just like a dancer. She had gentle curves in all the right places, her nipples pressing against the fabric of her shirt, her waist narrow, her blond hair hanging down her back.

By the time she returned, he had a cold bottle of water for her. He followed her into her room, handed her the water. "For the Xanax."

She swallowed the pill, set the water aside. "What

happens now?"

"You sleep. We'll talk about the rest of it tomorrow." He watched as she climbed into bed. Then he armed her surveillance camera. "Goodnight. Sleep well."

"Thanks, Thor. Today would have sucked a lot more without you."

"You're welcome." Thor stepped out into the hallway again, checked to make sure her door was locked. He lowered his voice so as not to be overheard. "Patty didn't die of natural causes. She was poisoned. Methanol. Her death was ruled a homicide."

"Holy shit."

"Oh, fuck."

"The US marshal stationed at McMurdo wants to deputize us and have us spearhead an investigation here, to be her eyes and ears."

Jones stared at him. "Tower will never go for that. We're not Sherlock Holmes."

"How much does she believe we can do in just a few days?" Segal asked.

"I don't know, but Hardin wants our help, too. I'll check in with Tower tomorrow first thing and bring him up to date. In the meantime, nothing about our mission has changed. We keep the package and Dr. Park safe."

SAMANTHA STARED up at her ceiling, waiting for the Xanax to kick in and grateful for the men who stood on the other side of her door. Like everyone else, she hadn't wanted the Cobra guys to come. She had worried that their presence would be disruptive to life on station. Now, she was glad they were here.

She couldn't imagine how this felt to Thor and his men. They'd come down here to do one job, and were now being asked to do another. Even so, Thor had stayed cool through all of it—getting the news, helping Samantha when she'd almost passed out, setting her up with a security camera, getting Kristi to check on her.

They only take men who can keep their heads in a crisis.

Well, Samantha believed that.

But Thor wasn't some detached, ice-cold automaton. When she'd kissed him, his reaction had been immediate and red-hot. It had been the best, sexiest kiss of her life. He barely knew her, and still, he'd been so kind to her, helping her pack Patty's things, putting up the fairy lights, making her a priority when he surely had more important things to do.

I know you're hurting.

She wouldn't have expected compassion like that from a military man. Then again, what did she know about military men? Apparently, nothing.

Oh, Patty, who did this to you?

Samantha ran through the staff, one by one, but that was too much like counting sheep, her thoughts unraveling as the Xanax finally kicked in.

THOR DIDN'T SLEEP WELL, his dreams shifting restlessly from Patty's murder to kissing Samantha. He woke at five with a hard-on and dragged his ass out of bed for a conference with Javier Corbray, Tower, and Elizabeth Shields, Cobra's top intel analyst. He'd already spoken with Tower last night, bringing him up to date before going to bed.

Shields' strawberry-blond hair somehow looked immaculate even though it was midnight in Denver. "Did you get any sleep?"

Thor could function pretty well on four or five hours. "Enough."

Tower looked as clean-shaven and pressed as ever. "That's why we have coffee. Corbray, are you there?"

Javier Corbray, a former Navy SEAL, was the company's other owner.

His face appeared on the screen. "I spoke with the DUSM at McMurdo—Reyna. Normally, we wouldn't take on something like this. We supply security. We don't do investigations. But she's right when she says there is no one else. Apparently, Hardin offered to take it on, but she's not confident in his abilities as a site manager to handle something like this, especially not when he has friendships with people on station."

That made sense. "So, now we're deputy US Marshals?"

Corbray nodded. "You'll be staying until the situation is resolved."

Thor had thought long and hard about how to get started on an investigation last night. "We don't have access to DNA tests or fingerprinting or any other forensic tools. There's no surveillance, so we've got no video evidence. We'll be asking people questions and relying on them to tell the truth. I seriously doubt that the person who poisoned Dr. Holcomb is going to confess."

Shields took over. "It's more complicated than you know. I've been on the phone with the medical examiner who did Dr. Holcomb's autopsy. I wanted to get the file for you because those details could be important. According to the medical examiner, the time it would take someone to die of acute methanol poisoning falls into a range that overlaps with the time of the satellite hack."

Thor stared at the image of Shields on his screen. "Then it's likely that whoever hacked the satellite is here and that this person is also the killer."

Shields stifled a yawn. "We know the hack came from south of the Antarctic Circle, and we know that Dr. Holcomb died the next morning from a poison that had to have been in her system for a while. It could be a coincidence, but I don't think so."

Thor didn't believe in coincidences. "What kind of skill set would a person need to hack a US military satellite?"

Shields was an expert on hacking. "He or she would need to be a top-shelf computer-systems expert with programming and networking skills and knowledge of military satellites and different hacking software. This person would also need access to a sophisticated computer setup with a fast satellite connection. This isn't something that the average geek could do from the station's computer lab."

That narrowed it down.

But Thor had another question. "Why would anyone commit murder in a closed environment like this one? It's not like someone could walk in off the street and kill her. There are forty-nine suspects. The killer would have to know we'd catch them eventually."

Shields raised an eyebrow. "Maybe, but you just told me there's no law enforcement, no surveillance, and no forensic technology there. Perhaps the killer was counting on that."

"How was she poisoned? Did the medical examiner say?"

"She probably ingested it."

Tower's face reappeared on the screen. "Methanol is tasteless, odorless, and colorless. In an alcoholic drink, it would be undetectable."

Thor knew it was used as a fuel source, a solvent, and an

antifreeze, so there was probably a lot of it on station.

"I've never done anything like this before. How do I get started?" He didn't have a problem admitting when he was in over his head.

Shields, who'd helped catch the man who'd murdered her husband's best friend in Glasgow last year, gave him a to-do list that started with interrogating everyone on station. She promised to scan the autopsy report and get it to him before she went to bed. Tomorrow, she would begin the long process of doing background checks on every person on station.

"Just watch your six, okay? We can't fly in on a helicopter to save your asses. Whoever killed her doesn't want to be found. The moment the three of you start asking questions, you could become targets."

"We'll be careful."

They had no choice.

In Antarctica, there were so many ways to die.

SAMANTHA ATE her breakfast in the small conference room, doing her best to remember Patty's last day, her brain still a little fuzzy from the Xanax.

"We recycled the fridges that morning and did some basic maintenance in the afternoon. We walked back to the station together and ate dinner in the galley. Lance sat with us—and Kristi. Then Patty and Lance left, and I went to my room to read. That would have been about ten o'clock."

Thor wrote down what she'd said. "Did she seem worried or upset about anything? Did she argue with anyone?"

God, had Samantha really kissed him?

Samantha took a sip of coffee, tried to focus. "Not that I saw, and I was with her most of the day. Well, except... But that's stupid."

"What?"

"Kazem asked her out a few times, and she turned him down. A few nights before she died, he showed up at her room, demanding to know if she'd refused to date him because he's Muslim. She told him she was already in a relationship and tried to close the door, but he stuck his foot inside to stop her. When she told him to knock it off, he left her alone, but that startled her."

Thor wrote that down, too. "Did he threaten her?"

"She didn't mention it if he did."

"Did you see her drinking the night before you found her?"

Samantha nodded. "We all split a bottle of wine over dinner that she'd bought from the store here. I drank it, too. She and Lance might have taken what was left to her room with them after dinner. I'm not sure. There was an empty wine bottle on her desk, the last bottle we shared with her. I set it aside for her shrine."

Then it hit her.

She got to her feet. "Come with me."

He stood, too. "Where are we going?"

"My room. There's a test I want to try. Do you have a lighter?"

"No, but I can borrow one."

They carried their trays from the conference room to the dish pit. Samantha grabbed a soup spoon from the galley while Thor stopped in the kitchen to borrow a lighter. Then they made their way to Samantha's room in silence.

Thor closed her door behind him. "What kind of test is this?"

"This is the box of stuff I set aside for her shrine." She pulled out the empty wine bottle, shook it, relieved that there was still a little left in the bottom. "I'm going to pour the dregs into the spoon. You light it on fire. If it's ethanol—regular wine—it will burn blue. If it burns yellow, it's contaminated by methanol."

She poured the last of the wine into the soup spoon, held it steady while Thor flicked the lighter.

The alcohol went up in a bright yellow flame.

"Oh, my God." Samantha stared, chills skittering along her spine. She hadn't wanted to believe it, but it was true. Someone had poisoned Patty. "But why am I still alive? Why are Lance and Kristi alive? We all drank this same wine."

"Maybe the methanol was added later—or maybe it's a different bottle with an identical label."

The flame sputtered out, but not before Thor snapped a photo of it with his phone. Then he grabbed a tissue from her desk and took the bottle from her. "Don't touch this. It's now evidence—our only evidence. I'll put it in a safe place."

But Samantha was still reeling. The thought that someone Patty had trusted had given her poisoned wine made Samantha sick. Death in the guise of friendship.

It was too hideous to contemplate.

"Do you know anyone on station with the computer skills needed to hack a military satellite?"

Samantha gaped at Thor. "You think her murder had something to do with that?"

"The time range for when she ingested the methanol overlaps with the time the satellite was hacked."

"Oh, God." This was all too surreal, too terrible. "Lance is our IT guy. Patty started in computer science. But I don't know the others' backgrounds. You'd have to look at personnel records."

"We're working on that." Thor moved toward the door, the bottle still in hand. "I'd like your help in the staff meeting here in a few minutes."

"Of course."

"Watch people's expressions. See how they react to the news that Patty was murdered. Jones, Segal, and I will be watching, too, but you know the people here better than we do. Until now, the killer might have hoped or believed they'd gotten away with this. This announcement is going to make someone very nervous."

"I'll do my best." She walked with Thor to the B1 Lounge, unable to shake a sense of dread.

Until yesterday, the station had felt like home, an oasis of warmth and life at the bottom of the world. But Patty's murder had shattered her sense of safety.

She sat toward the front of the room, Thor standing behind her, Malik and Lev beside him. People drifted in, cups of coffee or tea in their hands, curiosity on their faces.

Lance sat beside Samantha, stubble on his jaw, his salt-and-pepper hair damp from a shower. "Any idea what this is about?"

Samantha was still irritated about his actions last night. "It's about Patty."

"Sorry about last night." He held up Patty's ring. "I shouldn't have grabbed this, and I shouldn't have tried to take her journal from you."

"I appreciate the apology. Keep the ring. She cared about you."

Lance closed his fist around it. "Thanks."

Vasily and his crew drifted in, looking like they'd had too much to drink and too little sleep. He went to stand at the back and waved to her.

She had a hard time waving back. If they were involved

in hacking the satellite, that would make them partly culpable for Patty's murder.

"That's everyone." Hardin walked to the front of the room. "Yesterday, we got word that the medical examiner ruled Patty's death a homicide. Methanol poisoning."

Gasps. Shocked faces. Whispers.

Samantha's gaze moved over the faces, saw nothing but shock. Kazem. Charli. Jason. Ryan. Decker. Wei. The metal-working guys.

Kristi stared wide-eyed at Samantha. "Oh, my God!"

Lance leaned closer. "Did you know? Is this why Kristi gave you a sedative?"

Samantha ignored his question. "Shh. I'm listening."

"In response, the NSF and the US Marshal Service have asked our security friends from Cobra to investigate. I've assured them they'll get your full cooperation. This morning, they were deputized by the Special Deputy US Marshal at McMurdo. This gives them full law-enforcement authority on station. Do you want to say something?"

Thor nodded. "We'll be asking you all some questions in the coming days. In the meantime, the NSF has put together a list of new regulations for the station. No more alcohol sales. Curfew at ten each night. No one in the ice tunnels or service arches who doesn't work there."

"Curfew?" Jason blurted. "Why a curfew?"

Thor didn't bother to explain. "One of you—someone sitting in this room *right now*—murdered Patty. You gave her this bottle of wine after poisoning it with methanol. Yes, we've tested it. If any of you saw or heard anything unusual, please tell us. Patty was your friend and colleague. Help us catch her killer."

11

I f Thor had ever felt unequal to a task, it was now. He was used to acting when there was a crisis, not sitting around and talking. Give him a blizzard, a dog fight, an aggressive polar bear, his sled falling through sea ice, an enemy pointing a rifle at his head, an incoming grenade. He could handle those things.

But a murder investigation?

They knew how Patty had been poisoned, but they had no idea who the killer was or what exactly had driven that person to take her life. Shields had cautioned him against making assumptions—or excluding anyone, including Samantha.

"Don't share your progress with anyone. People living in a situation like this one develop close friendships. Everyone trusts everyone. Anything you say could get passed on to the killer."

"I understand."

He, Segal, and Jones had divided up the staff and had interrogated every person on station, asking them all the same questions, recording their answers and taking notes.

There had been a few confessions. One of the fuelies—a guy in his forties—was fucking around on his wife, who was back home, with Analise Weber, a kitchen worker in her twenties. The guy who ran the aquaponics greenhouse had smuggled in marijuana seeds and had a few plants in a secret grow operation in the back. Charli had taken books from the Quiet Reading Room, read them, and failed to return them.

Some people had their own theories. Lance said it had probably just been a bad bottle of wine. Ryan wondered if it might have been an accident, though how methanol could accidentally end up in someone's wine, he didn't know. Hardin and Wei had both wondered if it had been suicide.

Unsurprisingly, no one had admitted to killing Patty. More than that, no one had seen or heard anything unusual that night.

It had taken more than eight hours to interview everyone. Then Thor, Jones, and Segal had scanned their notes and uploaded both the scans and the recordings to Cobra's servers for Shields and the other analysts to study. The analyst team would cross-reference people's stories and look for holes and pieces that didn't fit.

Shields had already given them one bit of news. Vasily *was* former KGB, just as Thor had suspected. Whether he was actually a scientist or whether he now worked for the FSB—Russia's Federal Security Service—only Vasily knew.

All Thor wanted now was a drink—a beer, some whiskey, maybe cognac.

"Anyone else feel like we're stuck in a three-dimensional game of Clue?" Jones asked. "It's someone with a bottle of poison wine at the South Pole. But who?"

"That's the question." Thor sent his last scan and

glanced at his watch. "I'll meet you two in the galley. I need to escort Dr. Park back to the station."

He left Jones and Segal to finish and layered up. "Samantha, this is Thor."

She replied quickly. "Samantha here."

"I'm on my way to walk you back."

"Okay. I'll be ready."

She'd been out there by herself today. There hadn't been much choice, given the need to interview the staff as quickly as possible. Thor had checked in on her periodically, and she had kept the lab door locked, promising to call him on the radio if anyone came knocking.

He stepped outside, the cold reviving him, a chill wind helping to clear his head. The stars glowed above, the aurora flaring and ebbing across the sky, a tide of green.

Nature made sense. But not human beings. They were the only creatures capable of intentional malice.

He found Samantha waiting for him just inside the door.

She turned off the lights, put on her mask, and stepped outside. "How did it go?"

He started down the stairs, Samantha behind him. "I can't talk about it."

"Right. Sorry."

"How's the Cosmic Microwave Background?"

"I had a hard time concentrating. I couldn't stop wondering who poisoned the wine. I guess I freaked myself out. Every little noise made me jump."

Thor could understand that. "Knowing there's a murderer here has put everyone on edge."

Especially the killer.

Whoever they were, they had to know they were out of time.

"All I want right now is some supper, a glass of wine, and

an hour in the sauna. Sitting at the computer all day makes my neck stiff and gives me a headache."

"Sorry about the headache. How about two out of three —dinner and the sauna?"

"I'd like that."

But when they walked into the galley together—he, Samantha, Segal, Jones, and Kristi—the room fell silent.

"Do you feel like they're all giving us side-eye?" Kristi whispered.

Thor leaned down. "You and Kristi shouldn't sit with us. It might make people think you're getting special treatment."

It was probably a bad idea for them to be seen together, which put a damper on Thor's plans. He hadn't forgotten how sweet it had been to kiss Samantha. He'd meant what he'd said. They weren't finished.

But a lot of shit had happened since then, and his role here had changed. Until the killer was exposed, he needed to keep his distance from her.

Fuck.

Of course, the sauna was public. Anyone could walk in. But if he and Samantha just happened to be there at the same time...

SAMANTHA BRUSHED HER TEETH, combed her hair, and tried to decide. Bathing suit or towel? The bathing suit had padded cups and made her look curvier, but it also made her seem inhibited—which she was. Also, if by some miracle, Thor undressed her, he would discover how much was padding and how little was truly her. She should do what most people did and just wrap herself in a towel.

Make up your mind!

Thor was in the sauna. Right now. Waiting for her.

The thought sent excitement shivering through her—and made her nervous.

Of course, there was no guarantee that Samantha would be alone with him. And even if she was, it's not like they could just pick up where they'd left off. If someone walked in and saw them kissing, the entire station would know within hours.

Even so, she wanted to be with him. In all this chaos, he was the one person who'd gone above and beyond to support her.

So, bathing suit or towel?

You need to lighten up, be brave, let yourself go.

It was something Patty had said to her so many times over the years—when Samantha had been reluctant to try sushi, when she'd refused to join in karaoke night, when she'd turned down an invitation to go sky-diving.

Patty had always been the outgoing one, the brave one, the true adventurer.

You can do this.

Samantha picked up her bathing suit—and dropped it on her bed. Before she could change her mind, she slipped into her bathrobe, armed the security camera, and made her way down the hall toward the women's changing area. There, she traded her robe for a towel, wrapping it around herself and tucking the ends in between her breasts. Then she left the changing room and walked around the corner to the sauna, holding tightly to the towel.

Through the small window in the door, she saw him.

Oh. God.

He sat, towel low on his hips, his head leaning back, his

eyes closed, one long leg stretched out in front of him, sweat glistening on his skin.

Why was a man like Thor paying any attention to her?

Don't ask. Who cares?

She opened the door, stepped across the threshold and into the heat.

His head came up, and his eyes opened, his gaze moving over her. "Hey."

"Hey." She went to sit beside him, the wood hot against the backs of her thighs. "The heat feels good."

"It does."

"I thought there would be others here."

"There were until I showed up. When I walked in, they got up and left."

"I'm sorry. I know how it feels to be rejected. That was every day of my life in high school."

"It's fine with me. I'd rather be alone with you." Thor sat up straight, motioned for her to turn around. "Let's take care of that headache."

Headache? Oh, yes. She'd forgotten about that.

She held fast to her towel and turned her back to him.

He angled himself toward her, scooted closer, then gathered her hair, letting it spill over her shoulder, his fingers brushing against her nape, sending shivers through her. Big hands came to rest on her shoulders. "Your muscles are so tight."

Samantha couldn't help but moan as he found all the knots and tight places, his hands working magic. "Mmm."

A week's worth of stress and worry seemed to melt away beneath his touch, replaced by a different sort of tension, desire fluttering to life inside her.

He skimmed his hands down the length of her bare arms, his lips pressing hot kisses to her shoulder. "I can't promise you anything, Samantha. I'll be leaving soon. I'm not the kind of guy who gets married and settles down in the suburbs."

"I know." Nothing he'd said surprised her. "I appreciate your honesty."

Hookups down here didn't last. Everyone knew that. He didn't seem like a man who wanted a conventional life. If a little heartbreak was the price she had to pay for feeling like this, she would pay it—gladly.

"I meant it when I said we weren't finished." He teased her with feather-light kisses, heat searing her skin where his lips touched her.

"I... I hope so." Samantha's breath caught, her eyes drifting shut.

Then one hand moved to cup her right breast through her towel.

"See?" He nuzzled the sensitive skin beneath her ear, his voice deep and soft. "You fill my hand."

She opened her eyes, watched as he gently squeezed, his thumb rubbing over the bump in the terrycloth that was her nipple, making her belly clench. She arched into his hand, giving herself to him, wanting more. "*Thor.*"

Usually, she was too nervous to enjoy a man's touch, especially in the beginning of a relationship, but that wasn't true with Thor. She sank back against his chest, her head resting on his shoulder, his broad chest seeming to cradle her.

Voices.

Someone was coming.

Thor muttered something she didn't understand and drew away. "Can I come to your room?"

Samantha stood, moved toward the door, her heart thrumming as she weighed her answer. Would she be making a mistake? Would she regret it? He wasn't going to be here much longer, and she would probably never see him again.

You need to lighten up, be brave, let yourself go.

She would rather regret sleeping with him than spend the rest of her life wondering what she'd missed. "Yes."

She stepped out of the sauna, passing Ryan and a few of his firefighter buddies as she hurried back to the changing room.

THOR TOOK a quick shower and brushed his teeth. Then he dressed—jeans and a T-shirt—and tore through his gear, looking for his packet of condoms. "*For helvede.*"

Damn it!

He always carried some—just in case. Had he somehow unpacked them?

No, they were in his shaving kit.

He grabbed them, slipped two into the pocket of his jeans together with his phone. Then he armed his security camera and started toward the door, hesitating when his hand touched the doorknob.

What happened to your self-control, man?

He shouldn't do this.

He was in charge of a murder investigation, and he couldn't allow personal connections or hormones to interfere with his work. Although he knew Samantha hadn't killed Patty, he couldn't prove that. She, like everyone else, was still a suspect.

More than that, he didn't want to hurt her. He wasn't going to be here for much longer. How would she feel when he got on a plane and left her life forever?

She was vulnerable, alone at the bottom of the world, her best friend murdered, her life turned upside down. She also didn't have a lot of sexual experience. Hell, he wouldn't be shocked if she told him she was a virgin.

No, he shouldn't do this. It was reckless. It wasn't like him at all.

But Samantha had lit a fire in him that he couldn't put out with her intelligence, her directness, those blue eyes, her dancer's body. The way she'd reacted when he'd cupped her breast through the towel, arching against him...

He thrust away his doubts, opened the door, and made his way upstairs, careful not to be seen as he stopped outside her room.

Last chance to do the right thing.

Samantha *was* the right thing.

He knocked lightly.

Still wearing her bathrobe, she answered right away and let him inside.

He locked the door behind him, their gazes meeting, the sexual hunger he felt mirrored in her eyes. He dragged her against him and ducked down to claim her mouth with his, gratified by her little gasp of pleasure.

Fuck, yes.

She melted against him, yielding to his kiss, her body pliant, eager.

He willed himself to slow down, gentling the kiss, brushing his lips over hers, nipping them with his teeth, tracing their outline with his tongue. She tasted so good and felt wonderful in his arms, his second thoughts vanishing as she kissed him back.

He let her take control, her tongue teasing and tasting his, her hands sliding behind his neck, drawing him down.

He gave her what she wanted, his need for her rising as she grew bolder. Then he realized she was standing on tiptoe.

To hell with this.

He broke the kiss, scooped her into his arms, and carried her all of two feet to her bed, sitting her down on the edge. He had to ask. "Are you sure you want this?"

She looked up at him, pupils dilated, her lips wet and swollen. "*God, yes.*"

He wanted to strip off that shapeless bathrobe and whatever she had on under it and get down to sweet skin, but he remembered that she felt self-conscious about her body. Maybe if he got naked first, she'd feel more at ease.

He drew his T-shirt over his head, dropped it, watched longing spread on her face as her gaze raked over him. Yeah, she liked what she saw and—no lie—it turned him on even more, his cock threatening to split his zipper now.

He took her hand, pressed it against his chest, held it there, offering himself to her. "You can touch me however you want."

She sucked in a breath, her other hand joining the first as she ran her palms over his pecs, down his ribcage, over his abs, and back to his pecs, her thumbs running over his nipples, her touch like fire. "I've never met a man like you."

He pulled the condoms out of his pocket and set them on her headboard. Then he yanked down his zipper, kicked off his shoes, and stepped out of his clothes. Then he stood there before her, naked, his cock fully erect.

Her gaze went right where he knew it would, right where it had been the night he'd gone streaking on the ice.

But this time she reached out, took him in hand, stroked his length with cool fingers, her touch making his cock jerk. "Show me what you like."

He covered her hand with his, stilled it. "I'd rather learn about you."

Her gaze snapped to his, a hint of nervousness there. "I'm not special."

"Who put that idea in your head?" Thor wanted to punch the guy.

"Well, I..."

Thor pushed her robe over her shoulders, let it fall to the bed. "*Åh, skat.*"

Oh, sweetheart.

She was naked, nothing beneath the robe but silky skin. Her body was delicate, her breasts small but perfect, their pink tips puckered and tight, a thatch of dark blond curls between her thighs.

"You're beautiful, Samantha."

She started to shake her head, pink rising into her cheeks, but he caught her chin.

He looked straight into her eyes. "You're beautiful. I mean that. Do you think I'd be standing here, naked, with my cock about to explode, if I didn't truly want you?"

12

S amantha looked into Thor's eyes, his words, and the intensity of his gaze, making her heart thrum. She didn't know how to answer his question. But that didn't matter, because, in the next instant, he kissed her, his mouth hot and hungry against hers.

Oh. My. God.

No man had ever kissed her the way he did, a wild combination of fierce and gentle, his lips, teeth, and tongue assailing her senses. The thrill of it threw her off balance, left her breathless, turned her body to liquid. She forgot the nightmare of the past week, her world shrinking until it held only him—the clean scent of his skin, the heat of his body against hers, the minty taste of his tongue.

Thor pressed her back onto her bed and stretched himself out above her, supporting his weight with muscular arms, his lips never leaving hers, his erection brushing her bare belly as he settled between her thighs. She slid her hands up his body, turned on by the feel of him—soft skin, shifting muscles, the rasp of his chest hair.

He dragged his mouth from hers, sat back on his heels,

his brow furrowing as his gaze slid over her, his cock jutting upward, his chest rising and falling as if he were as out of breath as she was. He cupped a breast, caressed her nipple. "God, you're beautiful."

She might have objected out of habit, but something about the way he said it, something on his face, convinced her that he meant it.

He caught her wrists with his hands, pinned them above her head, his fingers threading with hers. Then he lowered his lips to the nipple he'd just caressed, moaning as he sucked it into the heat of his mouth.

"Oh!" The sensation shot straight to her belly.

But he was just getting started.

He moved from one nipple to the other, licking, nipping, teasing, until Samantha wriggled and writhed beneath him, aching and wet.

"*Thor.*"

He raised his head, leaving her breasts bereft, his gaze meeting hers, his lips curving in a smile as if her sexual anguish amused him. "Beautiful *and* sensitive."

Then he pressed a kiss to her breastbone and released her wrists, one hand moving to cup her breasts, while the other explored between her thighs, his mouth trailing fire across her throat, her shoulder, her ribcage, her navel. "You're so wet."

She was so turned on that it took her a moment to realize what he had in mind. She slid her fingers into his hair to stop him. "No, no. I've never really liked that."

He looked up at her, arched an eyebrow. "Seriously?"

She'd always felt too self-conscious. "Seriously."

"Will you give me a chance?" He scooted down the bed, kissed and nipped her inner thighs, soothing the sharp, little bites with his tongue. "Just give me one minute to taste you. Count to sixty. If you're not into it, I'll stop."

He truly wanted to taste her? That was a first.

The thought sent a shiver through her. "Okay."

"Don't start counting yet." He pressed a line of kisses across her lower belly, to the ticklish spot just above her hip bone, making her abdominal muscles tense.

Samantha wasn't used to this kind of attention. She wasn't used to having a man so focused on *her* pleasure. Sure, she had enjoyed sex before, but not like this. Every nerve in her body seemed alive, hypersensitive to his touch, his every caress, even the warmth of his breath as he exhaled against her skin.

"Ready?" He parted her with his fingers, made a sound that was halfway between an exhale and a moan. "Start counting."

"One..."

He licked her, making her breath catch.

"Two..."

He did it again, a little more firmly this time.

"*Threeee*..."

He began to torment her in earnest, teasing her clit with slick strokes of his tongue, flicking her, skimming circles over her.

"*Oh*..." Stunned by the sensation, she forgot to count.

It felt *so* good, pleasure shuddering through her, igniting a fire inside her, a burning need for release. The part of her mind that could still think rejected her previous hypothesis that oral sex was no big deal, because, oh, *hell, yes*, it was.

With Thor, it was.

Then he drew her clit into the heat of his mouth, suckling her just as he'd done with her nipples.

She cried out from the sweet shock of it, arching off the

bed, her hands fisting in his thick hair. He threw a strong arm across her hips to hold her still, leaving her no escape, no chance to catch her breath, no choice but to ride it out.

She couldn't keep her head above water, pleasure engulfing her, overwhelming her, dragging her under. Her breath came in ragged pants now, every exhale a moan, her trembling thighs spread far apart, her knees bent back, her inhibitions utterly gone. Then he pushed two fingers inside her, thrusting into her, stroking that deep ache.

Orgasm washed through her in a savage rush, a tidal wave of bliss, the shock of it tearing a cry from her throat, drowning her in pleasure and leaving her to drift as he finished her with gentle laps of his tongue.

Out of breath, her brain blank, she felt him shift and opened her eyes to find him reaching for a condom. He drew back his foreskin, rolled the condom down his length.

Her pulse skipped to think that his cock would soon be inside her.

He settled himself between her thighs, his gaze meeting hers. "Are you sure?"

God, was she ever. "Yes."

But how sweet of him to ask.

He nudged himself into her, filling her with a single, slow thrust, his eyes drifting shut, breath leaving his lungs in a rush. "You're so tight."

It felt good to Samantha, too, her body still hypersensitive.

He opened his eyes, pressed a kiss to one breast, held himself still inside her. "I don't know how long I'm going to last."

She ran her palms over his chest. "That's okay. I already came."

And it had *blown her mind*.

"You think that's it?" He chuckled, his smile sexy enough to melt winter. "Such low expectations."

He withdrew from her with excruciating slowness then inched himself into her again, his gaze locked with hers, that smile still on his lips.

"*Oh.*"

Over and over again, he withdrew slowly, only to enter her once more. And each time, it got better, the slippery friction hitting sensitive places inside her, arousing her, making her ache for the next thrust.

Little by little, he picked up the rhythm, his eyes drifting shut, his jaw tensing, muscles shifting beneath her palms. "You feel ... *so good.*"

How did he do that? How did he make her feel desired and beautiful with just a few words, a look, a kiss?

"*Thor.*" She moaned his name, her nails digging into his shoulders.

Faster. Harder.

She was losing herself again, losing herself in him, in the feel of him moving inside her—the hot glide, the sweet stretch, the deep, piercing fullness.

In her mind, she saw his cock pounding into her. The thought drew her gaze downward to where their bodies joined, those amazing abs contracting as he drove himself into her. A jolt of white-hot lust shot through her, the sight primal, erotic, *hot.*

He shifted, changing the angle of his hips so that his cock grazed her clit on the next thrust.

The sensation made her gasp—and moan. "*Oh!*"

The hint of a smile played on his lips as he watched her, his blue eyes dark. Sweat beaded on his chest, his hips keeping a relentless rhythm, each thrust driving her higher, pleasure winding tighter inside her. And then she was there, hovering on the iridescent edge of another climax.

Sexual need stripped her of control, left her moaning and whispering words that made no sense. *"Ooh. Thor! I want ... Oh! Yes. I need..."*

"Come for me, *skat*."

As if she had a choice.

Samantha shattered, orgasm burning through her like molten honey, scorching and sweet. Thor caught her cry with his mouth, driving her climax home with deep, hard thrusts. When her peak had passed, he shifted his hips again and let himself go, moaning against her throat as he, at last, joined her in paradise.

BREATHING HARD, Thor sank against Samantha, his heart hammering, his mind empty, his body floating somewhere between heaven and earth. For a time, he lay there, still inside her, orgasm fading into languid stillness. Bit by bit, his awareness returned.

Soft skin against skin. The silk of her hair. Her scent. The thrum of her heartbeat against his chest. The taste of her on his tongue.

He had the presence of mind to pull out before the condom slipped off. He tossed it, wiped off with a tissue.

"The beds here are tiny." Her voice was husky, sleepy.

"Come here." He shifted onto his side so that her head was pillowed on his bicep, her legs tucked between his. "Is that better?"

"Mmm." She snuggled against him. "What does *skat* mean in Danish?"

Had he called her *skat*? That ought to worry him, but

strangely it didn't. "It means something like 'honey' or '*sweetheart*.'"

"I like that." She laughed. "In English, *scat* is a term for animal poop."

"That's definitely not what I meant." He kissed her, trailed his fingers up the silky skin of her back, and found himself smiling.

One... two... threeee.

Yeah, she'd lost count pretty quickly.

"What is it? Why are you smiling?"

"For someone who doesn't care for oral sex, you seemed to enjoy it."

"That's only because you're so good."

"Yeah?" He wouldn't lie. That didn't hurt his ego *at all*.

"I've never come that way before. I've never come twice, either."

Thor found that hard to comprehend. She was as responsive as any woman he'd known—more responsive than some. "I think you need to stop sleeping with jerks."

She arched her head, looked up at him, and laughed, the sound putting a hitch in his chest. "I gave up men a few years ago."

"You gave up men? Last time I looked, I was a man."

"Yes, you are." She ran her palm over his bicep. "I mean, I quit dating. I gave up trying to meet someone."

Something told Thor this was about more than mediocre sex. It wasn't like him to want to hear about the previous lovers of the women in his bed, but this time he was curious. "What happened?"

"My first boyfriend was a guy named Scott. We met in chem lab my freshman year and started going out. He was the first guy I slept with."

Thor hated him already.

"One night afterward, he sat up in my bed and said he'd never really found me attractive. He said he liked curvy women who did feminine things. Then he got dressed and left, and that was it. I cried for a week."

Now Thor really hated him. "What an asshole."

"He wasn't the first person to say something like that. I heard it all the time in high school from boys and girls. 'Sam is flat-chested. She's a nerd. She thinks she's so smart. We hate her.' One football player grabbed my breast in the hallway and said he was just trying to decide if I was truly a girl."

"What a shitting bastard. Please tell me someone kicked his ass."

"I never reported it."

"You're *not* flat-chested." It hurt Thor to imagine a teenage Samantha enduring assault and taunts. He understood now why she had so little confidence. "They bullied you. Wasn't your mother a teacher? Didn't she try to stop it?"

Samantha shook her head. "I didn't tell her. Are you kidding? It would have been so much worse if I had."

Thor couldn't imagine that. "That's just wrong. In Denmark, children are taught not to bully as soon as they start school. They're also taught to intervene if they see another child being bullied. We believe that everyone has a right to be a part of things. No one should be left out."

"That's wonderful."

"If people can't learn at an early age how to be kind and get along with one another, how can you have a functioning society?" It seemed obvious to Thor.

She tilted her head back, looked up at him. "I like that."

"So, Scott was a bastard. Who else?"

"Nathan and I met in grad school. My parents thought we'd get married, but everything was a competition with him. If I got a better grade than he did, it made him angry. He would yell and tell me the professors were going easy on me because I was a woman. When I got the post-doc at the University of Chicago, he said it was only because of my sex. Then he packed and left. I was ... crushed."

The hurt in her voice made Thor want to punch the fucker. "What a fragile ego. He believed he had to compete with you. You're better off without him."

"After that, I stopped dating."

She'd been with two men—only two—and both times they'd hurt her badly and put her down. Thor couldn't undo the damage they'd done to her spirit, but, for the short time he was here, he could show her that not all men were like that.

He drew her close, stroked her hair. "Want to know what I see when I look at you? I see one of the most brilliant people I've ever met, man or woman. I see a woman with a sweet body, delicate breasts, a pretty face, and beautiful blue eyes. I see a loyal friend and a hard worker. I don't know what was up with the kids at your high school or those two men, but there's nothing wrong with you."

For a moment, she was silent. "You're not just saying that?"

"I never say things I don't mean." Thor kissed her forehead. "I also like that you're real."

"I'm *real*?"

"You don't wear makeup or talk about clothes or waste time on things that don't matter. You're not super... superfiscal." That was the word, right?

"I think you mean super*ficial*." There was a hint of laughter in her voice.

He repeated it. "Super*ficial*."

"Thank you. For some reason, I've never had an interest

in any of that. I thought most men like women who do all the girly stuff."

"I don't believe that. But who knows? My last girlfriend broke up with me because I didn't notice her new shoes."

"Are you serious?"

"She cried and told me I was cold and uncaring."

Samantha sat up. "But you're not any of those things."

Her distress on his behalf made him smile. "Thanks, but it wasn't a great loss."

Lying here beside Samantha, the end of that relationship seemed like nothing.

Thor drank in the sight of her—rosy nipples peeking out between strands of blond hair, the curve of her shoulder, guileless eyes. And the sexual thirst that had just been slaked flared to life again, blood filling his cock. He brushed her hair over her shoulder, exposing her breast to his touch. "See? I want you again already."

Her eyes drifted shut, her nipples drawing tight as he caressed her.

"Come here." He drew her onto him, helped her straddle his hips. "Now I can touch you anywhere I want."

She sucked in a little breath, her hands splayed against his chest for balance. "You have the most amazing body. I just want to play with it."

"Don't let me stop you." He let her explore him with her hands, her caresses striking sparks from his skin. It turned him on just to see how much touching him turned *her* on, lust in her eyes, hunger on her face.

But he was hungry, too.

He stopped her when she started to go down on him and drew her up the length of his body to kiss her. "Save that for another time."

Then he went to work on her, teasing her clit with one

hand, caressing her breasts with the other, until his fingers were drenched and her breasts were swollen.

He reached for the condom and tore the packet with his teeth, then sheathed himself and guided his cock into her tight body. "*Hold kæft.*"

Jesus.

Her head fell back on a moan, her hair tickling his thighs. "*Thor.*"

He let her set the pace, but it was pretty clear that she was used to doing this for the benefit of the bastards she'd dated and not for her own pleasure.

He gripped her hips, stopped her. "This isn't a rodeo. Do what feels good to you. Use my cock for your fun."

She looked surprised for a moment, then she began to experiment, rolling her hips, rubbing her pubic bone against his, canting her hips so that his cock stroked her inside where it felt best. He knew she'd figured it out when her eyes went wide and her nails bit into his chest.

"*Oooh!*"

He indulged himself, toying with her breasts and her clit, willing himself to relax, to hold still while she took what she needed from him. "God, you're hot."

She came fast and hard, Thor closing his hand over her mouth to still her cry.

When her peak had passed, he flipped her onto her back and drove himself into her, orgasm already uncoiling at the base of his spine. Climax hit him like a blast wave, pleasure shaking him apart, leaving him panting in her arms.

13

Thor was so deeply asleep that it took him a moment to realize that strange sound was his phone's alarm ringing. He opened his eyes to find Samantha still asleep in his arms, her face nuzzled against his chest. Warmth spread behind his sternum at the sight of her, a wave of tenderness welling up inside him.

Then he remembered.

For helvede. Damn it.

He reached over and turned off the alarm on his phone, trying not to wake Samantha. He'd set it to make sure he was ready for his early meeting with Tower and Shields. If he didn't haul ass, he'd be late.

"Thor?" She opened her eyes. "Is it time to get up already?"

"Go back to sleep. I've got a five A.M. meeting." He kissed her, climbed out of bed, and dressed. "One of us will walk you to the lab after breakfast. Don't go anywhere alone with Vasily. He's former KGB. Don't forget to arm your security camera and take your radio with you, okay?"

She sat up, her hair tousled, surprise on her face. "He's KGB?"

"He was. I have to go."

"Thank you for last night. Thanks for everything."

"Hey, thank you." He zipped his jeans, reached for his T-shirt, pulling it over his head before ducking down to kiss her again. "We're not finished."

He left her to get a little more sleep and made his way downstairs to his room, where Jones and Segal were waiting for him.

"The mighty Thor falls to earth," Jones teased. "We knocked on your door, man, and you weren't there. Keeping Dr. Park company?"

"Shut up." Thor unlocked his door, grabbed his laptop, and stepped out again.

Segal glared at him. "Am I the only one keeping my dick in my pants?"

Thor locked his door once more. "At least I didn't keep anyone awake."

They made their way upstairs to the small conference room, locking the door for privacy. While Segal made coffee, Thor booted up the computer, logged in to the satellite VPN, and found Tower and Shields waiting for him.

Thor took responsibility for their tardiness. "Sorry we're late. I overslept."

Segal rolled his eyes, while Jones smirked.

Røvhuller. Assholes.

"I'm glad someone slept." Shields had dark circles beneath her eyes. "The analyst team—all of us—pulled an all-nighter, going through the notes you sent, reading through transcripts of your interviews with staff, and finishing background checks on every person there. Based on all of that, we've come up with a short list of people for you to question again. I'm emailing it to you now."

Segal leaned in. "Do we know for certain the murder and the hacked satellite are related? Could Dr. Holcomb's death have been suicide or an accident?"

Shields spoke in the tone of voice she reserved for idiots. "We assess that the two events are related because of the time they occurred—and because a murder and the satellite hack are both extremely rare events there. Based on what we know about Dr. Holcomb, the probability of suicide is low. She had no history of depression and made it through austral winter last year without any psychological issues. Given that methanol was found in a bottle of commercially produced wine, I doubt it was accidental. Someone had to pour the methanol into that bottle."

Thor checked his email, opened the file Shields had sent him, and scrolled through the names, his heart giving a kick to see Samantha there. "I got your list."

It had details for each person and a set of new questions to ask.

"Let's go through the list one person at a time." Shields read the first name. "Kazem Hamidi. He certainly has the scientific background and capability to hack a satellite. He's an Iranian national. The Agency doesn't show any links between him and the Iranian government or any extremist elements, but that's not conclusive."

Thor hadn't forgotten what Samantha had told him. "He also had an interest in Dr. Holcomb and showed some aggression toward her."

"True—but there's more." Shields glanced at her notes. "He claims he was in the lounge the night she was poisoned, but no one else places him there. Not a single person you interviewed remembered him being there."

That *was* suspicious.

"And Bai Zhang Wei?"

"He's a Chinese national who worked on top-secret Chinese military projects before landing the job at UC-Berkeley researching neutrinos. He says he was in his room asleep the night Dr. Holcomb was poisoned, but Nick Pappas, his research partner, says Wei was still in the IceCube facility when he walked back to the station at midnight."

"What about Lance Barclay?" Thor didn't like the guy. "He and Dr. Holcomb were intimate. He's shown he can be aggressive and controlling."

"He's got the necessary computer skills, for sure, and he was the last person to see Dr. Holcomb healthy. He claims he went back to his own room to sleep. But Charli Ortega, the coms manager, remembers seeing him in the computer lab late that night."

"Kristi Chang, the nurse?"

"What?" Jones' gaze snapped to Thor's, disbelief on his face.

"She's a first-generation American, but her grandparents have ties to the highest levels of Chinese government. That in itself doesn't mean anything, but we found three bank transfers from her grandfather in Beijing to her account for a total of almost a hundred grand."

"You've got Jason Huger listed."

"Jason has a juvenile record. We were able to get the details unsealed. When he was a junior in high school, he was arrested for hacking and harassment after he doxxed a girl who turned him down for a date."

That didn't surprise Thor at all. "He hasn't changed much."

"He's only twenty-four. High school wasn't that long ago."

"And Dr. Park?" Thor fought to keep his expression neutral.

"She's got the skills, and no one remembers seeing her anywhere after dinner."

Thor knew that Samantha had spent the night in her room. She was too much of an introvert to hang in the lounge without her best friend. But he didn't say this.

Shields continued. "The FBI and the Agency have nothing on her. No suspicious bank deposits. No ties to foreign governments. But Lance Barclay says she and Dr. Holcomb argued that night after dinner."

Thor hadn't interviewed Barclay, so this was news to him. "She's also the person who found Dr. Holcomb—found her and got her medical attention."

"I agree it's unlikely, but I felt we had to include her."

Thor let it go—for now. "What about our Russian friends?"

"They might play some role in this. They could have a contact on station. What's the best thing to do if they're unsuccessful retrieving the technology from the crash site?"

"They stay with it and wait for a chance to acquire it," Segal answered.

Shields smiled. "Exactly. My guess? That's why they're there."

Thor wrapped up the meeting. "Thanks for this. Get some rest."

"Remember that we're outside the hacker-killer's game plan." Tower's face appeared on the screen again. "This is not how they expected things to go. They certainly didn't plan on Cobra showing up on the scene. They're going to get desperate, and desperate people do desperate things."

HER HAIR still wet from an extra stolen shower, Samantha stood in front of her mirror, looking at her naked body, trying to make peace with her reflection. Yes, she had small breasts, but they were sensitive. Thor had kissed and caressed them, driving her crazy. He'd called them beautiful, delicate.

She cupped one, ran her thumb around its nipple, remembering how amazing it had been to have Thor's attention focused entirely on her.

You're beautiful, Samantha. I mean that. Do you think I'd be standing here, naked, with my cock about to explode, if I didn't truly want you?

Until last night, she hadn't known how it felt to be desired. Now she did, and it changed everything.

She knew it was no better to base her opinion of herself on one guy's positive response than it was to base it on the taunts of high school kids and former lovers. She wouldn't take it seriously if someone called her stupid. She knew she was intelligent and would laugh in their face. Then why did she let other people's opinions determine how she felt about her body?

Her gaze moved below her breasts to the curls of her pubic area.

Give me one minute to taste you. Count to sixty. If you're not into it, I'll stop.

God in heaven.

Just thinking about how good it had been to have his mouth on her put flutters in her belly and an ache between her thighs. No man had ever made her feel the way Thor had. He hadn't rushed her. He'd put her pleasure first, taking his time with her. She'd come three times in one night, for God's sake.

You need to get to work.

It was time to get breakfast and then recycle the SPT fridges again.

Feeling lighter than she had in days, she dressed—long underwear, jeans, T-shirt, sweater, snow pants—and made her way to the galley, where Thor sat with Malik and Lev, the three talking quietly together. He saw her, acknowledged her with a nod, but there was a note of warning in his gaze.

He wanted her to be discreet.

She sat at an empty table on the other side of the galley. She had just stirred sugar and creamer into her coffee when a shadow fell across the table.

"Good morning." Tray in hand, Vasily sat across from her. "You are without your military guard dog this morning."

Samantha felt cornered. "They're not military, and they're not my guard dogs."

"The one—that big Dane—he has an eye for you. I see these things. Intuition."

A few months ago, over drinks at McMurdo, this would have seemed like a friendly conversation. But now that Samantha knew the truth about Vasily, she could tell he was fishing for information.

Samantha picked up her fork, her gaze meeting his. "Did you develop that intuition during your time with the KGB?"

She probably shouldn't have said that.

Vasily looked taken aback, but his surprise transformed into a grin. "Ah, so they are digging around. Yes, I served with the KGB, but it was dissolved almost thirty years ago, when I was still a young man."

"Was it truly dissolved—or just renamed?"

His eyes narrowed. "You Americans always ask the straight question. You would get more information by listening, being patient."

"That's not an answer."

Then Thor stood beside her. "Dr. Park, we need to schedule a time to run through some additional questions."

"Okay. Can I meet you in the small conference room in ten minutes?"

"That works."

Then Vasily spoke up. "I hear you are digging into me. Be sure to call my first wife and ask her what she thinks of me."

"Thanks for the tip. We just might do that." Thor returned to his table, but Samantha knew he was watching out for her.

"See? He is your guard dog."

"He's in charge of catching a killer. In case you've forgotten, my best friend was murdered by someone here on station. He's just trying to keep me safe."

Vasily leaned closer, a hint of alcohol on his breath. "I want you to be safe, too, so I will tell you if I hear anything about Patty's murder. I will show you that I am still your friend. If I find the killer, I will end him."

He stood with his tray and went to join his friends, leaving Samantha alone.

She finished her breakfast and went back to her room to brush her teeth, making sure to grab her radio and arm her security camera before heading to the small conference room. She found not just Thor, but Malik and Lev seated around the table, too.

She poured herself a cup of coffee and joined them. "You have more questions?"

It wasn't Thor who answered but Lev. "We had some people say that you and Patty got into an argument the night she was poisoned. Is that true?"

"What? No. We didn't argue." And then it hit her. "I'm a suspect?"

"Everyone who was on station that night is a suspect." Lev spoke as if she were a stranger, not someone who'd shared a perilous mission with him. "We have witnesses who said the two of you argued."

She looked to Thor, but he said nothing. His silence cut her. "No, she and I didn't argue. We had dinner with Lance and Kristi and then I..."

Then she remembered.

"Oh, Lance is such an idiot!" He must be the witness. "After dinner, Patty wanted me to ask Ryan McClain, the firefighter, to grab some popcorn and watch a movie with me. I didn't want to do it, but she kept pushing. She was always trying to hook me up with someone. We were whispering until finally, I said, 'No!' loudly. But it wasn't a fight. I was irritated, but I wasn't truly angry with her."

Lev then asked all the same questions they'd asked her yesterday, pushing her. Where was she when Patty was poisoned? What time did she leave the galley? Did anyone see her enter her room? Did she use methanol in her work?

Then he threw a new one at her.

"Were you jealous of Patty—her relationships with men, her accomplishments?"

Still, Thor remained silent.

"No, not at all." Samantha swallowed the lump in her throat, got to her feet, lacerated by Thor's indifference. "Patty and I balanced each other out. She was my best friend. I loved her. I would gladly trade places with her and be the one who died if it meant she could live. I need to get to the lab. If you have any more questions, you can find me there."

Thor got to his feet. "I'll escort you over."

She'd spent the night with him. She'd had the most mind-blowing sex of her life with him. Three hours ago, they'd been naked together in her bed. And yet he'd sat there and said nothing while Lev had interrogated her.

"No, don't. Work on finding Patty's killer. If you consider *me* a suspect, you've got a long way to go." She walked out of the room and down the main hallway toward the coatroom, fighting tears.

THOR HURRIED to catch up with Samantha. He told himself he was just making sure she made it safely to the Dark Sector Lab, but he knew that was bullshit. In truth, he wanted to explain, to take away the distress he'd caused her.

This is what you get for taking your dick out of your pants on a mission.

Yeah. Right. Thanks. He knew that. But knowing it changed nothing.

He hadn't meant for her to get hurt by this. "Samantha!"

She disappeared into the coatroom.

Fuck.

The last thing he wanted to do was hurt her.

He followed her inside, found his parka and boots, and began to dress for the cold. Because there were others in the room, he waited until they were outside and away from the building before he spoke.

"I'm sorry about that, Samantha, but we had to ask."

"You *had* to ask." She walked with fast, angry strides.

"Okay, well, you asked—or, rather, you let Lev ask while you sat there and said *nothing*."

"Segal and Jones know you and I were together. They were waiting at my door when I went downstairs. Because of that, I had to step aside and let Segal handle the questions, or someone might think I wasn't objective. That's the price *both* of us pay for last night. I didn't like it any more than you did."

She looked over at him, her expression hidden behind her mask. "So, that was just you recusing yourself because of our ... involvement?"

"Yes, and it could happen again. I know you didn't kill Patty."

"I'm happy to hear you say that. What kind of a man would sleep with someone he suspected of murder? And, for the record, I didn't like being interrogated."

He couldn't blame her—not when she was already dealing with grief. "I'm sorry, Samantha. I'm in command of this mission, but I don't get to call all of the shots."

He explained how all of Cobra's resources were being thrown at this investigation and how the analyst team used the interviews to come up with a short list of people for them to question a second time. "They don't know that you and I are involved, and they can't find out. I shouldn't have crossed the line with you, but I did."

She stopped still. "You're saying you regret last night."

"Not at all." Maybe he should, but he didn't. "I have no regrets—not one. Last night was perfect. But I'm walking a tightrope here, duty on the one hand, desire on the other. Try at least to understand that."

She started walking again but said nothing.

For helvede. Damn it.

They reached the Dark Sector Lab and walked up the

stairs and indoors. Thor probably ought to have gone back to the station, but he wanted to make this right. So, he stripped out of his cold-weather gear, needing to talk to her without the masks.

She hung up her hat and mask and looked up at him, the hurt in her eyes mingled with grief. "You mean it when you say you don't regret last night?"

"Yes." But words were cheap, so he decided to prove it to her. "Come here."

He drew her against him and kissed her. He meant only to reassure her, but the moment his lips touched hers, he wanted more than that.

He drew back, searched her face for any sign that she understood his situation. "I'm sorry you're caught in this awful mess."

She looked up at him, fragile hope in her eyes. "Duty versus desire?"

"That's it."

"And you still desire me?" Her lips curved in a teasing smile.

"So damned much that I'd be fired if my bosses knew what was running through my head right now." He lowered his mouth to hers and—

The alarm went off on both of their phones at the same time.

"Shit." He drew his phone out of the pocket of his snow pants, turned off the alarm. "Well, look at that son of a bitch."

She took her phone out, too, stared. "Lance? What the hell is he doing?"

"It looks like he's searching your room for something." Thor grabbed his radio. "Jones, Segal, this is Isaksen. You two seeing this?"

"Isaksen, Jones here. Affirmative, we see him. We're on our way there now."

"I just got Dr. Park to the Dark Sector Lab and am heading back to the station. Detain him. Remember, you're deputies. You have arrest authority. I'll alert Hardin."

Thor grabbed his parka, his hat, and his mask, and got ready for the trek back. "You stay here, lock the door, and don't open it for anyone but me, Jones, or Segal. I'll let you know what's going on. You just focus on your work."

"To hell with that." She grabbed her parka. "I'm coming with you."

14

Samantha followed Thor up the stairs, into the station, and down the hallway toward the AI berthing area, where she could see a small crowd gathered.

She stripped off her hat, gloves, and mask. "Why would Lance break into my room? Does he think you hid the... uh... package there?"

"I've got a few ideas about that, but we're going to find out."

She heard Lance shouting before they reached the AI pod.

"Get off me! You stupid bastards! You don't understand!"

"Dude, you're going to have lots of time to explain it to us." That was Malik.

Thor rested a hand in the middle of her back as they grew closer, the brief contact reassuring. People moved aside for him, letting them through. And there on the floor, hands zip-tied behind his back, was Lance, Malik holding his feet while Lev had a knee in the middle of his back.

Malik saw Thor, grinned. "Hey, man. He took a swing at me and tried to run, but, as you can see, he didn't get far."

The door to Samantha's room stood ajar, one of her dresser drawers dumped onto the floor, her panties scattered everywhere, the lamp on her desk toppled.

Rage flared inside her, white-hot. She stomped over to Lance, glared down at the back of his head. "What the hell were you doing in my room?"

"Samantha! Tell these bastards to get off me. I just wanted Patty's journal."

"You apologized for trying to take it from me, and now you break into my room to steal it? You jerk! That belongs to her family."

Thor walked up beside her, knelt, tilting his head to make eye contact with Lance. "Lance, buddy, you're under arrest."

"Under arrest? That's bullshit. Tell your lugnuts to get off me!"

"Lugnuts?" Lev snorted.

Thor got to his feet again. "Get him up. It's time for us to have a little chat."

Steve made his way through the crowd. "What the hell is going on here?"

Samantha pointed to her open door, trembling with rage. "Lance broke into my room and was searching it. He wanted to steal Patty's journal."

"Jesus, Lance." Steve rubbed a hand over his stubbled jaw, looking like he hadn't slept in a week. "What the fuck is wrong with you, man?"

Lev and Malik jerked Lance to his feet, the two keeping hands on him.

Red-faced, Lance craned his head to look at Steve. "Tell them to let me go."

"They're deputy marshals now, and breaking and

entering is a crime, even here." Steve turned to Thor. "You can take him to the small conference room if that works."

"Thanks." Thor faced Lance. "Did you take anything from Dr. Park's room?"

Lance gave Samantha a sullen look. "No."

"You two take him to the conference room. I'll meet you there. I need to get my laptop so we can film this. Dr. Park, do you want me to walk you back to the Dark Sector, or do you want to stay here and clean up?"

She started to answer, but Lance cut her off.

"Film it? Why do you want to film it? Wait. You think I killed Patty? Is that it? I had nothing to do with that!"

"Come on." Lev steered Lance down the hallway. "You know the way."

Hardin spoke to the crowd. "Okay, everyone. Back to work."

Samantha tried to regain her equilibrium, shock and rage giving way to an overwhelming sense of violation. She hugged her arms around herself. "I'll straighten things up and then get back to the lab."

Thor's eyes were warm with concern. "Come get me when you're ready to go."

Kristi made her way through the dispersing crowd. "I'll help, Sam. There's no one in the infirmary now. Decker can call if he needs me."

"Thanks." Samantha exchanged one last glance with Thor before he disappeared down the hallway. Then she stepped into her room. "It's not that bad."

"Why does he want Patty's journal?" Kristi knelt, picked up a drawer from the floor, and slid it back into the dresser.

Samantha scooped up her panties and began to fold them. "He said he wanted to see what she wrote about him. I told him it was none of his business."

"Is he insecure or what?" Kristi righted the lamp on Samantha's desk, then froze, a smile spreading on her face. "There are two condoms in your trash. It was Thor, wasn't it? Is he as incredible in bed as Malik?"

Heat rushed into Samantha's face. "I ... He..."

"I knew it!" Kristi picked up the papers Lance had knocked off Samantha's desk. "Malik is the best lover I've ever had. If Thor is anything like him... Sorry. You just had your space violated, and I'm getting into your business."

"I'm just more private than you are."

Kristi seemed to accept that. "After getting so many complaints about the noise, Malik and I snuck away to the greenhouse last night. That man knows what to do with his cock. That's for sure. I'm surprised I can walk today."

What was Samantha supposed to say to that? "I'm happy for you."

Kristi shrugged. "It will all be over when they leave. But in the meantime, I'm going to take what I can and enjoy myself. That's what you should do, too."

THOR STOOD outside the small conference room with Segal, going over their plan. "You're the one with the interrogation experience. You should take the lead."

Segal shook his head. "You start. Let me watch his reactions. I'll step in if I think it's necessary."

"Just remember this isn't a war zone. Lance is a civilian with legal rights. We can't touch him. If he asks for a lawyer, I'm not sure what we'll do."

There were no lawyers. Shields thought the stakes were so high and the situation so unusual that they might have more latitude than they would back home. Thor didn't know much about the US legal system and had to trust her.

"Keep him distracted and off-balance," Segal said. "Hammer him with questions, one after the other."

"Okay. Let's do this." Thor opened the door and walked inside to find Jones standing behind Lance, whose wrists were still bound. Thor sat across from him, Segal standing in the background. "Yesterday, you told us you went back to your room at midnight. You lied to us. You went to the computer lab. Why?"

"I just wanted to catch up on email. After that, I went to my room."

"He's lying," Segal said.

"Care to try again?" Thor leaned closer. "This time, give us the truth."

Lance glared at him, indignation on his face. "I did check my email."

"Lying."

"What else did you do?" Thor looked the bastard in the eyes. "If we have to, we'll confiscate your computer and your phone, hack in, and see what we find. I'm giving you a chance to tell the truth. You were caught red-handed breaking into Dr. Park's room. Do yourself a favor and come clean."

Lance was sweating now, perspiration beading on his forehead. "I'll lose my job."

"Oh, brother, that ship has sailed," Jones said. "You'll be lucky if you don't spend the rest of the winter locked in your itty-bitty room."

Lance looked from Jones to Thor. "Hardin wouldn't do that."

"He suggested it." Thor let that sink in. "What were you

doing in the computer lab late the night Patty was poisoned."

Lance's face crumpled, and Thor knew he was close to breaking.

Thor pushed harder. "You *lied* to us. Witnesses saw you there close to the time when the military satellite was hacked."

Lance went pale. "It was hacked? You think I ..."

"You're the IT expert on station. We know you lied about where you were that night. The Pentagon is very interested in you, man. It doesn't look good."

Lance broke. "I hacked into Patty's email."

That wasn't the answer Thor had expected. "You hacked into your girlfriend's email. Why would you do that, Lance?"

"I thought she was seeing someone else. I didn't go back to her room with her that night. She claimed she had work to do. Every night that week, she said she was busy. But she wasn't in the Dark Sector Lab, and when I went to her room, she wasn't there either—or she didn't answer."

Segal stepped forward. "What did you find in her email, lover boy?"

"Nothing—just the usual shit between her and Sam, emails from the university, messages from her parents."

Segal sat. "You hacked into your girlfriend's email because you were jealous. I find that interesting, don't you, guys?"

Thor had to agree. "A jealous lover."

"Jealous men do all kinds of reckless things," Jones said.

"Why did you lie to us about where you were that night?" Segal asked.

"I knew it would look bad."

Segal nodded. "Yeah, it does look bad. What did you do

after you hacked Patty's email? Did you confront her, pour some methanol in a nice bottle of wine for her?"

"No!" There was fear on Lance's face now. "No, I didn't kill her. I really liked her. I could never have done anything to hurt her."

Segal kept at him. "Hacking her email wasn't an act of love. You just admitted you were jealous. Today, you broke into Dr. Park's room to steal Patty's journal. That's stalker behavior."

"I just wanted the journal so I could see if she'd written about anyone else."

"That still matters to you even though she's dead?" Thor had never been able to understand why some men treated women like property. "Wouldn't you rather live with the good memories than dredge up more pain for yourself?"

Lance squirmed. "Wouldn't you want to know? What if this guy—whoever he was—had something to do with her death? Maybe she wrote about him. Maybe all the answers are there."

Segal got them back on track. "What did you do after you hacked Patty's email, Lance? Did you fight with her? Did you grab some methanol from the LO arch?"

"No! I went to her room. I knocked. She didn't answer. Then I went to bed—and that's the truth. The next morning, I heard that Sam had found her and taken her to the infirmary. I went to see what had happened, and ... she was dead. I couldn't believe it."

His shoulders slumped, and he began to cry.

Thor stepped out of the room with Segal. "What do you think?"

"I think he's telling the truth. Also, now we know that something unusual was going on with Patty—an affair or something else. We need to retrace her steps, find out what she was doing and who she was with that last week. We need that journal."

"It's locked away with the package."

"You already secured it." Segal looked pleased. "Perfect. When we're done questioning the rest of the people on Shields' list, we should read through her entries for her last week. Maybe she can give us the killer's name."

Thor was pretty certain Samantha wouldn't like this. "Let's get our stalker here back to his room and confine him there until we sort through this."

They had four more persons of interest to question if they were going to make it through Shields' list today.

SAMANTHA STRUGGLED to concentrate as she recycled the fridges on the SPT, her thoughts jumbled, her emotions tangled. When she wasn't trying to figure out who'd killed Patty, she was ranting at Lance in her head—or remembering the feel of Thor kissing her, touching her, driving himself into her. And, wow, was that a rare elliptical double-ringed galaxy?

Grief. Fear. Rage. Lust. Fascination.

It was like having a head full of ping-pong balls in constant motion.

She double-checked her work at every step as she performed the last calibrations to get the telescope scanning again and then verified the readouts on the computers. But still, her thoughts kept drifting.

Thor had called her beautiful. He'd made her *feel* beautiful.

It will all be over when they leave. But in the meantime, I'm going to take what I can and enjoy myself. That's what you should do, too.

Kristi's words came back to Samantha, a sinking feeling in her stomach.

She couldn't get too attached to Thor—or his kisses. He would be leaving soon, going back to his life of jetting around the world. She would be here until her flight back to Chicago in November. There was no chance that their relationship would outlive their time on the ice.

Thor is temporary. Science is eternal. Remember that.

Yes, but science didn't make her scream the way Thor had. If he hadn't covered her mouth, she wouldn't have been able to show her face in the galley for breakfast.

Sweet heaven.

She set the telescope to scan a new sector, raw data flowing into the computers, her focus slipping again.

Was Lance the killer? Part of her hoped he was because then the mystery would be solved. But the thought that someone Patty had loved might have ended her life was too awful. It was also terrifying to think that Samantha might have been friends with a murderer, sharing meals with him, splitting bottles of wine, talking about her research, trusting him with Patty's heart.

There was another thing. When the killer was caught, Thor would leave.

He's not going to stay here until November, so get that idea out of your head now.

Yes, she'd stupidly let herself fantasize about that. Months of nights with him—great sex, conversation, companionship. But it wasn't going to happen. Her time with him would end soon. This was just a fling, a few weeks of stolen joy.

A burst of radio static made her jump.

"Dr. Park, this is Isaksen."

"Samantha here."

"Are you ready to head back?"

She glanced at the clock, saw that it was almost six. "Yes. I'll wrap up."

"I'm on my way, over."

She rebooted a computer that had slowed to a crawl then checked all the connections between the telescope and the computers. By the time Thor knocked at the door, she was ready.

He stepped inside, removed his mask and hat. "We need to talk."

That sounded serious.

"Okay." She sat, motioned to Patty's chair.

But Thor remained standing. "I'm going to read the last week of entries in Patty's journal."

"*You* want to read Patty's journal?" Samantha stared at him.

He stood there, still in his parka, mask and hat in his hands. "It's for the investigation. I wish I could explain, but I can't."

"You can't even give me a vague idea?"

Thor seemed to wrestle with this. "We have reason to believe something unusual happened that last week of her life, something she didn't share with anyone—not you, not Lance. We're hoping she wrote about it there."

Samantha tried to remember the last week of Patty's life. It seemed like it had been so long ago now. Had something happened? Had Patty been caught up in something without Samantha knowing anything about it? "Why are you telling me? You have the legal authority, right?"

"You and I have a personal connection, so I'm telling you out of respect. Not telling you would feel like lying."

And that *right there* was as good as foreplay.

"Thanks." She stood. "That means a lot to me."

His gaze stayed on her chair, his lips curving in a smile. "I had a fantasy about you on that chair."

"You fantasized about me?"

"Oh, yeah."

She looked back at her chair.

He laughed. "It's not the chair, Samantha. It's you."

Samantha's heart skipped a beat. She walked over to him, slid her hands up the front of his parka. "What did we do in my chair?"

He wrapped an arm around her, palm in the middle of her back, a lop-sided grin on his face. "You straddled me and rode me until you came."

Heat flared between her thighs. "Well, the chair is here —and so are we."

He touched his forehead to hers. "I didn't bring a condom."

She was about to say something about how sad that was when she remembered. "Well, I have a similar chair in my room."

His lop-sided grin became a sexy smile. "Is that so?"

15

Thor sat in Samantha's chair, her back to him, her thighs straddling his, their gazes fixed on her mirror —and the erotic sight of his cock sliding in and out of her. "See how beautiful you are?"

She stared at their reflection as he withdrew then thrust into her again, burying himself completely. "Oh! That's so ... *hot*."

"Fuck, yeah, it is." It turned him on every bit as much as it did her, her body gripping him tightly, the slick friction muted by the condom—but still incredible.

He built up the rhythm stroke by stroke until he was pounding into her from below, one hand caressing her breast, the other reaching around to stroke her clit.

"Oh, *Thooooor*..." She moaned out his name, the nails of one hand digging into his forearm, the other reaching back behind his neck, her gaze still on the mirror. "*Yes*."

He willed himself to relax, to savor the sensation of being inside her, lust for her pounding in his chest, his nuts drawing tight. He needed to hold out, to last, to make this good for her, for Samantha.

He whispered her name, punctuating his words with kisses, his lips finding the curve of her shoulder, the sensitive skin beneath her ear, her earlobe. "*Åhhh,* Samantha. You're... too... much."

He could tell she was close, her breasts flushed and swollen, her breathing ragged, every muscle in her body tense.

Her eyes drifted shut, her head falling back against his shoulder, her body arching to press her breast deeper into his hand.

He couldn't help but groan, aroused to the breaking point by her gesture of sensual surrender, her head rolling back and forth on his shoulder now. Then her breath caught, her eyes went wide—and she shattered, biting her lip to keep from crying out.

His hips a piston now, he drove her climax home, falling over that bright edge with her, orgasm burning through him, white-hot and incandescent.

She went limp against him, laughed. "You're *so* good."

He wrapped an arm around her waist, kissed the top of her head, tenderness filling his chest. He couldn't bring himself to let go of her, wanting her even though his sexual hunger had just been satiated. What the hell was that about?

But they couldn't stay like this.

"I need to take off the condom while I'm still hard."

"Right."

While she crawled off him and into bed, he removed the condom, tossed it into her trash, and wiped himself with a tissue.

She reached for him, and he got into bed beside her, holding her close so the two of them could fit. For a time, they stayed like that, her cheek against his chest.

"These beds are too small," she said in a sleepy voice.

"You're telling me." His feet hung over the bottom. "We should complain."

That made her laugh, and she began to compose an imaginary letter. "Dear National Science Foundation: This letter is to inform you that the beds at Amundsen-Scott Station are too small to accommodate sexual intercourse and post-coital snuggling. Please address this problem soon."

"I'm sure they'll get right on that."

"Malik and Kristi had sex in the greenhouse last night. They didn't want to keep people awake."

"The greenhouse?" Thor had thought Jones had spent the night in his room alone. "If Cobra's owners were here, they'd kick his ass—and mine."

"Then I'm glad they're not here." She pressed a kiss to his sternum. "With all this terrible stuff happening, you and my work with the telescope are the only things that make me feel safe and grounded. Geez. Sorry. That might be the nerdiest thing I've ever said to a man."

"Hey, don't feel bad." He ran his fingers along her spine. "I'm honored to be mentioned in the same breath as the telescope—and I'm glad you feel safe with me."

She might not feel that way if she knew you better.

That had been war. It was in the past.

SAMANTHA SAT BOLT UPRIGHT, her face alight with excitement. "I forgot to tell you the news. I think we might have discovered a rare elliptical double-ringed galaxy. They make up only about ten percent of the galaxies in the universe. I haven't had time to analyze anything yet, but it looks a lot like Hoag's Object with young stars in the outer ring and older stars in the inner core."

Thor had no idea what a Hoag's Object was. He propped himself up on his elbow. "How can you tell the age of the stars?"

"Younger stars are typically hotter and emit more blue light, while older stars are often cooler and emit more red light." She shook her head. "Sorry, I don't want to bore you or come across as a total nerd."

"You're not boring me." He reached up, tucked a strand of hair behind her ear. "Your whole face lights up when you talk about your work. Samantha Park, discoverer of galaxies. That's pretty damned cool."

Her lips curved in a hopeful smile, something vulnerable in her eyes. "You really believe that?"

"Hell, yeah."

"Patty always said that men are intimidated by brainy women."

"Only if they're idiots." He leaned in, kissed a rosy nipple. "Intelligence is sexy."

A burst of static.

"Jones to Isaksen."

For helvede. Damn it.

He reached for his radio, which sat on Samantha's desk beside his pistol. "Jones, this is Isaksen. What do you need?"

"Uh, well, we're waiting for you."

Fuck. Right.

He'd lost track of time. He was supposed to meet Jones and Segal to remove Patty's journal from the vacant room. Rather than spending tonight with Samantha, he was going to spend it reading the private thoughts of her murdered best friend.

"I'm on my way." He sat up, caught Samantha's chin. "I

don't want to go, but I must. Will you be okay alone here tonight?"

Her room had been broken into today. He wouldn't blame her if she felt nervous about being alone in here.

"I'll be fine. If I get freaked out, I have a few more Xanax."

"Set that security camera after I leave and keep your radio handy. If you need me, call." He got dressed, tucked his pistol and concealed holster inside his jeans, and grabbed his radio. "*Sov godt, skat*. Sleep well."

It was almost painful to walk away.

SAMANTHA WASHED HER FACE, brushed her teeth, and combed her hair, her thoughts fixed on Thor. My God, the man was incredible. Not only was he the best sex she'd ever had, but he also seemed to care about her work, listening while she babbled about stars and galaxies.

Intelligence is sexy.

He certainly made her *feel* sexy—the intensity in his gaze when he looked at her naked body, the heat in his kisses, the way he said her name when he was fucking her.

Oh, Samantha. You're... too... much.

She'd spent most of her life feeling inadequate when it came to men. Sex had always come with anxiety. Would she come fast enough or at all? Would the guy find her disappointing in bed? Would she say something nerdy and turn him off?

With Thor, she forgot to worry. It all just seemed to come together—the emotional side of sex and the physical side. Was he even real?

She finished combing her hair and walked from the

restroom back to her room, hesitating at her door, chills skittering down her spine as if she were being watched.

"Samantha?"

She gasped, whirled, found Vasily standing behind her.

He hadn't been there a moment ago. "Sorry. I frightened you. I came to see if you are okay. I heard a man broke into your room."

"Y-yes." Samantha had left her radio in her room, so she couldn't call Thor. "He was trying to steal Patty's private journal, her diary."

"I brought for you something." He held out what looked like a pocket knife—except there was no blade that she could see. "This is the safety switch. Slide back, push this button."

In a millisecond, a stiletto knife appeared.

"A switchblade."

Vasily folded the knife down, clicked the safety button back into place. "I sleep better tonight knowing you have a weapon."

"I... I can't take that." She started to tell him she had a radio and a motion-activated security camera in her room but stopped herself.

He thrust it into her palm. "Please take it. I show you. You slide the safety back."

She tested the weight in her hand, slid the safety button back. "I don't know. I—"

"Push the button."

She did as he said.

Snap.

The blade appeared, fast and lethal.

But Samantha had never owned a weapon of any kind. She handed it back to him. "I appreciate your concern for me, but I can't keep this."

He tried to get her to take it. "You should keep it. I want to help you."

"What if a bad guy gets it away from me?"

His brown eyes looked straight into hers. "Do *not* let that happen."

"No, thank you, Vasily. I just can't."

Looking disappointed, he turned and walked away, leaving her to stare after him.

Unnerved, she stepped into her room and locked the door. The remaining Xanax were there, too, still in their blister pack. But she didn't take one. If something happened tonight, she wanted to be alert, not drugged and out of it.

Nothing is going to happen tonight.

She crawled into bed, turned off her light, and stared at the ceiling, but sleep wouldn't come, random images chasing each other through her mind. Malik and Lev pinning down a furious Lance. The reflection of Thor sliding in and out of her. Vasily holding the switchblade. Patty's body lying on the bed in the infirmary.

Oh, Patty.

Samantha threw back her covers and got out of bed. "To hell with this."

She put her bathrobe over her pajamas, stepped into her slippers, and left her room, remembering the radio this time. The hallway was empty and silent as she walked to the self-service kitchen next to the galley. There, she heated water in the electric kettle for a cup of chamomile tea.

Steve walked in, carrying an empty coffee cup. There were dark circles beneath his eyes, lines of fatigue on his face. "Can't sleep?"

"I'm just ... tense, I guess. How about you? You look exhausted."

"All this shit is happening, and I still have a station to

run." Steve set his cup on the counter and drew her into a hug. "I'm so sorry, kiddo. This has been tougher on you than anyone. Is there anything I can do?"

"Bring Patty back?"

He released her and stepped back, sympathy in his eyes. "I can do a lot of things, but not that. I miss her, too."

The kettle whistled.

Samantha found the chamomile tea and dropped a teabag into a clean mug. Then she filled the cup with steaming hot water and stirred in some honey.

"Milk?" Steve opened the fridge and took out a pitcher of reconstituted powdered stuff. "Or whatever passes for milk here."

"Thank you." She held out the mug. "Just a little."

"Whiskey would probably help more than tea." Steve poured the milk, then set the pitcher back in the fridge. "I thought you'd be with our resident god."

"Thor?" Steve's description made Samantha laugh, though given how good Thor was in bed, maybe he really *was* descended from Odin. "He has more important things to do than hold my hand when I'm feeling scared."

"I hope the tea helps. Goodnight."

She had to ask. "Are switchblades prohibited on station?"

"Switchblades?" He seemed to consider her question. "I don't think we have an official switchblade policy. Who has a switchblade? One of the Cobra guys?"

"Vasily tried to give me one tonight. He came out of nowhere, showed me how to use it, and told me to protect myself. That's part of the reason I can't sleep."

"Jesus." Steve rubbed his jaw. "I can see why you're tense. To be honest, I wish you all had gotten off the ground before the Russians realized they were stuck. They're a pain in my ass. Two of them got in a fistfight in the lounge tonight over a fucking game of darts, and they weren't even drunk. Just be careful, okay?"

"I will. Thanks, Steve. And goodnight."

THOR MET Jones and Segal outside their rooms. They waited until no one else was around. Then Segal opened the vacant room with his bump key so that Thor could retrieve Patty's journal.

"Thanks." He locked the door behind him. "We've got a meeting at zero-six-hundred. You two get some sleep."

Thor took the journal to his room and settled down for a long night. He decided to start reading with Patty's arrival on station to make sure he didn't miss anything. He'd gone only a few pages before he found himself smiling at her sense of humor and even laughing at her jokes.

"I've spent a winter here before, but when I stepped out of that plane and the cold hit me, a part of me wanted to hide under an airplane seat and sneak back to Christchurch. But Samantha would never forgive me if I left her here alone. Besides, she'd end up with a galaxy named after her, and I wouldn't. I can't let that happen, even if she is the smarter of the two of us."

Did Samantha know that Patty thought she was the smarter one? Possibly. Samantha had said something at the memorial service about helping Patty with one of her science classes while Patty helped her get out of her shell.

"Feb. 28: There's an obnoxious kid on station who keeps filming everyone and harassing the women. I swear this kid is an incel who somehow escaped his mother's basement. I predict that someone will punch this little shit in his filthy mouth before we fly out in November. I hope so, anyway. Is that wrong?"

Thor had to agree with her on that one. He wrote down the date of this entry in case he came across more conflict with Jason.

"*March 10: Lance and I hung out last night and talked until almost 1 a.m. He's the IT guy this winter. I wasn't too impressed with him at first. Okay, I won't lie, I didn't even notice him. Then we both ended up in the lounge watching* Citizen Kane. *He knew so much about it. We're having dinner tomorrow.*"

Thor hadn't imagined Lance as a classic film buff.

"*March 23: The sun dropped below the horizon today. We won't see it again until September 21. I wrote a little song in honor of the event and tried to play it on one of the guitars in the music room. I haven't touched a guitar since high school. Still, I think the lyrics were a smash hit.*

"'*There goes the sun, doo da doo doo/There goes the sun/And I say, it's all night.*'

"*Lance started banging on the cowbell and dancing. People shouted, 'More cowbell!' Poor Samantha stood there looking confused. 'Why more cowbell? What's the big deal with the cowbell?' Oh, my God, I laughed so hard. I just love her.*"

Thor could see why people described Patty as being full of life—and why Samantha missed her so much. He'd begun to feel it, too—a sense of loss.

He read through the rest of March and then started April, the next entry bringing him fully alert.

"*April 2: I saw something in the science lab here in the main building that I couldn't understand. It looked like someone was running hacking software on one of the desktop computers. I'm not a computer expert, but I know enough to recognize hacking software when I see it. I'm not sure whether to report it since I have no idea who was running that program or why.*"

Thor kept reading, a knot in his chest.

"*April 4: I lied to Lance again. I feel so bad about it. Poor guy!*

I'll have to make it up to the both of us soon. I'm sacrificing a night of sex for this, after all. Tonight, I'm going to hang out in the science lab and do busywork. If someone is up to something illegal there, my presence might prevent them from continuing. If it's all in my head, then I get ahead of our workload."

So, that bastard Barclay had told them the truth—at least about this. Patty had deceived him, but she hadn't done it to hook up with another man. She'd seen hacking software and had taken it on herself to figure out who was behind it.

For helvede! Damn it.

Some part of Thor wished he could warn her, tell her to stay with Lance and forget what she'd seen. The satellite would have been hacked anyway, but she would still be alive.

He came to her last entry.

"April 5: No one showed up last night, so I logged onto the computer that had been running the hacking software. I dug around a bit, and it looked to me like someone had been tracking a US military satellite. Maybe one of the other scientists is working on a secret project for the DOD. I don't know. I enabled logon auditing—it had been disabled—so that I could find out who is using that computer and when. I thought about telling Samantha and asking her to come with me. But if I'm wrong, I'd be wasting her time. If I find proof, I'll report it."

Thor stared at the page, dread hitting him in the chest as he realized how close Samantha had come to getting caught up in this—and possibly ending up dead, too. Patty had gone to the science lab alone that night, tried to get proof. But the person behind it—the person who'd brought down the satellite—had given her wine poisoned with methanol, using their friendship as a weapon against her.

Forbandet røvhul. Fucking asshole.

Anger and sadness welled up inside him, Patty's words enough to make him feel connected to her—and her murder. But now the truth would come out. Thanks to Patty and her journal, they had more information.

Thor set up the scanner, scanned the relevant pages, and emailed them to Shields, the sense of loss staying with him.

"I'll do my best to find this fucker, Patty. I promise."

16

Thor moved through the compound, rifle raised, night vision goggles turning the world a ghostly green. He and Jakob had already taken out six guys guarding the place, so whoever was inside knew they were here.

A man with an AK stepped out a side door.

Rat-at-at!

Thor dropped him with a three-round burst.

Women's screams. Children crying.

Jakob's voice came over his earpiece. "*Hvad gør vi så hvis al Harzi er gået?*" *What are we going to do if al Harzi is gone?*"

"*Han er her. Hold dig skarp.*" *He's here. Stay sharp.*

The muzzle of another AK peeked out from around the corner.

"*Han er min.*" *He's mine.* Jakob had the same right to avenge Lars, Mads, and Felix as Thor did.

A young man barely old enough for a beard appeared and ran at them with a cry, an AK-47 in his hands.

Rat-at-at-at!

Jakob fired, and the kid fell.

But the kid had been a distraction, a rush of footsteps coming up behind them.

Thor pivoted, dropped to one knee, and fired.

Rat-at-at-at! Rat-at-at-at!

Two combatants fell to the dirt, dead.

Weapons raised, Thor and Jakob crossed the courtyard and entered the main dwelling, frightened murmurs and the cries of children coming from a room to their right.

Jakob went through the door first, opened fire, dropping an older man.

Rat-at-at!

"*Er det ham*?" *Is it him?*

Rifle raised, Thor walked over to the man, lifted his NVGs, and shined the flashlight from his scope on the dead man's face. "*Nej.*" *No.*

He drew his goggles back down, glanced around to see a half dozen women, some very young, huddled against the wall, staring at him with horror on their faces. He didn't know Pashto, so he tried English. "We're not going to hurt you."

Then he saw her.

Samantha!

She sat on a bedroll in the corner, eyes wide, clearly terrified of him.

She screamed.

Thor jerked awake, sat up, found himself not in Afghanistan, but in his room at Amundsen-Scott Station. He got out of bed, his body drenched with cold sweat.

Fuck.

It had been a long, damned time since he'd had nightmares about Afghanistan. What the hell was Samantha doing in his dream?

He glanced at his watch, saw that it was zero-five-twenty. He had a meeting with Tower and Shields in forty minutes.

Knowing he wouldn't be able to get back to sleep, he dressed and hit the gym for a quick run before heading back to his room to change and grab his computer. By the time he had dressed, Jones and Segal were in the hall waiting for him.

Jones took one look at him. "You okay?"

"Yeah. Just a long night."

Jones grinned. "With the journal or with Dr. Park?"

"The journal." Thor headed up the stairs to the second level. "How was the greenhouse—or did you and Kristi find someplace else?"

"Jesus." Segal shook his head. "The greenhouse, man? Seriously?"

"How'd you hear about that?"

"Women talk to each other." Thor made his way to the small conference room. He logged in while Segal and Jones made coffee and traded barbs over Jones' sex life.

"I'm just saying it's unprofessional, man. Do it on your own time."

"You're just jealous because you're not getting any."

Segal laughed. "I just have higher standards for myself than boning the first chick who will have me while I'm on assignment."

"You two done?" Thor's finger hovered above the trackpad.

They shut their mouths and joined him at the conference table.

He clicked to start the meeting, sat, and took a sip of his coffee.

A moment later, Tower and Shields appeared on the screen.

"Great work yesterday," Tower said. "The analyst team has gone over the interviews and yesterday's events with Barclay, as well as the pages from Dr. Holcomb's journal. Shields?"

The view switched to Shields. "We can cross Jason Huger off our list. We were able to download the records from Huger's computer. He was where he said he was that night—hanging out online with his gaming buddies. We can take Dr. Park and Ms. Chang off the list as well. We assess that their answers are authentic. The money deposited into Ms. Chang's account was part of an inheritance from an uncle."

That left Lance Barclay, Bai Zhang Wei, and Kazem Hamidi.

Shields went on. "As for Barclay, the journal entries suggest he's telling the truth. I'm not ready to rule him out as a suspect entirely. He has the skills, and he lied about where he was that night. Also, his jealousy could be a motive. But I'm more interested in Kazem Hamidi. He hasn't admitted to his aggressive confrontation with Dr. Holcomb, and he still can't account for his whereabouts."

"What about Zhang Wei?" Segal asked. "He says he got the nights confused and changed his story to say he worked late."

"He's still on the list, too. No one you interviewed remembers seeing him, either."

Then Tower's face appeared on the screen. "Dr. Holcomb's journal confirms that her murder and the attack on the satellite are connected, as the analyst team believed. We know the killer's motive now. He wanted to silence her. It's our job to make sure he fails. The question is, what's our next move?"

Thor had thought about this. "We need to force the killer's hand, draw him out."

Tower nodded. "What do you suggest?"

"We can tell everyone that Jones and Segal are flying home with the package, while I'm staying to find the killer. We make it look real—flight schedule, all of it. This bastard wants the package. The moment it's in the air, he's lost his chance. He knows that. I'm betting he'll do whatever he can to get his hands on it before our fictional plane lands. With any luck, he'll get sloppy."

Tower considered it. "It's a risky plan."

"It is."

Desperate men were dangerous.

Samantha watched the readouts as the telescope finished observing four sky fields at declination minus forty-five degrees and then moved to the next four. She'd had time to look at yesterday's observations, the data from all thousand detectors coming together to create an image that was unmistakably an elliptical double-ringed galaxy. The work was a welcome distraction from the chaos that was life on station. This is what she was here to do, not obsess about murderers and hacked satellites and former KGB agents.

Still, her mind kept drifting to Patty's murder.

On the walk over, she'd told Thor about Vasily and the switchblade, and he hadn't been happy with her.

"I wish you'd let me know," he'd said, a grumpy frown on his face. "Vasily is not someone you want to hang with."

"For the record, I wasn't 'hanging with' him. He came up on me out of the blue."

Then Thor had warned her not to be alone with Kazem

or Bai. He hadn't given her an explanation, but it didn't take a doctorate to understand that Cobra must have narrowed their list of suspects and that both men were still on it.

It was hard for her to imagine either of them as a murderer. Both were scientists dedicated to their work. No, Kazem hadn't taken Patty's rejection as well as he might have, but he hadn't done anything violent. And yet someone here—someone everyone considered a friend and colleague —had killed her.

Samantha willed herself to focus, checking each amplifier channel's output before heading into the back to make more coffee. She reached for the canister and remembered it was empty. She'd used the last of the coffee grounds this morning.

She walked to the hallway and unlocked the door that separated the SPT control room from the BICEP half of the building. She made her way to the shared storeroom for another bag of coffee, Kazem's and Greg's voices drifting up from their control center.

"Try rebooting it now."

"I hope this works."

"Yes!"

She returned to her side of the building and brewed a fresh pot of coffee, carrying the steaming mug back to her desk, her thoughts drifting again.

None of this made sense to her. How could the killer possibly think he could get away with it? They were all here for the duration of austral winter in a closed environment. Under normal circumstances, no one came, and no one left. That meant the pool of suspects was small and static.

But what if the bastard hadn't planned it—or at least hadn't thought it through? Methanol poisoning was slow and easy to expose. All she'd needed was the bottle of wine and a lighter. Surely, the killer had understood that the autopsy would reveal...

Chills skittered down her spine.

Under normal circumstances, Patty's body would still be here. She'd be frozen solid somewhere in the service arches below the station, waiting for a flight home in austral spring. There would have been no autopsy until November, and by that time, no one here would have remembered what had happened that night. An investigation would be almost impossible.

Maybe the killer believed he *could* get away with it. No one on station had imagined that the Pentagon would risk sending a team of operators to retrieve components for the satellite. Or that Patty's body would go home on their plane. Or that those operators would take on a murder investigation.

The killer hadn't planned for any of that.

He hadn't planned for Cobra.

"Shit." She needed to tell Thor.

She picked up her radio but hesitated. He was probably busy. It's not like she had new evidence for him. This was nothing more than a few connected dots. It wasn't the kind of thing that would unmask the killer.

"Samantha?"

She gasped, dropped the radio, and turned to find Kazem standing behind her in his snow pants and a long-sleeved shirt. She must have forgotten to lock the door to the walkway when she'd returned with the coffee.

Shit.

She would have picked up the radio, but dropping it had broken the plastic casing, and the batteries had rolled beneath her desk. "Damn it, Kazem! Why the hell did you sneak up on me like that?"

"I'm sorry. I did not mean to scare you. I hoped we could talk."

She held up a hand. "Hang on a second. I was just about to call in."

"Okay."

She picked up her station-issued radio. "Charli, Charli, this is Samantha out at the Dark Sector Lab."

"Charli here, Sam."

"Hey, Charli. I'm here in the lab talking with Kazem." That was Samantha's insurance. "Can you please let Thor know I need him to come out here?"

"Will do. Is everything okay?"

"Yes, I think so. Tell him it's urgent."

"Got it. Over."

It would take Thor fifteen minutes to make it here, which meant she was alone with Kazem until then. But now Charli knew he was here. If anything happened to her...

Samantha set the radio aside, gestured toward Patty's chair, and did her best to look like she wasn't unnerved by Kazem's presence. "What's going on?"

He stayed where he was, his expression crumpling into misery, a pleading look in his eyes. "Please help me. I didn't kill Patty, and I didn't hack the satellite. They think I did it because I am from Iran. But it wasn't me."

Samantha didn't know what to say. "Did you tell them this?"

"Yes, but they do not believe me because I have no proof. You must talk to them. Explain to them that I would never hurt her."

"Kazem, you're going to have to do that yourself. I don't know where you were or what you were doing that night. They're not interested in anyone's opinion. They just want facts."

His shoulders slumped. He walked to Patty's chair and sat. "I told them I was in the lounge with the others, but it was a lie. I wasn't there."

"Where were you?"

"If I tell them, people in Iran might find out. I would be ... I would be hanged."

"What do you mean?"

He looked toward the hallway.

Samantha followed his gaze to find Bai Zhang Wei standing there, the same pleading expression on his face.

"Kazem can't tell them where he was because ... he was with me."

THOR RAN the kilometer between the station and the Dark Sector lab, the cold air burning his throat even with the mask. He and Shields had been going over his plan for drawing out the killer when he'd gotten word from Charli that Samantha was in the Dark Sector Lab with their top suspect. Why he'd heard it from Charli and not via radio from Samantha he didn't know. But if she'd forgotten her radio again, the two of them would have a little talk.

Coughing, he reached the stairs and took them two at a time. He drew his pistol, looked through the small window in the door, and saw Samantha sitting at her desk and talking with both Kazem Hamidi and Bai Zhang Wei.

Hva' fanden? What the hell?

He holstered the pistol, stepped inside, and pulled off his mask. "Are you okay?"

Samantha stood, walked to the door, grabbed her parka. "We need to talk."

She opened the door and stepped out into the cold, zipping her parka to her chin.

"Why didn't you call me directly on your radio?"

"I had the radio in my hand to call you for a different reason." She wasn't wearing a hat or a mask, her breath rising in a cloud of ice crystals. "Then Kazem came up behind me, and I was so startled that I dropped it. The batteries rolled under my desk. I did the best I could at the moment, okay?"

"Okay." Thor coughed, his throat raw from his run through the cold. "What the hell are they both doing here?"

"That's what I wanted to tell you. They're lovers. They say they were together the night Patty was poisoned."

"What? Jesus!"

"Kazem is terrified that if he tells you the truth, the Iranian government will find out he's gay. Apparently, people get hanged for that in Iran. That's why he lied about being in the lounge and Bai lied about being in his room."

Thor shook his head. "I don't buy it. Wei was at the IceCube lab that night."

"Yes." Samantha huddled deeper into her parka. "That's where they hook up. They're afraid of being seen together, so they meet there after hours. They bring food from the galley and have romantic dinners. There's a sofa bed. They can hold hands and kiss and ... stuff without being seen."

"Didn't Kazem try to ask Patty out more than once? Why would a gay man ask a woman for a date?"

"Isn't that obvious? Patty was supposed to be his cover—proof that he's not gay."

Thor wasn't sure he could buy any of this. "Why did they come to you?"

"I guess they thought they could trust me. Kazem is terrified to the point of tears. You have to find a way to keep what he tells you out of the official record. I don't want to be the reason he ends up swinging from a rope."

Thor's gaze moved over the skin on her face. "You shouldn't be out here without a hat and mask. Let's get you back inside."

She stopped him with a hand to his chest. "Please, Thor. I believe them."

"Trust me, okay?" Thor opened the door, held it for her, and followed her inside.

Kazem sat in one of the office chairs, dread on his face, Bai behind him, his hand on Kazem's shoulder.

"Dr. Hamidi. Dr. Wei." Thor took off his mask, unzipped his parka, and met each man's gaze. "Samantha has just shared what you told her. I understand your situation."

Kazem shook his head. "I don't think you can understand, Mr. Thor. You are from Denmark. Bai and I have been to Denmark. We visited last summer. It is a paradise for gay men. Men can get married and walk together on the streets, like other couples. But in Iran, I would be arrested, tortured, and hanged. If the wrong person finds out..."

What he'd said about Denmark was true. It was one of the world's most progressive countries when it came to gay rights and had been for nearly a century.

"Then you know that I wouldn't do anything to put you in danger." Thor bent down and gathered the broken pieces of Samantha's radio. "I need the truth from you both, but there's no reason the details need to be a part of the official record. Cobra can protect you, but you need to tell us the truth."

They all walked back to the station together. While Samantha went to the galley for dinner, Thor met with Jones and Segal in the conference room to question Kazem and Bai separately. Segal handled most of it, going at them hard while Jones taped it to send back to Shields.

Afterward, Thor sat with Jones and Segal in the conference room, going over what each man had said. There were no holes in their stories, no red flags.

"They could have worked this out ahead of time," Jones said.

Segal nodded. "They could have, but there was nothing rehearsed about their answers. We'll have to see what Shields says, but I think they're telling the truth."

"There's one way to find out for certain." Thor glanced at his notes. "They said they visited Denmark last summer. I'm going to give Shields their passport and credit card information and see if their story checks out. If they really did spend a week together in Copenhagen last summer, there's no reason not to believe the rest of their story."

"Fuck." Jones leaned back in his chair, bent his arms behind his head, laced his fingers together. "You know what this means, don't you?"

Thor nodded. "We're back where we started."

17

Still breathing hard, Thor lay on Samantha's bed, his gorgeous body glistening with sweat. He reached for her, drew her down against him. "Where did you learn to do that? That was ... incredible."

"You sound surprised." She moved up his body, snuggled against him, rested her head on his chest. "I used science."

"Science? I fucking love science—especially now."

She did her best to explain. "Penises enjoy the stimulation of vaginas, right?"

Thor couldn't disagree. "Right."

"I theorized that oral sex would feel best for men if their partners made their mouths and hands work together to feel more like a vagina, while focusing on the most sensitive parts of the penis."

Thor grinned. "So, you just logicked your way through sexual physics and dick anatomy and came up with ... whatever you just did? A world-class astronomer reasoning her way to giving incredible head. Do you have any idea how *cute* that is?"

"Cute?" She raised her head, looked up at him. "Why are you laughing?"

"You amaze me, Samantha." His brow furrowed. "By the way, why does everyone call you Sam? Patty called you Samantha—at least in her journal. I call you Samantha. It's a pretty name. Should I call you Sam instead?"

"I prefer Samantha, but it seems to be too much for most people to say." She'd tried correcting people her first winter here, but it hadn't worked.

"You should tell them, let them know not to call you Sam any longer."

"It seems like a lot of fuss over something trivial."

He stroked her hair. "It's not trivial. It's your name, and you're worth the fuss."

"I suppose you're right." She threaded her fingers through his chest hair. "I'm glad you're not leaving yet."

"So am I."

He'd told her this evening that Cobra was flying Jones and Segal home when the next weather window opened in about a week, but that he would be staying to finish the investigation. She knew he'd be leaving eventually, but she'd take every day—and every night—she could get with him.

Are you falling for him?

No, of course, she wasn't. She'd given up on men. She was doing what Kristi was doing—taking what she could and enjoying herself.

"You should know that things could become more dangerous when the killer or his contacts hear that Jones and Segal are leaving and taking the package."

She propped herself up on her elbow, saw that his expression was serious. "You think the killer might try to stop them?"

"The person who brought that satellite down loses any

chance to profit by that action the moment the plane leaves. Yes, I think they'll try to stop us—or try to get the package from us. And then there are the Russians—or whoever is paying this guy. The people who wanted those components might become a threat, too. Be extra careful, okay? I'll get you another radio in the morning."

At the mention of her radio, it came back to her.

"Oh! I remembered what I wanted to tell you earlier." She sat up. "I realized this afternoon that the killer probably believed he could get away with murder. He—or she—thought that Patty's body would stay here on station until November. If you Cobra guys hadn't been sent down here, she would still be lying in a body bag in the LO arch. The autopsy wouldn't have happened until everyone who's here now had gone home. That would make it almost impossible to investigate, wouldn't it?"

Thor sat up, his brow furrowed. "Say that again."

"The killer probably thought they could get away with it because Patty's body wouldn't have gone back to the US for an autopsy until November. They counted on being gone before the autopsy results came back. Whoever loaded her body onto your plane and sent it home unknowingly ruined those plans."

Thor seemed to consider what she'd said. "I need to pass this along to Shields."

"I doubt that helps with anything, but…"

"It might. Thanks. You're right. If we Cobra guys hadn't come down here and those men in the service arch hadn't taken it upon themselves to load her body onto that outgoing plane, she would still be here, and we would have no idea that she'd been murdered. We'd be focused on the satellite hack and nothing else."

She ran a hand up his chest. "I want to thank you for

listening to Kazem and Bai today. I told them they could trust you."

Thor lay back, drew Samantha with him. "I'm waiting to get confirmation on elements of their story, so I can't write them off as suspects just yet. But, yeah, I don't want anyone getting hanged for being gay. I shouldn't be discussing this with you."

"Am I still a suspect?"

He kissed her hair. "No—but I shouldn't tell you that, either."

"What was it like reading Patty's journal? You don't have to tell me what she wrote or anything related to the investigation. I just … I miss her so much."

For a moment, Thor was quiet. When he spoke, there was a note of sadness in his voice. "I feel like I got to know her a little. She seems like a fun person and a good friend. When I finished, I felt grief, like I'd lost a friend, too. She loved you."

Samantha's throat went tight. "Did she write that?"

"Yeah, she did." Thor kissed her forehead.

Samantha blinked back tears. "Thanks for telling me."

"I promised her I'd find the bastard who killed her. They won't get away with it."

Samantha hoped that was true. "Just don't get killed yourself, okay?"

He kissed her again. "You got it."

THOR INVITED Ryan McClain into the small conference room. "Have a seat. We just have a few extra questions for you."

"Sure." McClain sat across from the computer. "Are you filming?"

"Yes." Segal explained. "It's hard to take in everything that's said while we're talking, so we film it in case we need to check back later."

Thor sat across from Ryan. "I spent the morning down in the LO arch talking with the guys about Patty's body and how it ended up on the airplane. Dean, Bob, and Walt said you were the guy who made that happen."

"Oh. Yeah. Well, I helped carry her down there. We all felt awful about losing her. Patty was a friend to all of us. When I heard a plane was coming in, I talked with Hardin about sending her body back, but he wouldn't approve it. He said there wasn't enough time because the pilot had to get airborne right away. I told him we could be standing there when the plane landed, but he cut me off."

This was all news to Thor. "So, Hardin refused to let her body go on the plane?"

"Yes. I got to talking with some of the guys down in the LO arch, and we figured we could handle it ourselves. During the summer, the guys down there are responsible for all of the outgoing shipping. They filled out the shipping form and emailed it to the authorities in Christchurch. Her ID and passport were already in the body bag with her, so we just carried her out and waited for you to land."

Thor had been standing right there when Hardin had gotten the news that Patty's body had gone out with the plane, and Thor couldn't remember him being particularly upset or angry about it. But Barclay had been. He'd shouted at Samantha. "What did Hardin say to you afterward when he found out?"

Ryan let out a breath. "Man, he was pissed at first. He reminded me that he was the site manager and said he couldn't run a station if we didn't follow protocols. Then he calmed down and said he appreciated what we'd done for Patty. He said he ought to have taken the time to hear me out when I initially suggested sending her back and that he was happy she was on her way home."

Thor wasn't sure what to make of that. "Did anyone else confront you about sending Patty's body home?"

"No one spoke to me, but I heard that Lance lost his shit in the hallway and started shouting at Samantha. She had nothing to do with it."

"Yeah, I witnessed that myself." Thor had gotten the information he wanted. "Thank you for speaking with us again."

Ryan stood. "Happy to help. See you all at the meeting this evening."

"Meeting?" Thor hadn't heard about that.

Segal turned off the camera. "Hardin called a meeting for seven—something about water usage with extra people on station or some shit."

"See you all later, and thanks for your help." Ryan left the room.

Thor waited until the door was closed. "What do you think?"

Jones stood, stretched. "I think we need to get Hardin in here."

"Has Shields gotten back to you about Kazem Hamidi and Bai Zhang Wei?"

Thor shook his head. "I talked with her early this morning, and she was still working on it. I asked her to take a second look at Hardin. Here's the thing that keeps coming back to me. Who wanted to keep her body on station? And who's the person she would have gone to if she had something suspicious to report?"

"Hardin," Jones and Segal said almost at the same time.

"Exactly." Thor glanced at his watch. "Let's upload all of this and check in with Shields to see if she's got anything new for us. It's about seven p.m. in Denver."

They caught Shields at home having dinner with her husband, Quinn McManus.

"You're keepin' my wife busy. You boys must be freezin' your bawbags aff. It's pure Baltic down there."

Most of the time, Thor had trouble understanding McManus' Glaswegian accent, but he got this one. "Believe it or not, they have heat down here. Our nuts are fine. Thanks."

"Quinn!" Laughing, Shields turned the screen away from her husband. "I was going to ping you after dinner. Bai's story checks out. Credit card records show he was definitely in Denmark when he said he was. But I can't prove anything where Kazem Hamidi is concerned. If Hamidi entered the Schengen Area through a different country, that would explain why there's no record of his entering Denmark. I need his flight information if you can get it."

"We're on it." Thor brought her up to date. "Anything on Hardin?"

"Not yet, but I'm working on it."

Quinn stuck his face in front of the camera. "She does need to eat and sleep and spend a wee bit of time wi' her husband, aye?"

Shields shook her head, but she was smiling. "Hey, you three be careful. We did a threat assessment this afternoon about your situation."

"Let's hear it." Thor had learned to respect Shields' judgment.

"We believe there's an eighty-percent chance the killer

will react with violence when he hears that the package is leaving Antarctica. Watch your backs."

KRISTI POKED AT DINNER—CHICKEN fried steak, biscuits, and mixed frozen veggies. "You're so lucky, Sam."

"It's Samantha, please." Samantha got the words out despite the awkwardness of her request. "I've never liked being called Sam."

"Oh. Okay. Samantha." Kristi didn't seem bothered. She looked up from her plate. "You're so lucky that Thor is staying longer. I wish Malik weren't leaving. It's going to be so hard to say goodbye."

Samantha glanced around the galley, but Thor, Malik, and Lev weren't there yet. "You've only known him for a couple of weeks. What happened to just taking what you can and enjoying yourself?"

"Malik happened." Kristi leaned in. "He's just too good in bed, and he's sweet, too. He's ruined me for other guys."

A week ago, Samantha would have thought Kristi was exaggerating or being overly emotional, but now she understood. She couldn't imagine getting together with anyone but Thor. He wasn't just a fantastic lover. He also saw her for who she was. His kindness had carried her through some of the toughest days of her life. "Maybe you two can reconnect after you get home."

"I'm not sure he would want that. We agreed there would be no strings."

"And now you want strings?"

"I want the *option* for strings."

Samantha wasn't sure what that meant. She hadn't let herself think about Thor leaving, but this conversation pushed her mind in that direction—and her stomach sank. It was hard to imagine six more months down here without him and Patty. "Maybe you should talk with him about it. Maybe he feels the same way."

"You think so?"

"You're both adults, right? Talk to him."

Of course, there was no chance that Samantha would take her own advice. Thor lived in the mountains west of Denver, while she worked in Chicago. There was no way for them to be together once they returned home.

She tried to change the subject, but Kristi couldn't get her mind off Malik. By the time she'd finished her meal, Samantha felt she knew more about Malik than she did Thor. "Are you sure he'd want you to tell me all of this?"

Then Hardin walked up to their table. "Hey, Sam, Kristi."

Kristi corrected him. "She prefers Samantha."

"Ah. Okay." He knelt beside the table and leaned in. "Samantha, can you do me a favor? I got an email from Patty's parents. They've got questions about her last week. You knew her a lot better than I did. Can you help me answer them?"

"Sure. See you later, Kristi." Samantha carried her tray to the dish pit and followed Hardin out of the galley toward the administrative offices.

"I really appreciate this," he said. "It was hard enough having to tell her parents that she was gone. But I just don't have the answers they want."

"I'm happy to help." Samantha meant it. "I can't imagine what it's like knowing their daughter was murdered."

"Neither can I. They seem like good people." He opened the door to his office, gestured her inside, then closed the door behind him. "Let me wake up my computer. It's on the screen. You can take my seat."

She sat. "I hope they find some kind of peace when—"

A sharp jab in the shoulder.

She gasped, jumped to her feet, saw Steve holding a hypodermic needle in his hand. Ice slid into her blood, the pieces coming together with a chilling *click*. "Oh, my God. It was *you*."

A rush of dizziness.

"Patty wouldn't mind her own fucking business. She kept poking around the computer I was using to hack the satellite. I made a special bottle of wine for her. When she came to report what she'd found, I offered her a drink. But I didn't want to kill her. I liked her. I don't want to kill you either. I just need to get information from your lover boy— and then I can get rid of him and his two goons."

"What did you give me? Was that methanol?" Dizziness left her unsteady on her feet, his office closing in around her.

"No, idiot. It's midazolam—a sedative. I stole it from the infirmary. It won't kill you. It will just make it easier for me to get you out of the building."

Out of the building? Where was he taking her?

"There's nothing out there."

"There's ice and cold and darkness."

"You ... bastard! You acted like you were grieving! You stood up at Patty's memorial and talked about how wonderful she was, but *you* killed her. Liar! Murderer! Dick!" She lunged for the door, but he caught her easily, pushing her back into the chair as if she were a child. "What are you ... going to do to me?"

The drug was acting fast.

His face swam before her as he put on his parka, a hat,

gloves, and mask. "We're just going for a little walk out the back fire escape. Oh, don't worry. I disabled the alarm. I'm hoping I got the dose right and you can still walk, but if you can't, that's okay. I'll carry you or drag you by your hair. I don't care."

She screamed. "Help! Help me!"

Steve laughed, took her phone and station radio. "They can't hear you."

"I need ... my parka... my hat. Please!"

Darkness dragged her down, the world around her blurring.

"No parka for you." He slipped an arm around her waist, opened the office door, and walked through the dark administrative wing toward the rear fire escape. "Everyone's gathering for the meeting. I'm sorry you're going to miss it."

He pushed open the fire escape, frigid air blasting her in the face, burning her skin, searing her throat. "It's eighty-five below, so it should be quick."

He was going to leave her to freeze to death.

The thought snaked its way through her mind, brought an adrenaline rush.

"No!" She tried to scream again, tried to jerk free of him.

Steve half-dragged, half-carried her down the stairs, then threw her in the snow. "I've heard that hypothermia is a relatively painless way to die—unlike methanol poisoning. Oh, yes, I kept Patty in my office after she drank the wine to make sure she couldn't go for help. It took hours of stomach pain before she finally lost consciousness. When I was sure she was beyond help, I carried her to her room and left her."

Samantha's heart shattered. "Patty."

"You'll see her soon enough." Steve dragged her somewhere, the Aurora Australis flashing overhead, the Milky

Way bright. "Your Norse god will be joining you before too long."

Thor!

"L-leave ... h-him... a-alone."

It was so cold, unbearably cold, the ice chilling her through her jeans and sweater.

Then the stars disappeared. Was she beneath the station?

"I-I'm s-so c-cold. Please..."

"Sorry, Sam—oh, I mean *Samantha*." He tied her up, trussed her like an animal. "I can't risk you crawling anywhere. Now, be a good girl and die."

"*Steve*."

He walked away, leaving her on the ice.

Her teeth chattered, cold making her bones ache, her throat raw, her skin on fire.

Had Patty felt alone like this? Had she felt this afraid and desperate?

Tears filled Samantha's eyes, her eyelashes instantly freezing together.

She didn't have the strength to force her eyes open again, the cold seeming to devour her, the wind gnawing through her with icy teeth.

Her last conscious thought was of Thor.

18

Thor locked up the laptop and took the stairs two at a time, heading for the BI Lounge, already late for Hardin's damned staff meeting. Jones and Segal were there, waiting for him. The three of them had spent the rest of the afternoon questioning Hamidi and Wei again, and Thor had just finished uploading the video to Cobra's server.

Wei and Hamidi claimed that Wei had paid for their hotel and meals with his credit card and that Hamidi had paid him back with cash. Hamidi said he'd entered the Schengen Area through Frankfurt and had then taken a train to Copenhagen. Shields would check with German authorities to confirm his date of entry, but since he'd taken a train, there was no way to prove he'd been to Denmark.

Wei had shown them selfies of the two of them eating at a café on Strøget, in front of Rosenborg Castle, and standing on Langelinie with the Little Mermaid sculpture behind them. Thor had sent those photos to Shields, too. They looked real to him, but someone who could hack a satellite would have no difficulty faking selfies.

Thor wished Shields would get back to him on Hardin.

The more Thor had thought through the evidence, the more uncomfortable he felt about the site manager. Hardin could go anywhere in the station at any time without arousing suspicions. He had access to the entire facility and its computer resources and coms. He had denied Ryan's request to send Patty's body home. Also—and this was important—people trusted Hardin. Patty had trusted him, and if she'd decided to report what she'd seen, she would have gone straight to him.

Also, the perpetrator had to be a stone-cold sociopath and extremely intelligent, capable of concealing his true emotions and intentions behind a mask of friendship. Barclay wasn't capable of that. Jason Huger couldn't control his mouth or his temper. Hamidi and Wei had both broken down during questioning.

There had to be something in Hardin's background, something the analyst team had missed.

Down the hallway, Thor saw Hardin standing just outside the BI Lounge. Hardin spotted Thor, waved to him, met him halfway.

"Can we talk for a second? It's about Sam... Samantha. That's what she prefers to be called, I guess. I'm worried about her."

Hva' fanden? What the hell?

"Okay."

"My office. It will only take a second."

Thor's instincts told him something wasn't right. He pulled out his radio, called Jones and Segal just to let them know where he was going—and who he was with. "I'm meeting briefly with Hardin in his office. I'll be there in a minute."

He hoped they understood the subtext.

If Hardin shows up at the meeting without me, kick his ass.

He followed Hardin through the warren that was the admin offices, noticed ice on the plastic mat just inside the emergency fire exit. There was also ice on Hardin's boots.

Hardin had just come through that door.

This was fucked.

Thor reached down, loosened his pistol in its holster, kept his hand at his hip, ready to draw.

Hardin opened his office door, gestured for Thor to enter, his gaze dropping to Thor's right hand. "Go on in."

"You first." Thor stood his ground.

Hardin's pupils narrowed, but he smiled. "Are you getting paranoid? It's the twenty-four-seven darkness. It happens to all of us."

Thor followed him inside. "What is this about?"

Hardin sat on the edge of his desk, a grin sliding over his face. "I'm going to need your pistol, your radio, your phone, and the location of the Golden Horde components—or Samantha will die."

Thor drew, pointed his weapon at the bastard's head. "Where is she?"

Hardin didn't flinch. "Check the webcam."

Thor hazarded a quick glance at Hardin's screen, the green glow of a night-vision camera showing... His heart gave a hard knock, a single, sickening thud. "*Samantha.*"

SHE LAY STILL on the ice, tied up without a parka or any cold-weather gear. Thor couldn't identify where she was, exactly, and he couldn't see her face or tell whether she was breathing. But he recognized the sweater—and her long hair.

Fuck! Son of a bitch!

Rage such as he hadn't felt since Afghanistan surged

through him, made his face burn, blood lust pounding through his veins.

Thor grabbed Hardin by his hair, slammed his face into his desk, jammed the pistol into the fucker's temple. "Where the *fuck* is she? Tell me, or I'll splatter your brains around this office."

"You've got one chance to save her, and you're wasting it. If you kill me, she dies. If you delay, she dies. She's already been out there for, oh, I'd say, about five minutes. Even if you mobilize everyone on station to search for her, she'll be dead before you find her. Give me your radio, your weapon, and the location of the Golden Horde components, and I'll tell you where she is. And don't say the goods are in my safe. I already looked. That's all fucking Legos and scrap metal."

For Satan! Damn it to hell!

Thor knew he had no choice. If he killed Hardin, the bastard couldn't tell him where she was. It was eighty below out there right now. If Thor didn't get to Samantha soon, she'd be dead. "You fucking bastard! If she dies, you die, too. That's a promise."

He lowered the pistol, handed the weapon, his phone, and his radio to Hardin. "The package is locked in the vacant room across from mine. It's locked in a biometric case hidden in the ceiling—check the rear corner tile above the bed."

Biometric safes were easy to crack.

Hardin laughed. "Clever."

Jones and Segal would know the moment Hardin entered the room. The security camera would ping their phones, and they would know Thor was in trouble. They would act to keep the components and the rest of the people on station safe, no matter what happened to Thor and Samantha.

But Thor needed to hurry. "You got what you wanted. Where the hell is she?"

Hardin pointed Thor's pistol at his chest. "Move."

Thor walked out of the office, careful to keep Hardin in his peripheral vision. "Do you think you'll get away with this? There's nowhere to run. You're already at the top of our list of suspects. They'll catch you."

"I have buyers willing to do almost anything to get their hands on this. They'll come for me." He gave Thor a shove. "Head out the emergency exit."

"Give me your parka." If Thor was going to save Samantha, he'd need a way to keep her warm.

"No way. I can't even the odds like that. You'll have to do without."

Hardin intended for him to die, too.

Thor pushed open the door, sucked in a breath at the blast of cold air, the wind chill cutting through his clothing. He felt the barrel of his pistol against his back. "If you pull that trigger, everyone on station will hear it."

"Not if I close this door first."

Thor didn't hesitate but jumped over the stair rail to the ice two stories below just as the shot rang out. Pain sliced through his left shoulder.

Shit!

He hit the ice hard, rolled beneath the stairs, leaving blood on the snow. "Where is she, Hardin, you fucker!"

Bam! Bam!

One of the shots creased Thor's thigh, the sting barely registering over the blistering chill as he crawled beneath the cover of the station. "Where is she, Hardin?"

"Fuck you!" Hardin stood at the top of the stairs for a moment as if trying to decide whether to come down and finish Thor. Then he turned and opened the door. "I hit you!

I see your blood on the snow! You're done, Isaksen, and so is Sam!"

The fucker walked back inside, shutting and locking the door behind him.

STEVE SHOVED the pistol into the back of his jeans, locked the door, and ran back to his office. He'd gotten the bastard. He'd put at least one bullet in him, maybe two. It didn't matter how big or tough Isaksen thought he was. No man could survive bullets and temps of eighty below for long.

He logged onto his computer and into the station's emergency control panel, then punched in his admin code and sealed the BI Life Pod to keep the two surviving Cobra guys from getting out. Just to be safe, he locked the station down. Every entrance, even the doors to the service arches and ice tunnels, was secured now. If Isaksen didn't die from his gunshot wounds, he'd die of hypothermia, trying to find a way back inside.

Either way, Thor Isaksen was a dead man.

Steve stripped out of his parka, drew a breath to compose himself, and made his way downstairs toward the Cobra guys' rooms. He ought to kill all three of those Cobra assholes, but he couldn't risk that. If Isaksen had lied to him, he would take the other two, one at a time, until someone told him what he needed to know.

They'd fooled him. He'd believed the Golden Horde components were secure in his office safe this entire time. He had reached out to his contact, told him he had the goods when all he'd had was junk.

Fucking assholes!

If the components had been in his safe, he wouldn't have

had to kill Sam or Isaksen. He could have taken the package —that's what the Cobra guys called it—and handed it over to his contact at any time.

Who gives a shit?

Steve was smarter than all of them and good at thinking on his feet. Every time something had gone wrong, he'd found a way around it. He'd brought the satellite down to take his revenge against Titan. Then, thanks to Cobra, he'd seen a way to make some money by selling the technology to a power that would appreciate it—and his skill.

God, he would love to see his former supervisors' faces at Titan when they found out *he* was behind the satellite hack. He'd brought their pet project crashing down, and now he was going to sell it to their enemies and pocket millions. Living in exile for the rest of his life was a small price to pay for destroying the men who'd fired him, taken his research, and gotten rich by selling it to the Department of Defense.

Golden Horde had been *his* vision, and the sons of bitches had cut him out of it.

All these years of planning were finally going to pay off. He'd rebuilt his identity, taken bullshit jobs that were far beneath his intelligence, and dealt with more idiots than he could count—people like Jason and Charli.

Fuck them. Fuck all of them.

He reached the room, grabbed the keys on his belt, and unlocked the door. Isaksen had told him it was hidden behind the rear corner tile above the bed. Steve would know in a moment whether the bastard had lied to him.

He climbed onto the bare mattress, pushed on the tile, felt something heavy weighing it down. He lifted the tile out of the way and drew the steel lockbox out of the ceiling.

Yes!

Isaksen had told him the truth—and all to save Sam. These Cobra men had more testosterone than brains and thought with their dicks. That had made Steve's job easier.

Steve shut down his emotions. He could celebrate later when he was far away from this frozen, godforsaken continent. In the meantime, he needed to stash this in a secure location and move to the next phase of his operation, which was getting the hell away from the station.

He walked along the empty corridor back to his office, where he locked the case in his safe. That was probably unnecessary, as he had control of the station, but he hadn't gotten this far by being careless or taking chances.

When the lockbox was secure, he logged into his personal VPN and sent an encrypted email to his buyer.

```
I have it. Deposit the funds, and send a
plane during the next weather window and
it's yours.
```

Steve sat back, waited for the reply. He could keep the staff locked up in the B1 Lounge for as long as was necessary. The life pod had water, food, videos, toilets—everything they needed. Until his ride arrived, the station was his.

Chuckling, he got to his feet and walked to the B1 Lounge. He wanted to see Jones' and Segal's reactions to the news their leader was dead.

He found them standing at the door, looking out at him.

"Where is Isaksen?" Jones shouted through the small glass window. "We know he went with you."

"Where the fuck is he?" Segal shouted. "And where is Dr. Park?"

Steve grinned, amused by their helplessness. Their brawn and bullets couldn't help them now. "They're dead. I drugged her, shot him, and locked them out in the cold without parkas. I'm sure they died quickly—or faster than Patty did anyway."

The two men looked at each other.

"Did you hear that, brother?" Jones laughed. "This sick fuck locked Isaksen and Dr. Park outside without parkas. He thinks they're dead. He doesn't know the Viking. He's not someone you want to piss off, Hardin."

Segal leaned closer to the glass, peered out at Steve, his gaze hard. "Jones, you know what I'm looking at?"

"A dead man."

This wasn't the reaction Steve had expected, his disappointment mingling with anger. "I don't care how tough he is. No man can survive out there for long."

The others came up behind Jones and Segal, anger on their faces.

"Hardin, what the fuck?" Ryan glared at him. "*You're* the murderer? Jesus!"

Kristi pushed her way to the front, tears on her cheeks "Where's Samantha, you bastard? What did you do to her?"

"Hardin's the killer?" Lance was there, his face red. "You fucking piece of shit!"

"Is he going to kill us, too?"

"Hardin killed Sam and Thor!"

But Steve didn't have to put up with this—the questions, the demands, the anger. These people weren't worth his time. "You'll all be locked in there until I'm gone, so make yourselves comfortable."

He walked back to his office, sat at his desk, savoring the quiet. Then he logged onto his computer, driven by a morbid sense of curiosity. If Isaksen hadn't bled out under the stairs, he was probably lying beside Samantha on the ice.

How perfectly romantic.

Hardin clicked on the webcam and stared. "What the...?"

There was nothing but rope.

Sam was gone.

The bitch was gone.

Isaksen.

THOR STAGGERED across the ice toward the structures that the staff called Summer Camp, doing his best to ignore pain and cold, Samantha in his arms.

Let her be alive.

If Samantha was alive, he might be able to save her.

If she wasn't...

The thought almost split his chest wide open.

Thor had found her almost right away. Hardin hadn't tried very hard to hide her, perhaps because he'd planned to kill Thor with his own firearm. Too bad for him that he was such a lousy shot.

Samantha had patches of white skin on her face and fingers, a sign of early frostbite. But it was the tears frozen on her eyelashes and cheeks that had crushed him—and unleashed that sickening, deadly rage.

You don't have the energy to waste on emotion. Keep moving.

Fighting to put one foot ahead of the other, Thor kept his gaze on the nearest building, pushed himself to go faster. He thought he remembered Samantha telling him that the first two structures were still in use—one as a climbing gym and the other as a café and nightclub. He hoped to God they had heat—and a cold-weather first-aid kit.

Not that the gunshot wounds posed any real threat to his life. The bullet had lodged deep in his left shoulder and hurt like hell, making it hard to hold Samantha's weight. But he didn't yet have to worry about blood loss, as both wounds had frozen.

The immediate threat to her life and his was the cold.

He focused on one step and then the next and the next, the blue building with its white door only a hundred meters away now. He was almost there. A hundred meters was a little more than a hundred steps for him. He counted them down, the wind chill seeming to suck the life out of him.

Seventy to go. Sixty. Fifty.

If he collapsed, if he gave in to hypothermia now, they would both die.

Forty-five. Forty. Thirty-five.

He had never been this cold in his life, not even during the worst snowstorms in Greenland. Temperatures never dropped this low, and he'd always had shelter with him.

Twenty. Fifteen. Ten.

He reached the door, shifted Samantha in his arms so he could grab the doorknob.

It was unlocked.

Gudskelov! Thank God!

He turned the knob, lifesaving warmth hitting him in the face. Careful not to bump Samantha's head, he walked inside, kicking the door shut behind him. He would need to secure it in case Hardin came looking for them to finish them off, but for now, his priority was saving Samantha's life —if she wasn't already gone.

He didn't flick on the lights. In the Antarctic darkness, the windows would shine like a beacon and tell Hardin exactly where they were. Instead, he walked through the darkness into the next room. There, a bar ran along one wall, a handful of tables arranged in a narrow space. This was the café.

He carried Samantha over to one of the heat registers that ran along the floor and laid her down on the carpet, tucking his numb fingers into his armpits to warm them enough to feel for a pulse. "Samantha, can you hear me? Wake up, *skat*. I'm going to take care of you."

He wished he'd been able to bring her inside the station, but he was pretty sure Hardin would anticipate that move. Thor had decided against giving the bastard another crack at the two of them. But that had meant exposing Samantha to the cold for much longer. She was so still, so pale, her skin cold.

He pressed a finger to her carotid, let out the breath he hadn't realized he'd been holding, almost weak with relief. Her pulse was faint, but she was alive.

Now the hard work began.

His body sluggish, he willed himself to stand, and walked behind the bar, searching in the dark for things that could help him. Bar rags. A coffee maker. Hot cocoa mix. Teabags. Ground coffee. Powdered milk. Biscotti. Lots of bottled water.

There was also a large plastic box beneath the counter. He opened it and could have shouted for joy. A flashlight. Matches. Emergency candles. Several cold-weather first-aid kits.

He grabbed all of them, carried them to Samantha, and dug inside, taking out what he'd need. Hand warmers. Body warmers. Foot warmers. Several Mylar emergency blankets. A trauma kit for his shoulder. When he had everything arranged, he stripped Samantha out of her clothes. The radio he'd given her spilled out of her jeans pocket.

He would test it later. For now, she was his priority.

Using the flashlight, he checked her for frostbite. The skin on her cheeks, nose, forehead, and fingertips was white, but her ears, which had gotten some protection from her hair, and her toes seemed fine.

He stumbled to his feet once more, went to the bar, and grabbed several clean bar rags, making his way back to Samantha's side. He couldn't put the body warmers on her skin without risking burns, so he wrapped each one in a rag as he activated it and set them on her chest, abdomen, and throat, even tucking one beneath her head. Then he covered her with a Mylar blanket and walked to the nearest table with the trauma kit to treat his shoulder, which had begun to bleed heavily.

He groaned between gritted teeth as he pulled off his shirt, the pain in his shoulder radiating down his arm and into his chest. There was no exit wound, so the bullet was still inside him. Well, it was going to be there for a while.

He cleaned the area with an antiseptic cloth, then ripped open a QuikClot dressing and pressed it against the wound before fixing it in place with a pressure bandage. Next, he peeled off his snow pants and jeans and cleaned the graze wound on his thigh, sucking in a breath at the burn of the antiseptic.

When he had triaged the graze, he checked on Samantha, then went to the bar and made a pot of coffee. Warm drinks would go a long way toward helping with the cold. While the coffee brewed, he moved one of the tables so that it sat over Samantha and then draped another Mylar blanket over the table, creating a sort of tent to hold in the radiator's heat—and hide the light from the flashlight.

He drank a cup of coffee as quickly as he could but didn't pour one for Samantha. She needed to be conscious to drink. Now, there was one last thing he needed to do before he could get beneath the blanket beside her.

He walked to the entrance with a chair to bar the door.

As it turned out, the door also had an old-fashioned bolt. He slid it into place and tucked a chair beneath the doorknob. Then, at last, he crawled into the Mylar tent, got beneath the emergency blanket with Samantha, and held her close, doing his best to warm her.

"I'm right here, *skat*."

19

S teve had no idea how many bullets remained in Isaksen's pistol—hopefully enough to kill the bastard. He must not have hit him in any critical organs. Somehow, Isaksen had gotten to Sam, untied her, and disappeared.

Well, he couldn't have gotten far.

Steve dressed for the cold, tucked the pistol in his pocket, then grabbed a flashlight, unlocked the rear fire escape, and headed out into the dark. The wind had picked up, creating whiteout conditions. But this wouldn't take long. The Dane was probably lying dead outside one of the doors, Sam beside him.

But if they weren't dead, it would be an act of mercy to finish them.

Steve headed down the stairs, gritting his teeth against the bitter cold. The wind had scoured Isaksen's blood away. There was no sign of footprints, either.

Damn it!

Beneath the station, which functioned like a fucking wind tunnel, the ropes were gone, too, probably blown into a drift somewhere.

He shined the flashlight around. He didn't see any bodies, but visibility was limited, the light reflecting off the flying snow. He walked out from beneath the station and made his way from one entrance to another. They weren't at the main entrance. They weren't at any of the fire exits. They weren't at the B1 power plant exit.

They weren't anywhere.

Chills that had nothing to do with the cold shivered down his spine.

No, this couldn't be. They couldn't have disappeared. There was no one to help them. Sam had been drugged, Isaksen wounded. No, the bastard was dead, and so was Sam. They were probably buried in blowing snow somewhere.

He must have missed them.

Steve walked around the station a second time, looking for telltale mounds of snow, a bit of fabric, anything to show him where their bodies were. The wind cut through his parka, his gloves, his snow pants, his boots, cold seeping into his bones.

Nothing.

"Goddamn it!"

Where the fuck were they?

Maybe Isaksen had made it to the entrance of the service arches. Or perhaps he had tried to get to Summer Camp or one of the labs, where they would have heat.

If he had, he was dead out there. It took just a few minutes to become hypothermic in this weather, and the labs were about fifteen minutes away. Summer Camp was much closer, but Steve wasn't about to head out there. There were no flags to guide him, and in this weather, he might wander off and not find his way back.

Still, he could walk part of the way, keep the station in sight, and see if there were any lights on out there.

Keeping the station to his back, he walked toward Summer Camp, leaning into the wind, panning back and forth with the flashlight, watching for bodies buried in the snow. But all too quickly, the station began to disappear, swallowed by darkness and whiteout. He couldn't see Summer Camp at all.

"Shit." Painfully cold now, he made his way back to the station, up the back stairs, and into his office, where he sat, shivering, rage building in his gut.

Why would Isaksen's buddies be so certain he was alive?

They're just fucking with you.

Where the *fuck* had Isaksen gone, and how had he managed to take Sam with him? She was dead weight—in more ways than one. She'd been out there for at least six or seven minutes before he'd gotten to her, lying exposed on the ice.

Steve peeled off his parka and logged into his VPN to check his email.

Finally! A response from his buyer.

He clicked the email.

```
Situation too hot. We are being watched.
Deal is off. There will be no further
contact.
```

Adrenaline hit his bloodstream, panic making his pulse rocket. "No! No, no, no! You can't do this to me!"

If they didn't send a plane, he was fucked! He'd be arrested for triple homicide and spend the rest of his fucking life in SuperMax—if he wasn't executed for treason.

"Jesus!" He bit back a sob, his stomach in knots.

He fired back a response, demanding that they send someone as soon as the wind died down and reminding them of everything he'd risked for this.

The email bounced.

"Fuck!" Bile rose in his throat, his stomach rebelling. "Oh, God!"

He couldn't frame anyone because he'd bragged about killing the three of them to the two Cobra guys. He could kill them, too. He could kill everyone on station. But they had probably contacted their boss by now.

People know.

That's why his buyer had backed out.

No, there had to be a way out of this. He was too smart to be caught by a few hired guns. He would find another buyer. Or smuggle himself off station in a shipping crate. Or fake his death and make his way to McMurdo and onto a container ship. Or hold everyone on station hostage in exchange for safe passage.

Another buyer. That was the easy answer.

If China didn't have the balls for this, Russia surely would. And it just so happened that he had a team of Russians right here, locked in the B1 Lounge. He was certain they'd faked the shit about their plane so they could steal the components. Maybe he could interest them in buying the goods instead.

PAIN BROUGHT Thor awake with a jerk.

For helvede! Damn it!

When had he fallen asleep?

He must have been hit harder by the cold than he'd realized.

He reached up slowly with his left hand, pressed his fingers to Samantha's throat, felt her pulse. It seemed stronger now, and some color had come back to her cheeks. The patches of skin on her face that had frozen were red—a good sign.

He cupped her cheek, her skin warmer now. "Samantha, can you hear me? It's Thor. I want to give you some hot cocoa or coffee, but you need to wake up first."

She turned her head toward the sound of his voice, her eyes still closed.

He glanced at his watch, saw that he'd been asleep for about an hour. He reached for the radio. Last time he'd checked, it wasn't working, probably a result of extreme cold. He turned it on, relieved to hear a little *beep*.

But who was listening on the other end—Jones and Segal, or Hardin?

For all Thor knew, Jones and Segal were hostages—or dead. The last thing he needed was for Hardin to overhear him and come out here to finish him off. He had no weapons and was already injured, while Hardin had his pistol.

Instead of speaking into the radio, he pushed the talk button a few times, sending out three bursts of static. Then he waited—but not for long.

"Isaksen, this is Jones. Is that you, man?"

"Jones, Isaksen here. Are you and Segal safe?"

"We told that bastard you weren't dead." Jones' words were almost drowned out by cheers in the background. "Is Dr. Park with you? Is she alive?"

"Yes, but she's dangerously hypothermic and has mild frostbite. I found shelter and treated her as well as I could, but I think she might be in a hypothermic coma. She's still unconscious."

"Hardin drugged her. That's what he told us. I don't know what he gave her, but if she's still unconscious, Decker here says it might be the drug."

Hardin, you fucking bastard.

"How are you?" Jones asked. "He says he shot you."

"Yes, with my own damned weapon. I've got a round in my shoulder and a graze on my thigh and a bit of frostbite, but I'm okay for now."

He'd get an infection if the bullet didn't come out, but that was a worry for later.

"Damn, brother, you are hard to kill."

"What's your situation?"

"We're fine. Hardin has us all locked in the lounge. He's got the package—and the run of the station. I have no clue what he has planned, but he's got control of the doors. So far, he hasn't shown aggression toward anyone here. We haven't seen him for about an hour."

Thor tried to remember what Hardin had told him about the B1 Lounge as a life pod. It had its own power plant. It had food, restrooms, and a kitchen, as well as medical supplies, sleeping bags, its own coms and computers. The staff would be safe there—at least until the food ran out.

"Jones, Segal—Hardin said the station could be run from the lounge. Does anyone on staff know what he meant or have access to the station's systems?"

"I'll ask."

"Isaksen, Segal here. I've kept Tower apprised of our situation. I just gave him an update to let him know you've checked in. They're working on a rescue op, but that's likely some time off, thanks to the weather."

Then Jones was back. "Lance, Ryan, and Charli from coms say they both have access to the system. McClain says that power for the heating can be rerouted to the lounge, cutting off the rest of the station. But doing that might drive Hardin to attack us—or to seek shelter elsewhere. That might bring him out to you."

Those weren't the only risks.

"Can Hardin override that command and cut off power to the lounge?"

The bastard was capable of almost anything.

"Lance says he thinks they can lock him out of the life pod controls altogether. Lance and Charli are working on it now. The life pod's systems operate independently, so if they get in there first and establish admin control—"

"Do it. Will they be able to open the doors to the rest of the station?"

"They don't know, but the lounge's powerplant has its own exit on the ground floor. The guys from the service arches think they can force it open if this doesn't work. But we still won't be able to access the rest of the station."

"Would Decker or Kristi be able to bring me some kind of weapon and get medical aid to Dr. Park?"

"When it comes to weapons, all we've got is our concealed carry pieces. Everything else is locked up in our rooms."

Fuck. "Right."

Jones continued. "Between the fifty-six of us in the lounge, only one has a parka, and no one has gloves or hats or masks. I'd be willing to borrow the parka and take my chances, but the wind has picked up. We've got whiteout conditions outside. I'm not sure I'd find you."

"No, stay there. It's too risky."

The good news was that whiteout conditions would keep Hardin indoors, too.

Samantha whimpered.

"Work on cutting off power to the rest of the station. Check in before you throw the switch. We need to come up with a plan that gets me back into the station and gives us access to our weapons. The three of us would have no problem taking out Hardin. But I need to go. I think Dr. Park might be regaining consciousness."

"Copy that. Jones out."

SAMANTHA TRIED to open her eyes, but couldn't, the sound of Thor's voice lifting her out of the darkness. "Thor?"

"I'm right here, *skat*." Warm lips kissed her forehead. "You're safe. Do you hear me? You're safe, and you're going to be okay."

"So ... cold." Her skin seemed to burn—on her face, her fingertips.

"I'm going to make you some hot cocoa, okay? Will you drink it for me?"

"He ... killed me."

"He tried."

The next thing she knew, Thor lifted her head. "Samantha, I need you to drink. This will help warm you up."

Something warm touched her lips, the scent of chocolate tickling her nose.

She drank, sweet, warm cocoa sliding down her throat.

"Good."

It felt so good, but she was so tired.

"Stay awake, *skat*. Keep drinking. That's right. Another sip."

She did as he asked.

"Jones says Hardin drugged you."

"A shot. Mida...zolam."

"Midazolam?" A burst of static. "Jones, this is Isaksen."

"Isaksen, Jones here."

"Can you ask the doctor or Kristi about midazolam? Samantha is coming around. She says that's what Hardin used to drug her."

"Copy that."

The conversation seemed to be happening somewhere far away, the words drifting around Samantha, her mind unable to capture them for long.

"Isaksen, Jones here."

"Jones, go ahead."

"Decker says it's a strong sedative. She probably needs oxygen. He says they keep portable oxygen canisters in all of the buildings in case someone gets sick from the altitude. McClain here says to look beneath the bar."

We're just going for a little walk out the rear fire escape. Oh, don't worry. I disabled the alarm. I'm hoping I got the dose right and you can still walk, but if you can't, that's okay. I'll carry you or drag you by your hair. I don't care.

"No!" Samantha cried out, tried to fight. "Don't!"

"Samantha, honey, it's me, Thor. You're safe here. Can you open your eyes?"

She tried but just couldn't do it. "My skin… It burns."

"You have mild frostbite. The burning is a good sign. I'm going to give you some oxygen. Just breathe, okay?"

A plastic mask over her mouth. A hiss. A puff of canned air.

"That's it. Keep breathing."

Every time she inhaled, there was another hiss.

But it was the sound of his voice, deep and reassuring, that held her.

She tried to tell him that. "Talk to me."

Hiss. Hiss. Hiss.

"Okay. You keep breathing, and I'll keep talking."

He told her how he'd found her and carried her out to Summer Camp and how they both had hypothermia. "When I saw you lying there, I was so afraid I was too late, that you were already gone. I don't think I've ever been more afraid in my life."

He'd been afraid for her?

Hiss. Hiss. Hiss.

Then he told her how the coldest he'd been before this evening had been after a snowstorm in Greenland.

"There was more than a meter of new snowfall, more than the dogs could handle. My partner had twisted his ankle that morning, so it was up to me to ski ahead of the sled and break trail for the dogs. After a while, the snow that got into my clothes melted from my body heat. I got wet down to my skin. It was only forty below, but I became hypothermic. We had to stop and make camp."

More than a meter of snow?

Hiss. Hiss. Hiss.

He drifted from story to story. "People think that being in Sirius was all about the weather, but it was really all about the dogs. I can't tell you how many times I had to break up fights between horny male dogs because one of the females was in heat."

As her head began to clear, his words painted vivid images in her mind.

She remembered the scars on his wrists. "They're big dogs, aren't they? Wasn't that dangerous?"

"I suppose it could be. We made sure the dogs never forgot that we humans were the pack alphas."

Hiss. Hiss. Hiss.

"Malik said ... you saw polar bears."

"Lots of polar bears." He told her how a bear had

followed them, showing up every night when they made camp, but keeping its distance as if waiting to see whether they'd do something stupid and become a snack. He told her how a bear had broken into one of their emergency shelters and eaten all the food, leaving a big pile of shit with candy wrappers in it as a thank you. He told her how he and his partner had dug into a snowbank for emergency shelter, only to realize there was a mother polar bear denning in that same snowbank.

"We heard her snoring. We decided to take our chances with the weather, got the hell out of there, and made camp a short distance away."

"That sounds ... scary."

Hiss. Hiss. Hiss.

"Greenland wasn't scary. It was ... freeing. When you're with one other person on the ice for weeks at a time, you run out of things to talk about. Then, after enough silence, you run out of things to think about. Your mind is just ... empty. You live moment to moment in a way that's impossible when you're surrounded by cities and crowds of people. Your pain and all your burdens just fall away."

Hiss. Hiss. Hiss.

She opened her eyes, looked into his. "What pain were you carrying?"

"Afghanistan."

20

"What happened in Afghanistan?" Samantha took the canister of oxygen from Thor and began administering it to herself. "Can you tell me?"

Thor had never told a woman what he'd done that night. His fellow Cobra operatives knew the story. They were all veterans who'd served in special operations forces, and Thor had trusted them at least to understand. He'd also felt they deserved the truth about him since they were all going to be working together.

But Samantha...

She knew very little about war. She was logical and rational, and there had been nothing logical or rational about his actions that night. Still, a part of him wanted her to know. He'd been more open and naked with her than he'd been with a woman in a very long time, and he'd almost lost her today.

"Thor?"

He brushed a strand of hair off her cheek. "It's not a pretty story."

"It hasn't been a pretty day."

"I told you about the IED blast that killed my friends—
Lars, Felix, Mads."

"Yes. You were thrown clear. Mads and Felix were killed.
Lars died while you held his hand. I remember."

"Three died. Three of us survived. We were airlifted
back to our base, along with the bodies. I was out of my
mind with rage. I wanted blood. I wanted to make al Harzi
pay for what he'd done. Jakob, one of the other survivors,
felt the same. So, we waited until night, and we comman-
deered a vehicle and snuck off base, armed to the teeth."

"You went AWOL?"

"AWOL? What's that?"

"Absent without leave."

"Yeah, and stole a vehicle."

"Okay. Wow."

"We drove through the night back to those poppy fields.
It was a crazy thing to do. AQ operatives and Taliban fighters
were everywhere. But we made it to al Harzi's hideout,
passing the crater in the dirt road that was left by the IED.
The blood of our friends was still there in the dirt. We
parked about a half-mile away and walked the remaining
distance, weapons ready."

"Weren't you afraid?"

"I was too out of my mind with grief and anger to be
afraid." Thor told her how they'd taken out six armed men
to get into the compound and then made their way through
a courtyard into the main structure, killing every fighting-
age male. "Some were teenagers—just kids. Others were the
real deal—AQ combatants. We killed every last one of them
in front of screaming women and crying children."

"Oh, Thor."

Thor couldn't meet her gaze. "It wasn't war. Warfighting
is supposed to be controlled, targeted. It was a rage-fueled

massacre. I had become a Berserker, a monster. All I wanted to do was kill and kill and kill."

"Did you kill the women, too?"

"No women or small children."

"Thank God." Samantha whispered the words, but Thor heard them.

"We found al Harzi hiding in the back. He let all of his men die for him and then hid behind women. We killed him, dragged his body back to our vehicle, stripped him naked, and dumped him in the crater left by that IED. We wanted all of the AQ forces in the area to know who had killed him—and why. Then we drove back to base, parked the vehicle, and snuck back into our beds. I didn't sleep at all that night."

"You could have been killed."

Thor nodded. "In the morning, word got around that US forces had found al Harzi's body in the exact spot where our men had died. Our commanding officer called us into his office, asked if there was anything we'd like to tell him. We shook our heads. He let us go. And that was the end of it."

"But it wasn't the end." She reached up, touched Thor's face. "You carry this with you still. I can see it in your eyes."

"I thought I had let it go while I was in Greenland, but I had a nightmare about it a couple of nights ago. You were there. You watched me kill a man. You looked at me with horror on your face, and you screamed."

"I'm not screaming, Thor. You haven't scared me away. I can't judge you for what you did that night. Besides, you've already judged yourself."

He looked into her eyes, saw only compassion. "I turned into a monster, Samantha. Do you understand? That beast still lives inside me. Tonight, when I thought you were dead,

I felt that same rage, that same bloodlust. I wanted to kill Hardin. I wanted to rip him to pieces."

Samantha sat up, took his hand. "That doesn't make you a monster, Thor. That makes you human."

Her gaze shifted to his shoulder, and her eyes went wide. "You're hurt."

"Yeah. Hardin shot me with my own damned pistol."

"He *shot* you?"

Thor realized she had no idea what had happened, so he told her what the bastard had done. How he'd used her to get Thor into his office. How Thor had seen her lying motionless on the ice on Hardin's webcam and had given Hardin everything he wanted without a fight. How Thor had found her, untied the ropes, and carried her here.

She glanced around their Mylar tent. "Where are we?"

"The café out in Summer Camp. We were both hypothermic and have early frostbite. You were drugged, too, and in a lot worse shape than I was."

She was staring at him. "You carried me all the way out here with no cold-weather gear and a freaking bullet in your shoulder?"

He slid his fingers into her hair, his fingertips still tingling from frostbite. "I wasn't going to let you die."

"Malik said you're the toughest man he knows."

"Jones talks too much." Then Thor kissed her.

Samantha savored Thor's kiss, the warm brush of his lips against hers proof that they were both still alive. "I can't believe I'm not dead. You could have shot him. You could have killed him. But instead, you came for me."

He cupped her cheek in his palm. "Of course, I did."

What he'd suffered was written on his body. Lines of pain and exhaustion on his face. Patches of red skin on his cheeks, forehead, nose, chin, and ears from frostbite. The bloody bandage covering the bullet wound in his shoulder.

"And now he's got the Golden Horde components?"

"Yeah. I'm not sure what he's planning to do next. He's stuck here just like everyone else."

Then it came to her. "Where are the others?"

"Locked in the life pod. Hardin has the station locked down."

"That bastard!"

"He didn't take your radio, which is the only reason I'm in touch with them." Thor reached for the replacement radio he'd given her.

"He took the other one—and my phone. He didn't know about this one." She shivered, the horror of what the bastard had done snaking through her. "He was so *cold* about it. He lied to me, told me he needed help answering some questions from Patty's parents. But when I got there, he injected me with that sedative. I tried to fight him, but the drug made it hard to think, hard to stand."

"There's no way you could have fought him off, even if he hadn't drugged you."

"I begged him for a parka, a hat, gloves. I was so afraid. He told me that hypothermia was a relatively painless way to die compared to ... compared to methanol poisoning." Tears filled her eyes, anguish sharp in her chest. "He told me he kept Patty in his office to make sure she couldn't get medical help. She suffered, Thor. She suffered while that *bastard* sat there waiting for the methanol to incapacitate her. She must have been *so* afraid."

Thor's jaw went tight, his blue eyes going ice cold. He

drew her against him, held her close with his good arm. "I'm so sorry. He won't get away with this. I promise."

"Why? Why did he do this? Why would he betray his country?"

"I don't know." Thor looked into her eyes, smiled. "You need to rest and get back to huffing that oxygen. You're still hypothermic. Lie back and let me get you tucked in with those body warmers. I'll make more hot cocoa."

He got to one hand and his knees to crawl out of their little tent, his left arm tucked against his chest, a bloody bandage on his thigh.

"Oh, Thor. He shot you in the leg, too?"

"I'll be fine." He crawled out, and she heard him rummaging around at the bar.

She went back to using the oxygen, a puff every time she inhaled, a kind of numbness settling over her. She let the **numbness** take her, grateful just to be alive.

She was alive. Thor was hurt, but also alive.

You'll get through this.

He returned with two cups of cocoa, one for himself and one that he insisted on holding for her. "I want you under that blanket."

She indulged him, letting him give her sip after sip. It *did* make her feel better, though she wasn't sure she'd ever feel warm again.

A burst of static.

"Isaksen, this is Jones."

Thor reached for the radio. "Isaksen here."

"We're doing all communication with you from the life pod's command center—the computer room. We don't want to risk someone overhearing and betraying us to Hardin. Can you update us on your medical situation?"

"Dr. Park is conscious. Our frostbite will heal. My shoulder still has a bullet in it. What's going on there?"

"Lance and Charli have been working on the life pod computer system with help from Shields. They can shut down the power to the station and transfer it to the life pod, but that would cut off the power to your building and all labs around the station. All of them run off the main power grid."

It was all surreal to Samantha.

Thor didn't look happy about this news. "Okay, so that's out. Can they lock him out of their system and prevent him from turning off the power to the life pod?"

"Affirmative. They've already done that."

"Good. What about the doors?"

"Lance hacked those controls. We can open the doors now, but Hardin will know it. There's no way for us to get out of here without alerting him. When the wind dies down, we could bring you one of our pistols and some medical aid, but it would likely lead him right to you."

"Okay, then what's our play?"

"Before we get into that, there are two other things."

"Go ahead."

"Steve Hardin is actually Stephen Michael Delaney. Fifteen years ago, Delaney was a researcher for Titan, the defense contractor. He did the preliminary development for the Golden Horde systems. Apparently, he had a falling out with his bosses over workplace behavior. They fired him, and then he disappeared. It turns out he created a new identity for himself. Shields thinks he wants to get back at the company."

Samantha stared at Thor, stunned.

Thor didn't seem shocked at all. "I wish she'd discovered

that a few days ago. Thanks for the update. What we need now is a plan. It's time to take back the station."

THOR LOOKED SAMANTHA OVER, made sure the emergency blankets were duct-taped into place. Beneath the Mylar were body warmers taped on top of her clothes like a vest.

"We look like Antarctic mummies or something." Her words and her laugh were muffled by the dish towel that covered her nose, cheeks, and mouth like a mask.

Thor appreciated her spirit, but she was still hypothermic—they both were—and they were heading back outside. As plans went, this one sucked. But it was their best chance.

Thor, Jones, and Segal had gone over every possible scenario, trying to find the one with the highest probability of success. No one could get out of the life pod without Hardin knowing. They couldn't cut off the heat and let him freeze to death without also cutting off the heat to Summer Camp. As long as Thor and Samantha stayed here, they would get no medical help, and Thor would be without a firearm—a real liability if Hardin **showed up.**

But there was another consideration, one Thor hadn't shared with anyone. He was running a fever, and the bullet wound had begun to bleed again, more heavily this time. He'd changed the bandages several times. He was pretty sure the bullet, or a fragment of it, had nicked an artery. Either way, his strength was fading.

If he didn't get Samantha back to the safety of the station soon...

"We move as efficiently as we can to the emergency hatch. I'll shovel the snow away and lift the cover. Then we head down the ladder to the ice tunnels and warm up in the machine shop before heading into the station."

"It's minus sixty in those tunnels."

"That's better than minus a hundred and ten." He handed her the dish towel for his face and sat. "Can you help with this? My shoulder … I don't think—"

"Of course." She took the duct tape, fastened it into place. "I think you're good."

Then she helped him cover his head with Mylar and taped that on, too.

He could see in her eyes that she was smiling. Yeah, okay, so they looked ridiculous. "We move quickly to the hatch and down the ladder. The longer we're on the ladder and in the tunnels, the worse the hypothermia will be."

"I understand."

Ryan, who knew the station well, had suggested using the ice tunnel emergency hatches to gain entrance to the station. Intended for emergency use from the inside or outside, the hatches were marked with green flags. They were covered only by heavy steel lids that didn't lock. Most of the time, the lids stayed covered with snow. The ice tunnels led into the unheated service arches, and the service arches were connected by several flights of stairs through the Beer Can to the warmth of the station.

The only thing this plan had going for it was that Hardin believed they were dead. He wouldn't see them coming. Once inside, Thor would get their rifles from their rooms and head with Samantha to the life pod. Then the staff inside would force open the doors. Samantha would stay with Kristi and the doctor and get care, while he, Jones, and Segal went after Hardin—or whatever his name was.

"Remember to keep your hands as close to your body as you can."

"Right."

Thor grabbed a shovel that stood inside the door, handing her the flashlight. "Put that somewhere safe so you don't drop it."

She tucked it into the back of her jeans. "Ready."

Thor opened the door, icy wind hitting him in the face. "Let's move!"

Samantha hurried along beside him. "Shit, it's cold!"

"Keep going. Don't run."

The wind had died down enough that he could see the lights of the station. He veered to his right, watching for the flags that marked the lids to the escape hatches. Ryan had said it was only fifty yards from the door of the café but in this darkness...

"There!" Samantha saw it first.

A dark flag fluttered in the wind.

Thor gritted his teeth against the pain in his shoulder and walked faster, wanting to get out of this wind as soon as possible. He began shoveling, moving snow as fast as he could with one arm.

"Give me the shovel!" Samantha took it from him and went to work, cussing the whole time. "Damn it! Fuck!"

Then the shovel hit steel.

Samantha stepped back, tossed the shovel, reached down, but struggled to remove the heavy lid. Thor took over, shifting it to the side to reveal a dark, square hole with a wooden ladder leading into the depths of the ice, a faint light shining at the bottom.

He fought back a wave of dizziness. "I'll help you down and then follow."

She looked over the edge, teeth chattering. "O-okay."

He gripped her hand with his good arm as she dropped

down, turned around, and felt with her foot for the first rung of the ladder.

"It's such a long way." She started down.

"You've got it. Just keep going. Ryan said the ladder goes all the way to the bottom without a gap."

Shivering, Thor let her get a body-length ahead of him then followed, the wooden rungs creaking under his weight. Instantly, it was warmer, the wind chill gone. But still, he shivered almost uncontrollably.

Down they went until it seemed they must be halfway to hell by now, but the ladder kept going, walls of ice surrounding him.

"I'm d-down!" Samantha turned on the flashlight, flooding the space with light.

Thor dropped to the ice beside her, pulled out his radio. "J-Jones, this is Isaksen. W-we're inside the ice t-tunnels."

21

S amantha didn't think she'd ever feel warm again, the cold making her shiver uncontrollably. She hurried as fast as she could through the narrow ice tunnel, leading Thor to the unheated LO Arch, desperate to reach the machine shop. After that, they still had to walk to the Beer Can and then up all those stairs to reach warmth and the station.

Not to be a baby, but Samantha wasn't sure she'd make it.

You have no choice.

Shit. Shit. Shit.

She came to a fork in the tunnels and stopped, body shaking from the cold.

"Which w-way?" Thor was shivering, too.

She hesitated, uncertain. If she took a wrong turn and got them lost, they would die. She shined the flashlight down both tunnels, then recognized the Buzz Aldrin shrine cut into the tunnel on her left. "Th-there."

She didn't remember the ice tunnels being quite this long, but then she'd been dressed for the cold when she'd gotten her tour. She led Thor past the shrines, following large pipes that carried fuel, water, and waste leading them toward the service arches. Then ahead, she saw the exit and, beyond it, the cavernous space of the LO Arch.

"S-stop." Thor walked to the exit, looked up and down the length of the arch, as if checking for Hardin. "The s-stairs to the station are that way, r-right?"

But Samantha's gaze was fixed on the door to the machine shop. "Th-there's the machine sh-shop. We can w-warm up th-there."

Thor nodded. "Hurry."

They crossed the corridor, the thirty-foot-high ceiling and flickering lights lending a creepy feeling to the space. Its hundreds of meters of steel shelves were covered with boxed supplies, giving a person so many places to hide.

Don't think about that.

Samantha took the stairs as fast as she could with muscles that had begun to slow down, and then stepped into the warmth of the machine shop. Her body ached with cold, the heat barely registering. She might have sat, but Thor took her arm, kept her standing.

He pulled down the towel that covered his face. "S-stay on your f-feet. Let's see if th-they've got anything w-warm to drink here—or anything I c-can use as a w-weapon."

Samantha pulled down her makeshift mask, too, moving on pure adrenaline now, her mind barely registering all the equipment and tools that sat on shelves and workbenches.

"C-coffee." Thor motioned toward a coffee maker that sat on a nearby table.

The machine was on a timer and set to make a fresh pot in the morning. Thor got it brewing with the push of a button, and then walked off, searching shelves and tool-boxes. He picked up a hammer, tested its weight.

"Th-that's fitting. A h-hammer."

He didn't laugh.

Samantha stumbled after him, some thought in her head about not being helpless if she ran into Hardin again. She saw a narrow chisel, picked it up.

Thor saw her, raised an eyebrow. "Be c-careful with that. If you're cl-close enough to use it, he m-might take it from you. I th-think that coffee is done."

He poured them each a cup, handed one to her. "Don't b-burn yourself. It's hot."

Samantha sipped, the bitter liquid sliding down her throat and into her stomach. By the time she'd finished it, she had stopped shivering, some sense of warmth flowing back into her body.

"We'll stay for a few more minutes." He tucked a finger beneath her chin, lifted her gaze to his. "We're almost there. We just need to make it to the end of the arch and up four flights of stairs. That's nothing compared to how far you've already come. When we get to the life pod, Kristi and Decker will take care of you."

"What about you?" She could tell he was suffering, too, his face lined with pain.

"I'll be fine." He set his empty cup down and drew her close with his good arm.

For a time, they stood there in silence, sharing body heat.

"We should get moving." He kissed her forehead. "You can do this, Samantha. In five minutes, you'll be in the life pod."

Samantha nodded, but she couldn't shake a sense of foreboding.

He didn't bother covering his face this time, so she didn't either, the two of them moving back the way they'd come, the chisel in Samantha's pocket, her hands clutching the body warmer taped to her chest as she steeled herself to face the cold once more.

Thor opened the door, frigid air flooding in, making Samantha gasp. "Don't rush. Move efficiently."

She followed him back down the stairs to the main hallway of the LO Arch, the flickering lights adding to a growing feeling of dread. "That way."

They moved quickly, the cold stealing back into Samantha's bones.

Thor opened the door to the Beer Can, motioned for her to wait while he cleared it. "Okay. Let's go. Time for a workout."

Was it ninety-nine steps or seventy-seven?

Samantha couldn't remember, her body starting to shiver again. "W-we could take the freight elevator. It's f-faster."

The car stood empty and wide open, available for them.

"Hardin might hear it and know exactly where we are. It's safer to walk."

"W-why did I know you were going to s-say that?"

Thor's radio squawked.

"Isaksen, Jones here."

"Jones, this is Isaksen."

"Be on the lookout. That bastard just raided your room. He took your rifle and some ammo. He's acting like he's in a hurry. I'm betting he knows you're there."

Thor muttered something in Danish, shivering now, too. "B-blow those doors, get your gear, and find him. K-keep everyone else locked down, including the R-Russian team. I'm taking Samantha b-back to the machine shop. If he's coming this way, he'll c-cut us off at the top of the stairs. I'm t-turning off my radio so it doesn't give us away."

"Copy that. See you soon."

Thor turned off the radio, slipped it into his pocket. "We n-need to hurry."

Then, from the top of the stairs above came the creak of cold, steel hinges.

∾

THOR HAD JUST PUT his foot on the first stair when he heard the door to the station open four stories above them.

Hardin.

If he and Samantha tried to make it back to the machine shop, the bastard would see them. He might even get a clear shot. With only a split second to act, Thor grabbed Samantha's wrist, pressed a finger against her lips for silence, then drew her with him beneath the stairs and into the open freight elevator.

Footsteps on the stairs.

Hardin seemed to be in a hurry.

In one corner of the elevator, Thor saw a pile of quilted moving blankets. He grabbed them and lowered his voice to a whisper. "I'll c-cover you with these. Curl up in the corner. You'll be warmer. Stay quiet and still, no m-matter what happens."

She lay on her side, drew her knees up to her chest, her gaze on his until he covered her with the first blanket. She mouthed the words, "Be careful!"

Thor did his best to disguise the shape of a human being beneath the blankets, placing the last on top, still folded. After that, he pulled off the Mylar blanket that was taped around his body and shoved it beneath the blankets with Samantha, knowing it would give him away and hamper his movements. Yes, it would make his hypothermia worse, but he was beginning to think it was over for him anyway. His heart pounded as if he'd been running, and he felt out of breath—both signs of serious blood loss.

He stepped back into the opposite corner and waited, hammer ready. If Hardin came at them, he would have one shot at neutralizing the fucker. After that...

If he'd been here by himself, uninjured and armed, Thor would have taken Hardin from behind as he walked into the LO Arch. But, given the situation, it would be tactically wiser to let Hardin enter the LO Arch and then bolt up the stairs—or take the elevator, which would get them up to the station faster.

The footsteps drew closer.

Thor fought another wave of dizziness, his body wracked with chills, whether from hypothermia or fever, he didn't know. It didn't matter. All that concerned him was getting through the next few minutes alive so he could return Samantha to the safety of the station and get her the care she needed.

And then Hardin was down, his footfalls landing on concrete now, instead of the steel grating of the stairs.

Thor stayed motionless, sure the bastard would have the rifle raised.

Cautious footsteps drew closer. The muzzle of the rifle appeared inside the elevator door first, then Hardin's head came into view. He bent down, poked at the pile of blankets with the rifle.

Thor let loose his rage, unleashed his inner monster— and brought the hammer down on Hardin's skull with as much force as he could with one arm.

The bastard grunted, dropped to his knees, stunned.

Thor kicked him in the face, flinging Hardin backward out of the elevator, the rifle clattering to the elevator floor.

But the action threw Thor off-balance, dizziness landing him on his back, making it hard for him to regain his feet.

Hardin lay on the floor, moaning, blood gushing from his nose, freezing on his face. He rolled onto his hands and knees and staggered to his feet. "Why won't you die?"

"Why d-did you betray your c-country?" Thor managed to stand, too, but blood loss and cold were taking their toll.

Hardin kicked him, the bastard's boot connecting with Thor's wounded thigh and throwing him off-balance once more.

Thor fell back, one hand landing on the barrel of the rifle. He grabbed it, fought with all of his strength to stand just as Steve drew the pistol from his pocket. Thor didn't give Hardin time to aim but threw himself against him. The two of them crashed to the floor beneath the stairs, and the pistol flew from Hardin's hands.

"You f-fucking son of a bitch!" Blood lust pounded inside Thor's chest. He wrapped his hands around Hardin's throat to choke the life from him.

But Hardin went for Thor's wounded shoulder, digging deep with his thumb, pain making Thor's left arm useless.

Hardin threw him off, crawled over to the pistol. "You're tough, I'll give you that, but I've got the brains."

"Really? How are y-you getting out of this, genius? The P-Pentagon knows you're a t-traitor." Thor fought his way to his feet once more, reached for the rifle with his right hand, warm blood spilling from his shoulder to freeze on his skin.

But Hardin moved faster. He aimed the pistol at Thor's face. "Don't. You have nowhere to go this time. I can't miss."

A shriek.

Samantha lunged at Hardin, drove her chisel into his cheek. "You piece of shit!"

Hardin backhanded Samantha hard enough to knock

her to the floor and clutched his bleeding face. "You fucking little bitch!"

It was the break Thor needed.

Fighting dizziness, he picked up the rifle and aimed it at Hardin's head. "Drop the p-pistol! On the g-ground! Hands b-behind your h-head!"

"You heard him, you m-murdering sack of sh-shit!" Samantha got to her feet, clutching the chisel in her hand once more, fury on her face. "Get d-down!"

Hardin dropped the pistol, looked from Samantha to Thor. "What's the matter? Is the cold getting to the two of you?"

"T-take the elevator upstairs. G-go, Samantha!"

"N-not without y-you!"

Above them, a door opened, footfalls echoing through the space.

Jones and Segal, at last—and it sounded like they'd brought back-up.

"Drop the weapons now!"

Thor looked up, saw Vasily standing with the other Russians on the stairs, their rifles pointed down at them. "Fuck."

STEVE GAGGED on the blood running down the back of his throat, the pain in his head excruciating, his broken nose throbbing, the wound in his cheek a sharp ache. He ripped the rifle out of Isaksen's hands. "Like I said. I've got the brains."

He rammed the butt of the rifle into Isaksen's gut.

The fucker doubled over with a grunt, lost his balance, and sank to the floor.

"St-stop!" Samantha threw the chisel and grabbed a moving blanket off the elevator floor, then covered Isaksen and sat behind him, cradling his head against her shoulder. "Th-Thor, are y-you okay? H-he needs the d-doctor."

"Fuck him!" Steve pointed the rifle at Sam's head. "I should shoot you both!"

"L-let her g-go." Isaksen's face was unnaturally pale. "She's done n-nothing to you, Delaney."

Hardin flinched. "The name is Hardin."

"Stephen M-Michael Delaney." Sam glared at him, her cheek red where he'd struck her. "You g-got fired by T-Titan. You w-wanted revenge."

Blood rushed into Steve's head, his finger moving to the trigger.

"Wh-what good does it d-do to kill us now?" Isaksen asked. "Everyone kn-knows. You w-won't get away with it."

Vasily reached the bottom of the stairs and walked over to Steve, followed by his men. "I see you do not need our help. Put the rifle down. They are no threat."

Steve supposed Vasily was right. "It took you long enough."

Steve had returned the Russians' rifles days ago—a gesture he'd hoped would win him their favor. It had worked. A short time ago, Vasily had promised him a flight out of here, safe harbor in Russia, and ten million US dollars in exchange for the components. He'd hoped for more, but they'd known he was desperate.

"Y-you said you w-were my f-friend." Sam glared at Vasily, looking like someone had just killed her puppy. "Y-you said you were P-Patty's friend."

"Aw, poor baby. Do you feel betrayed?" Steve cupped his gloved hand over his injured cheek. "The fucking bitch stabbed me."

Vasily leaned in, examined the wound. "That little scratch? That is nothing."

Snap.

At first, Steve thought Vasily had punched him in the gut, a friendly jab. Then his heart started to slam in his chest, blood rising in his throat, black spots dancing in front of his eyes. He looked down and watched as Vasily withdrew a stiletto switchblade from his solar plexus. "Wh-what...?"

Vasily leaned in close. "You murdered Patty, and you tried to kill Sam. You are lower than shit, a traitor to your friends and your country. You truly believed we would make a deal with you?"

Steve tried to inhale, tried to speak but couldn't, his knees buckling as the pain hit. He collapsed onto the floor, found himself staring up at the frost-covered ceiling four stories above, his heart flailing in his chest.

He was dying.

He was going to die here on this fucking continent and lie, frozen, in the LO Arch in a body bag just like Patty. "No!"

Vasily leaned over him. "For traitors, hell is ice cold."

Steve felt the life leave his body, the world fading to black.

SAMANTHA STARED in mute horror as one last strangled breath left Steve's body, blood spilling from his mouth, freezing in a pool around him. She looked from Steve to Vasily, who walked back to his men.

With a smile on his face, he said something to Vlad in Russian—and then slit Vlad's throat with one clean swipe of the blade. He wiped the blade on Vlad's snow pants and turned to Samantha. "He overheard your men. Then he sent a text to this bastard and told him where you were. He betrayed you against my orders."

Samantha was too terrified even to scream as Vlad fell to the floor, clutching his throat, blood spilling between his fingers.

Vasily walked over to her, making her recoil. He put the switchblade away, stripped off his parka, put it over her and Thor. "I told you I am your friend. Now I have proved myself, I think."

Then the doors from the LO Arch flew open, and Malik and Lev rushed through, weapons raised.

"Nobody move!"

"Hands above your heads!"

Samantha gasped, raised one hand, but kept her other arm wrapped around Thor, doing her best to put pressure on his wound.

"Not you, Samantha, sweetheart." Malik knelt beside them, reached for his station radio. "Ryan, this is Jones. Ryan, do you copy?"

"Jones, Ryan here."

"Hardin and Vlad are dead. We're bringing Isaksen and Samantha up in the freight elevator. They're both in bad shape. Isaksen has lost a lot of blood, and both are severely hypothermic."

"EMS is responding, out."

"Thor?" He lay still in Samantha's arms. "Stay alive. Please, stay alive. Help him. Malik, please!"

Thor was dying. He was bleeding to death.

While Lev disarmed the Russians, Malik felt for Thor's pulse. "His pulse is weak and thready. We've got to move. Help me get him into the elevator!"

"Is he going to be okay?"

Malik's face showed only worry. "I don't know."

Thor spoke, his voice barely a whisper. "A... p-pos."

"A pos," Malik repeated. "We've got you, brother."

It took Samantha a moment to realize they were talking about his blood type—A positive—but then she was so sleepy.

"We are here to help," Vasily told Lev. "I killed that whoreson."

Lev knelt beside Samantha, examined her aching cheek. "Is he telling the truth?"

"Y-yes." Samantha struggled to keep her eyes open. She'd stopped shivering and no longer felt the cold. She knew that wasn't good, but she couldn't seem to care. "Don't worry about me. Save Thor."

Then Lev and Malik lifted Thor and carried him between them into the elevator, Lev staying with him, keeping pressure on the gunshot wound.

Samantha tried to stand but couldn't. She was so sleepy, so painfully tired. She wasn't even cold any longer.

Vasily moved toward her, but Malik stepped in.

"I've got her." He scooped her into his arms and carried her into the elevator.

And then they were moving, machinery humming.

"You'd better not die on us, Viking," Lev said.

The words brought Samantha's eyes open. "Thor?"

Please, let him survive!

When the doors opened, it was organized chaos.

Malik lay Samantha down on a stretcher, concern on his face.

Someone covered her with a heated blanket.

"Stay awake, Samantha!" Ryan seemed to be in charge. He was talking into a radio. "They're both hypothermic, but it looks like Isaksen has a bleeder in that GSW. Tell Decker to prep for emergency surgery. We're on our way to medical."

"He's A positive." That was Malik. "Do you have blood?"

"Yes, but I'm not sure we've got enough."

Their words swirled around Samantha, but she understood, panic trilling through her. "Thor! Is he... Will he be okay?"

She couldn't lose him—not Thor, too. She loved him.

"You're going to be okay, Samantha." Malik was there, one of four men carrying her stretcher toward the infirmary, the lights of the hallway sliding by overhead.

The next thing she knew, she was lifted onto a bed, something warm beneath her.

"You came to the right place to be treated for hypothermia. That's one thing we do well here at the South Pole." Ryan covered her with another warm blanket. "I'll get an IV going for heated fluids. Start warmed oxygen."

From nearby, she heard Decker. "Open those fluids wide. Warm all the A and O we have on station. Let's prep for surgery."

"Thor!" She couldn't lose him.

Then her eyes closed, and her awareness faded.

22

Thor opened his eyes, fluorescent light above his bed making him blink, an oxygen mask on his face, the pain in his shoulder sharp.

"Thor?"

Samantha.

"Hey." Warmth swelled in his chest at the sight of her, the sound of her voice.

She sat beside him, her hand resting on top of his, a blanket around her shoulders, a woolen hat on her head. One cheek was bruised and swollen, and there were patches of red on her face from frostbite. "How do you feel?"

"*Det gøre fanden ondt.*" *It hurts like hell.*

"In English maybe?"

"It ... hurts."

"I bet it does." She raised her voice. "Kristi, when can he get more morphine?"

"Is he awake?" Kristi appeared wearing blue scrubs, a wide smile on her face. "Welcome back. I am so happy you're still with us. Are you in pain?"

He nodded.

"I'll be right back."

Samantha stayed with him. "They got the bullet out, along with some fabric from your shirt. The bullet nicked a small artery. That's why you lost so much blood."

"The posterior humeral circumflex artery," Kristi said from the other side of the curtain. "We had to give you six units of blood."

"They said that your carrying me, going down the ladder to the ice tunnel, and fighting with that *bastard* did more damage and made the bleeding worse."

Kristi ducked inside the curtain, injected something into his IV. "You had also developed an infection, so you're getting IV antibiotics for that. Luckily for you, you had the best medical team at the South Pole at your side."

Samantha rolled her eyes, a hint of a smile on her lips. "That's the *only* medical team at the South Pole."

"But, hey, we're top-notch. Decker's a trauma surgeon. I'm an ER nurse. I have to say, I never thought I'd be treating GSWs—gunshot wounds—here."

The pain in Thor's shoulder began to fade. "Thank you, Kristi—for all of it."

"You're welcome. Now that you're awake, maybe you can tell Samantha to get back into bed. She's been sitting at your side all morning, so I made her wear a wool hat. She's still a little hypothermic. Hardin or Delaney or whoever he was fractured her cheek, so she'll be our guest for another day or so. You are both lucky to be alive."

It touched Thor to think that Samantha cared enough to sit by his side, but she needed to heal, too. "How do you feel?"

"Now that you're awake, I'm fine."

"Liar." Kristi put a pulse oximeter on Thor's right forefinger.

"Okay, so my cheek hurts. I've got a perpetual headache. My fingers are all tingly, and I can't seem to stay warm."

That didn't sound good to Thor. "You should do what Kristi tells you to do."

"See? You're a smart man, Thor. Do what the RN tells you to do."

"I'm fine. Besides, every time I fall asleep, I have nightmares."

"Aw, sweetie. I'm so sorry." Kristi rested her hand on Samantha's shoulder. "But that's why God invented sedatives."

"He injected me with that midazolam. I don't want to feel helpless again."

"Fair enough." Kristi turned to Thor. "Do you want me to let Malik and Lev know you're awake?"

"I want a few minutes alone with Samantha first."

Kristi nodded. "I'll be out here charting and pretending I can't hear you."

Samantha looked down at him, tears filling her blue eyes. "I was so afraid I'd lost you. I ... I care about you, Thor."

Maybe it was the morphine, but he heard the words she'd intended but *hadn't* spoken. They struck something tender inside him, unleashing emotions he'd never felt for a woman. "I care about you, too, *skat*. I'm so happy to see your face. I thought it was over for me. I just wanted to stay alive long enough for Jones and Segal to reach you."

A tear slid down one cheek. "I would never have gotten over it if you'd died. I would never be able to forgive myself."

"None of this was your fault—or Patty's."

She nodded, but the anguish on her face remained.

"I'm sorry about the nightmares." He knew from personal experience how rough bad dreams could be. He reached up with his good hand, brushed a strand of blond hair off her bruised and swollen cheek. "I should have kept you safe. I should have—"

"You almost *died* saving my life." She turned her head, kissed his palm. "If it weren't for you, I wouldn't be here."

"You saved my life, too, so we're even."

"When did I...? Oh. When I got him with the chisel."

"Yeah." Her scream as she'd jumped out of the elevator echoed through Thor's mind. "He was about to pull that trigger."

Her face crumpled. "I wanted to *kill* him for hurting you. I aimed for his eye, but I got his cheek instead."

"I'm glad you missed." He wasn't sure how Samantha would have handled having a man's death on her hands. "It's not easy to live with taking a life."

She sniffed. "It was awful—Vasily stabbing Hardin and cutting Vlad's throat with that switchblade, watching them bleed and die."

He wiped a tear away with his thumb. "I'm sorry you saw all of that—the fighting, the killing."

Her lips curved into a wobbly smile. "I certainly appreciate your job now. You're my hero, Thor Isaksen."

She stood, leaned down, kissed his forehead.

From beyond the curtains came Kristi's voice. "He's awake if you want to see him. Just don't wear out your welcome."

Then the curtain was pushed back and Jones and Segal were there, the two of them staring down at him with worried looks on their unshaven faces.

"Hey, brother, how do you feel?" Jones asked.

"Like I got shot in the shoulder."

"It was touch and go there for a while, man," Segal said. "You are one tough son of a bitch."

Then Jones and Segal filled him in.

Life on station was returning to normal. Jones and Segal had liberated the package from Delaney's office safe, verified its contents, and secured it once again. Lance was no longer confined to his room. Shields was beating herself up over failing to uncover Delaney's deception. Tower was waiting for Thor to be healed enough for the long journey home before trying to set up extract. Vasily and his buddies had fled the station a few hours ago on an unauthorized flight to Bellinghausen, a Russian station off the Antarctic Peninsula. They'd taken Vlad's body with them.

"We heard the plane land," Jones said. "We got outside in time to see it take off."

"Were they Delaney's contacts?"

"Delaney's emails showed that he tried to make a deal with China, but his buyers backed out," Segal said. "Then he turned to the Russians. Vasily cut a deal with him but intended to kill him. Vasily hoped to get his hands on the components, I'm sure, but we'll never know what his true motives were."

"How did Delaney know Samantha and I were in the LO arch?"

"Vlad overheard us and shot Delaney a text to warn him that you and Dr. Park were still alive and headed back into the station."

"That's why Vasily killed him—for betraying us," Samantha said. "I still don't know whether Vasily is a good guy or a bad guy."

"Oh, he's definitely a bad guy," Segal answered. "But he's a bad guy who cares about you—and Patty. This time, that's what mattered."

Thor remembered Jones and Segal rushing through the doors after Vasily had already killed Delaney. "What took you two so long? How did Vasily and his crew get there first? Didn't you lock them down?"

"Sorry, man." Jones explained. "After we left, they over-powered Ryan and his guys, went for their rifles, and ran straight to Delaney. You said you were backtracking to the machine shop, so we went outside and came back in through the door to the LO Arch, thinking we could get ahead of Delaney. But he had already found you."

"Better late than never." Thor struggled to keep his eyes open.

"Okay, guys, he needs rest." Kristi motioned for Jones and Segal to leave. "Samantha, either you get back into your own bed, or I'll have these two strong men pick you up and put you there."

"Listen to her!" Samantha stood. "She's so bossy."

Thor drifted into a dreamless sleep.

SAMANTHA WAS DISCHARGED two days later and spent the next few days doing her best to catch up on work. It seemed like an impossible task. She wasn't sleeping well and was tired all the time. Typing with her healing fingers was uncomfortable despite ibuprofen and the aloe gel Kristi had given her. Worse, her body couldn't tolerate extreme cold, not even with all of her layers. The moment she stepped outside, she began to shiver, her frostbitten skin to ache. She had no choice but to operate the telescope remotely, doing what she could from the science lab on station and getting help from the other astronomers—Kazem, Greg, Bai, and Nick—with tasks that needed to be performed in the Dark Sector Lab.

Everyone on station seemed to know what had

happened. They had been incredibly kind to her. They got her coffee, brought her snacks, carried her tray to the dish pit. Analise Weber, a young woman she barely knew who worked in the galley, gave her a pair of hand-knitted socks to keep her feet warm.

Jason had come up to her in the galley to apologize. "Sorry I was such an asshole. I'm really glad you're going to be okay."

"Thank you, Jason."

She saved her breaks and free time to be with Thor.

Kristi and Decker said he was recovering quickly, but she knew he was frustrated.

"Go easy on yourself," she'd told him this morning when the pain of his physical therapy exercises had left him tight-jawed and angry. "Three days ago, you almost died. I know you're not used to physical limitations, and pain really sucks. But you can't storm your way through healing. Your body needs time."

Kristi had ducked inside the curtain, holding a tiny paper cup with two pills in it. "Or he could take his oxycodone an hour before starting his exercises like his excellent nurse suggested."

"Fine!" Thor had snatched the cup from her hand, tossed the pills back, and swallowed them without water.

Kristi had winked at Samantha. "For a Viking, he's a teddy bear."

It was both touching and distressing to know that what he suffered now, he suffered for her sake.

But the hardest part of Samantha's day came at bedtime. Every night, she had nightmares, not just once a night but two, three, or four times. It had gotten to the point now where she dreaded going to bed.

After supper, she tried procrastinating in the lounge,

watching some weird B-movie with a few of the others until it was late. Then she made her way to the infirmary, hoping Kristi would let her visit with Thor—or sit beside him if he was asleep. When she reached the infirmary, she discovered that Kristi had already gone to bed in the adjacent sleep room and Thor was awake and sitting up, reading something on his phone.

He smiled when he saw her. "Hey, what are you doing up?"

"I just wanted to check on you."

He arched an eyebrow. "At midnight?"

She leaned down, kissed him. "Why not?"

He set his phone aside and took her hand. "You're having trouble sleeping. Nightmares?"

She nodded, sat. "It's not like most bad dreams, where you wake up and then go back to sleep. They come again and again."

"Have you talked to Decker or Kristi? That's post-traumatic stress."

She shook her head. "It seems stupid."

"It's not stupid. It's real." He seemed to study her. "Can you tell me about it?"

"Do you think that will help?"

"It can't hurt. You need to talk to someone."

Samantha drew a breath, steeled herself. "In one of the dreams, I'm trapped beneath the station alone and my body starts turning into ice. I try to get away, but the ice creeps up from my fingers until my entire body is encased like a piece of fruit stuck in an ice cube. I can't run. I can't scream. I just lie there, terrified and trapped in the ice, until I wake up."

He took her hand, held it fast. "That's not far off from what almost happened. I'm so sorry, Samantha."

"The other dream is worse."

He didn't push her, but waited.

"You and I are in the ice tunnels running from Steve, who has a knife stuck in his abdomen. He should be dead, but he's not. He chases us and then shoots you. You fall to the ice, and your blood spreads around you." Tears filled her eyes, her throat going tight, the horror of the dream only too real. "I try to gather it up so I can put it back inside you. I claw at the ice, trying to get it all, but... Then I wake up feeling sick."

"Hey, come here." He drew her against his chest with his good arm, kissed her hair. "I'm safe. We're both safe."

"I know they're just dreams, but when I wake up, I'm so afraid. I don't want to go to sleep, Thor. I don't want to be alone. I don't want to close my eyes. I'd rather try to sleep in this chair tonight than go back to my room alone."

Thor released her, scooted to his left, and patted the mattress. "Climb in. We slept in your tiny bed. We can make this work."

"I don't want to hurt you."

"Just don't punch my shoulder."

Samantha kicked off her shoes, climbed in beside him, drew the blankets up over the two of them to her chin. "God, you're warm."

"Good." He pulled up the safety rail behind her and turned off his overhead light.

She curled up against him, her head pillowed on his uninjured shoulder. "I wouldn't blame you if you regret it."

"Regret what?"

"Coming after me. It almost got you killed."

"The only thing I regret is that I wasn't the one to kill that fucker." He kissed the top of her head. "Sleep, angel."

Samantha inhaled his scent, closed her eyes, feeling safe in his arms. Before she knew it, she was sound asleep.

~

"IT's good to see you alive." Tower looked out at Thor from his computer screen. "Jones and Segal have kept me up to date on your recovery. How do you feel?"

"It's good to be up and around again." He hadn't yet regained his full strength, and his shoulder hurt, especially if he didn't wear the damned sling. But he kept this to himself. "I'm grateful for the care I received here."

"I hear they're treating you like a hero."

This was, unfortunately, true. Since his discharge this afternoon, everyone he'd passed in the hallway had thanked him.

"Their attitude toward us has definitely improved, sir."

"Glad to hear it." And the small talk was over. "I've already gotten a full report from Jones and Segal, but there are questions they can't answer."

Thor recounted what had happened, ending with losing consciousness moments after Jones and Segal had arrived on scene. He was careful to refer to Samantha as Dr. Park. "I woke up the next morning after surgery. By that time, Jones and Segal had secured the package, and the Russians were gone."

Tower asked him questions, breaking it down—standard for a debriefing.

Had he thought about asking Jones and Segal to come with him to Delaney's office? What had he been wearing when Delaney forced him to go outside? How far was it from the station to Summer Camp? How had he been able to tell from the webcam image that Dr. Park was even still alive?

"I couldn't." It was the truth. "She might have been dead already, but I had to act on the hope that she was alive and that I could save her. I didn't know for certain she was alive until I got her to Summer Camp and checked her pulse."

Tower rubbed his jaw, a concerned frown on his face. "You gave your weapon and the location of the Golden Horde components to Delaney and risked your life on a *hope* that Dr. Park was still alive."

Thor had known this was going to be an issue.

He explained his thought process—not that he'd had much time to think. "Jones and Segal knew where I was. I knew they'd be warned if Delaney went after the package. Even if he got hold of it, he wasn't going anywhere. It seemed right to leave Delaney to Jones and Segal and to go after Dr. Park. I believed Delaney would give me her location. I was wrong about that. As it turned out, he planned to kill me outright after getting the intel he wanted. She was just bait."

"With others on hand, why did he choose Dr. Park?"

Thor answered carefully. "I can't be sure, but because Dr. Park went with us to retrieve the components, the three of us know her better than anyone else on station."

That wasn't the whole truth. Everyone on station knew that Thor and Samantha had slept together. Delaney had gone for Thor's vulnerable spot—and it had worked. Even so, Thor didn't regret it.

Then it hit him right in the face.

Did he love her? Was he in love with Samantha?

"Why did you carry her all the way to Summer Camp? Four hundred meters is a long distance in wind chill of minus a hundred. Wouldn't it have been faster to head back into the station?"

"When I heard that door lock, I figured Delaney would lock the other doors, too. With everyone in the life pod, no one would have heard me knocking. I would have wasted precious minutes trying to find a way in. Instead, I went to the closest shelter I could find, a place I thought might be off Delaney's radar."

Tower seemed to consider this. "When you're armed and the bad guy makes demands, it's an unusual strategy to give him what he wants. You gave him everything—your weapon, your means of communication, access to the package—to save someone who might already have been dead. In the process, you were shot, got hypothermia and frostbite, and nearly died. But you also saved Dr. Park's life."

"Dr. Park could have been anywhere out there. I didn't have time to fight Delaney or interrogate him. I either needed to find her—or give her up for dead. I couldn't do the latter. I just couldn't."

Tower nodded. "You made some strategically question-able choices, but now I understand why. It all worked out in the end. You saved Dr. Park's life. The package and the station are secure. Dr. Holcomb's murder is solved."

"Yes, sir."

"You know, I'm tough, and I've done a lot of extreme shit. But I'm not sure I could have done what you did. I'm not sure any of us could. You've got unusually high endurance. When Corbray and I decided to bring you on board, we knew we were acquiring a somewhat different skillset. Our decision has paid off on this mission. Well, done, Isaksen. Now, heal up, and I'll do my best to get you all home quickly."

Thor wasn't sure he wanted to go—yet. "Thank you, sir."

Relieved to have the debriefing behind him, Thor disconnected from the satellite VPN, left his room, and made his way upstairs to the galley. The meeting had gone on a little longer than he'd expected, and he was a few minutes late joining Samantha for supper. She'd stayed with him in the infirmary these past few nights—with Kristi's approval—and had at least gotten some sleep.

He walked through the door—and people got to their feet, clapping and cheering.

Hva' fanden? What the hell?

An amused smile on her bruised and beautiful face, Samantha walked over to him and spoke for his ears alone. "Hey, it's okay. You look like a deer in the headlights. They're happy to see you on your feet and grateful for what you did."

Thor wasn't sure what a deer was doing inside headlights, but he forced a smile onto his face. "Can we eat fast and get out of here?"

She picked up a tray for him. "Oh, come on. Don't tell me a big, tough guy like you can't handle a little adoration. Lasagna or beef stew?"

23

"You don't have to go down there." Thor drew Samantha's hood up over her woolen hat. "It's bound to trigger bad memories."

"Patty was my best friend. I *need* to be there. The rest of it doesn't matter." Then it hit her that this might be hard for Thor, too. He'd almost died down there. "You never met her. If you'd rather wait here in the station, I don't think it will take long."

"I feel like I have a connection to her through her journal—and through you." Thor kissed her forehead. "I won't let you face this alone."

"I won't be alone."

"You know what I mean." He slipped into his parka.

God, she loved him.

He'd been by her side every day of the past two weeks, supporting her recovery, both physical and emotional, in any way he could. He wasn't going to back out when she needed to go down to the ice tunnels.

Samantha picked up her mask with a gloved hand, while Thor grabbed a small box of things she'd set aside. Then the two of them walked together toward the Beer Can freight elevator, where a group was waiting for the car to return.

"Hey, Samantha, Thor. Let me carry that." Ryan took the box from Thor. He had taken over running the station as acting winter site manager. "If either of you start feeling chilled, let us know."

"Thanks, man."

"We will—and thanks." Samantha had hand warmers in her pockets and was wearing her warmest woolies. At this point, she was more concerned about her fingertips and the patches of frostbite on her face than she was about getting hypothermia again. Her skin was healing, and there hadn't been any deep-tissue damage. Still, she couldn't risk injuring those areas further.

A bright *ding* announced the arrival of the elevator, the doors sliding open, releasing a burst of frigid air. The others entered, talking with one another about their work, about the weather, about news from home.

Samantha's pulse picked up, but she slipped the mask over her face and followed them, Thor behind her. She would be living here for the next six months. She couldn't be afraid of this area. The bastard who had tried to kill them was dead.

Then her gaze fell on the moving blankets that were folded and stacked in the corner, the same corner where she'd tried to hide—and her pulse raced.

Thor wrapped an arm around her shoulders, turned her away. "Look at me."

She looked up at his masked face. "I'm acting like a baby."

"No, you're not. You're a badass warrior chick with scars."

The ride down to the bottom of the Beer Can was quick. She followed the others out, trying not to see the spots where Steve and Vlad had died on the floor. Then they stepped through the door and into the LO Arch with its creepy, flickering lights.

She feared she'd be stepping into her nightmares, but the space was crowded with people she knew. More than that, it had been transformed. Someone had strung white fairy lights along the shelving to mark the occasion, the sight of it putting a lump in Samantha's throat. Everyone knew how Patty had loved fairy lights.

"You okay, *skat*?"

"Yeah."

People moved together toward the entrance to the ice tunnels.

Samantha tucked her arm through Thor's, needing his reassurance, not just because they were walking through the ice tunnels, but because of what they were about to do. The LO Arch crew had created a shrine for Patty, carving it out of the ice walls of the tunnel. Tonight, they were dedicating it to her.

When Samantha saw it, she gasped. "Oh!"

Somehow, they'd connected a short strand of fairy lights to electricity, the lights making the ice glisten. A plaque of recycled metal was frozen into the ice above the shrine, Patty's name, the dates of her birth and death, and the words "Daughter, Friend, and Astronomy Badass. Rest in Peace" engraved in it.

"What do you think?" Thor asked.

She blinked back tears. "It's perfect."

Ryan called out to everyone, box still in his hands. "Get as close as you can. Keep each other warm. It's hard to fit fifty-one people in this space. Let Samantha and Thor through. I'll try to speak so you can all hear me."

Ryan talked about how much people loved Patty and

shared what most people didn't know—that she'd realized someone was trying to hack the satellite and had taken that information to Delaney. "Patty is a hero. Samantha, do you want to take over?"

Samantha scooted into his place. "A lot of Patty's stuff is in the Skua area. Some of it will go to her parents. But I saved some things for her shrine."

Ryan tilted the box so she could see inside.

She drew out the framed photo of the Milky Way that had the words "You Are Here" written on a little tag in Patty's handwriting. She held it up, swallowed hard. "This was on Patty's wall when we were in grad school together. She brought it with her last winter, too, and now it will stay here."

Samantha set it in the back of the shrine, then reached inside the box for Patty's coffee mug. She held it up for everyone to see, her throat too tight to speak.

Ryan took over. "It says 'Astronomers Do It in the Dark.'"

"It was her favorite mug." Samantha set that inside, too.

"I've got something." Lance threaded his way over to her, a bottle of wine in his hand. The charges against him had been dropped, and Samantha had forgiven him. "It's a bottle of wine that she bought for me. I can't drink it without her."

Lance set it into the shrine, too.

"I've got something to add." That was Jason.

"This ought to be interesting," someone muttered.

Jason nudged his way through the tightly packed bodies and held up what looked like a plastic snake. "I printed this with my three-D printer and painted it. If you can't tell, it's a cobra. I thought it belonged here because it was the Cobra team who found Patty's killer. They should be a part of this, too."

"Hell, yeah!" someone called out.

Ryan nodded. "Thanks, Jason."

Jason handed the plastic snake to Thor. "Maybe you should do the honors."

"Thank you." Thor set the plastic cobra next to the mug.

Tears streamed down Samantha's face, though no one could see them because of her mask. "Thanks, Jason."

"Rest in peace, friend. We all miss you. A moment of silence?" Ryan bowed his head. When the moment had passed, he made an announcement. "Tomorrow night, we're having a special dinner in honor of the Cobra team. They'll be flying out the next morning if the weather holds."

Not for the first time, Samantha hoped the weather *didn't* hold.

THOR KNELT next to the bed and sucked Samantha's clit into his mouth, stroking her with his lips and tongue the way she liked it. He did his best to memorize her taste, her scent, the sound of her sighs. Her body was as precious to him now as his own—the mole next to her navel, her sweet breasts, her beautiful eyes.

Don't think about leaving tomorrow. Be in the moment.

He pushed aside thoughts of his departure, focused on giving her pleasure, sliding his fingers inside her, stroking her, focusing on that sensitive spot right *there*.

Her hands fisted in his hair, her breathing ragged, her thighs quivering. "*Thor!*"

She arched off the bed as she came, her muscles clenching around his fingers.

He kept it up, gave her everything she could take until her body slowly melted, the tension draining away, the rush of orgasm slowing into ripples.

She exhaled, a long, drawn-out sigh. "How do you want me?"

Thor stood, grabbed a condom, slid it over his erection. "Face to face."

He needed her tonight, needed to fill himself with her.

She scooted up the bed, a smile on her lips, her gaze locked with his, her blond hair tangled around her shoulders.

Without breaking eye contact, he climbed in at her feet, crawled up to her, settled his hips between her thighs.

She reached down, took hold of his cock, and guided him inside her, the two of them moaning in unison as he buried himself in her slick heat.

But this wasn't about fucking or getting off—not for Thor, not this time.

This was different.

He moved slowly at first, doing his best to draw this out, to make it last, unable to take his gaze off her face. She felt so good—the way her body gripped his, the silky feel of her skin, her softness. "Samantha."

She wrapped her legs around his waist, her eyes drifting shut.

"Look at me."

She opened her eyes again, her gaze locked with his.

It was the most intimate thing he'd ever experienced, seeing the effect he had on her, letting her see inside him. It felt more like sharing souls than sex, their bodies joined, their hearts pounding together, their breath mingling.

But soon their bodies took over, his hips thrusting into her hard and fast, her eyes going wide as she came again, her cry sweet. A few more thrusts and he was flying with her, bliss washing through him, hitting him straight in the heart, as pure as sunlight.

He tossed the condom in the trash and drew her with him, the two of them lying in a tangle of limbs as heartbeats slowed and sex cooled into tenderness.

She broke the silence. "I wish I could freeze time and make tonight last forever."

He kissed her hair. "Yeah."

"That was a really nice dinner. Prime rib at the Pole. You guys looked so embarrassed when people stood up and cheered for you."

"We're not used to that. We were just doing our jobs."

She was quiet for a moment. "What's going to happen after you leave?"

"You'll be able to focus on your work discovering galaxies, and I'll probably make a half-dozen trips to the Middle East." That was *after* he completed physical therapy and was medically cleared.

"No, I meant what's going to happen to *us*? Most relationships on the ice are over when people get on the plane, but I don't want this to end."

How like Samantha to come right out with it, to be so open.

"Neither do I, but six months is a long time. You might not feel the same way in November. Crisis situations can make people feel close quickly, but the emotion doesn't always last once the adrenaline is gone."

She sat up. "Are you saying you don't want to stay in touch?"

The absurdity of it made him laugh. "God, no. That's not what I mean at all. I want to stay in touch—email, Zoom, whatever. I just don't want you to feel burdened."

"Burdened?"

"I know you're going to be lonely without Patty, and if

you need to take comfort with someone, I hope to be a big enough man to accept that."

She gaped at him. "Are you giving me permission to have sex with other men? That's a Danish thing, isn't it?"

He supposed it *was* rather Danish of him. "You don't need my permission."

Her expression fell. "Does that mean you want to have sex with other women?"

Okay, he wasn't doing a very good job with this.

He sat up, too, tucked a silky strand of hair behind her ear. "I don't plan on having sex with anyone until I see you again. But I'm not the one who lost my best friend and was almost murdered by someone I trusted. You've been through hell, Samantha. I just want you to do what you need to do to take care of yourself. I don't want you to be lonely or afraid at night. If you need someone to hold you, I will do my best to understand. I care too much about you to see you unhappy."

He didn't tell her that he'd changed his will so that she was his beneficiary if the plane went down on his way home or he were killed in action on another assignment. He had no heirs and no siblings, and his parents sure as hell didn't need the money. He felt good knowing that she would be taken care of should anything happen to him.

She seemed to consider his words. "God, you're sweet, but the only man I want is flying out on a damned plane tomorrow."

He cupped her cheek, kissed her. "Then don't talk about tomorrow. Let's make the most of tonight."

Samantha stood with Thor inside Destination Alpha,

fighting not to cry. "You'll let me know when you're safely back home?"

"Count on it." His brow furrowed. "You have friends here, Samantha. These people care about you. You don't need Patty to open doors for you any longer. Ryan and Kristi both promised to look after you. Let them help you."

Kristi stood not far away, crying, she and Malik locked in an embrace.

Samantha nodded, tears coming at last. "You stay safe. Do you hear me? No heroic sacrifices, no more getting shot."

His lips quirked in a lopsided grin that melted her heart. "I'll do my best."

From outside the station came the sound of the approaching plane, and staff began to gather to say goodbye.

If only she could freeze time. If only she could replay last night.

At least he'd left her one of his T-shirts. It smelled like him.

Lev stuck his head through the door. "He's landing. Let's move out."

"They have to refuel," Jones fired back. "Chill, man!"

Thor kissed Samantha, soft and slow, then wiped the tears from her cheeks with his thumbs. "You're going to be okay."

"I know. I'm just going to miss you." She hesitated then blurted the words. "I love you, Thor. There. I said it, and I won't take it back."

He kissed her again, a tender sweet kiss—but he didn't tell her that he loved her.

She told herself she wasn't surprised. He'd been straight with her from the start. He wasn't the kind of man who played for keeps. Still, a woman could dream.

This is the price you pay for getting involved. You knew this day would come.

Yes, and it had been worth it.

Lev stuck his head in again. "They're refueling. Time to roll."

Thor drew her into his arms, held her tight for one precious moment. Then he touched his forehead to hers, his gaze warm. "We're not finished, Samantha."

Her heart held onto those words. "I hope not."

Then he and Jones put on their masks, picked up their duffel bags, called out their goodbyes to the staff, and left the station.

Samantha and Kristi rushed into the coatroom, put on snow pants, hats, gloves, masks, and their parkas, and hurried outside and down the stairs. They watched as the LO crew loaded Delaney's body and his and Patty's personal belongings onto the plane. Then Thor, Malik, and Lev boarded, Thor glancing back and waving to her just before the doors closed. The fuelies stepped away, and the plane was ready to depart.

Please don't crash. Please don't crash. Please don't crash.

Kristi took Samantha's gloved hand in hers, neither of them speaking as the plane headed down the skiway. Then the rockets fired, and the plane left the ground.

Kristi sniffed. "Well, I just said goodbye to the best sex of my life—and the nicest man I've ever known. I'm going to miss Malik so much."

But Samantha couldn't speak, tears freezing on her face, her heart breaking, as the plane's lights disappeared in the distance.

24

July 10

Thor's face appeared on Samantha's computer screen, his jaw covered with a short beard, his skin tanned. "Happy Birthday, *skat*."

God, she missed him.

The sound of his voice was like an elixir, her heart seeming to swell, contentment warming her like sunshine. "Thanks."

"Damn, you look good." There was a note of longing in his voice.

Somehow, he always made her feel beautiful, even when she hadn't washed her hair for two days and was dressed in sweats.

"They threw a little surprise party for me with cake and ice cream." She told him how Kristi had persuaded her to go to the lounge to watch a movie. "When she switched on the lights, everyone shouted 'Surprise!'"

"You deserve that."

"I got your present." She reached for the little white gold

daisy pendant hanging from her throat on its white gold chain. "Thank you. I love it. It's so delicate."

"It's probably the most Danish thing I could give you." Thor explained that the Danish queen's nickname was Daisy and that a Danish designer had created a line of jewelry in her honor when she was a child. "I wanted to give you something that couldn't come from anyone else, something that would make you think of me."

"I love it even more now. But how did it get here?" There was no postal service between Antarctica and the rest of the world during austral winter.

He gave her that sexy smile that made her melt. "I know some people who know some people who know the guys who fly the planes. They got it into the last airdrop."

"Connections. I'm impressed." But there was something she needed to say to him, something serious. "You're the reason I got to celebrate another birthday. Thank you."

That would be true for the rest of her life.

"I had pretty selfish reasons for doing what I did."

"What do you mean?"

"I couldn't bear to lose you."

Samantha's heart melted. No man had ever made her feel loved the way Thor did, even though he'd never told her he loved her. "How's your shoulder?"

"It aches sometimes, but otherwise I'm back to normal." Thor changed the subject. "What else is going on? Ryan says he taught you to play chess and that you crushed him."

"Are you checking up on me?"

"Always."

"Yes, I beat the pants off him. You know what's crazy?"

"What?"

"For as long as I knew her, Patty told me there was more to life than science. It took her death for me to learn what she meant." Samantha told Thor how she'd kept mostly to herself her first winter here and how she'd forced herself to socialize after he'd gone. "At first I did it to keep from feeling depressed and lonely—and because you pushed me. But now I'm actually having fun. I've made friends."

"You're special, Samantha. They all see that."

She brought him up to date on the rest of the news. Bai and Kazem were determined to marry. They had applied to Denmark and Sweden for jobs and visas. Lance was back to his old self, and he and Charli were together. The galaxy she'd discovered was, indeed, an elliptical double-ringed galaxy.

"I've started a campaign to get it named after Patty rather than assigned a catalogue number. Some of our former professors at UC-Berkeley are helping. I'm also working with them to establish an endowment for women doctoral students in Patty's name. We haven't raised much money yet."

"You've been busy. I'm certain Patty would be touched."

"It gives me something positive to do, a way to turn my grief into something tangible that will ensure that Patty is never forgotten."

"That makes perfect sense."

"Remember the ladder we came down—the one that led into the ice tunnels?"

"How could I forget?"

"The guys who work down there now call it 'Thor's Ladder.'"

He frowned. "Why my name? Why not 'Samantha's Ladder'? You were the first to see the flag that marked the escape hatch, and you were the first one down."

"Yeah, but I'm not named after a deity. 'Thor's Ladder' just sounds better, doesn't it?" But Samantha had saved the best news for last. "I haven't had a nightmare for a couple of weeks now."

Relief spread across his handsome face. "I'm so glad to hear that. The therapy is helping then?"

At Thor's request, Cobra had connected Decker with a PTSD specialist who combined therapy with controlled doses of ketamine to help people process traumatic events without retraumatizing them. As a scientist, Samantha had insisted on reading the research before she'd agreed to go along with it.

"I'm loopy for a few hours after every therapy session, but it seems to be working. I'm less jumpy. I don't think about what happened all the time like I did at first, and I'm able to concentrate on my job again."

He smiled. "It makes me happy to see you doing so well."

She was doing well, but this was still so *hard*. "I miss Patty. I miss you so much."

"I miss you, too, *min elskling*."

My love.

She loved it when he called her that. No, it wasn't the same thing as him saying that he loved her, but it was close.

"How's life wherever you are?" Samantha had never told Thor this, but nowadays she kept an eye on international headlines. She saw global politics from a different perspective, knowing Thor was out there somewhere, risking his life.

"We're wrapping things up and flying out tomorrow."

"Nothing scary or dangerous happened?"

He grinned. "Not this time—unless you count McManus hitting his head on a low stone archway and needing stitches."

"Ouch!"

They talked for more than an hour, time slipping through Samantha's fingers. Then Thor had to go. They said their goodbyes.

"Be safe, Thor."

"I'll do my best. Talk to you again soon."

THOR WATCHED out the window as Cobra's jet flew over the Atlantic, carrying them home from a long assignment in Yemen. Apart from the occasional cloud, there was nothing but blue above and blue below. What he wouldn't give right now for a few hours in the starlit darkness of Antarctica.

Long-distance relationships sucked.

Get used to it.

It would be easier when she was back in Chicago. The time difference wouldn't be so extreme, at least when he was in the US, and Denver to Chicago wasn't a long flight. He'd be able to visit her whenever he had leave, and she could come to Colorado when she was on break.

No, it wouldn't be the same as living in the same space, but it would be a hell of a lot more manageable than this set-up. Given how often he was away from home, it seemed right that she should have her own home and her own life.

"*¡Hijoeputa!*" Dylan Cruz yelled at the TV.

He and his bride, Gabriela Marquez, were watching some Spanish-language film with Jones, who needed translations once in a while. In the row of seats behind the newlyweds, McManus talked quietly with Shields, a bandage on his forehead. Segal sat behind Thor, reading an Israeli magazine.

Then Jones stood, grabbed two beers out of the refrigerator, and came to sit beside Thor, offering him a bottle. "You talk to Samantha lately, man?"

"Yeah. We talked last night."

"How's she doing?"

"She's better." Thor opened his beer, took a drink. "It's been a hard stretch, but the community there has pulled together to help her through it."

"Did she mention Kristi?"

"Kristi?" Thor fought back a grin. "Oh, right. Kristi. Um... I think she said Kristi helped throw a surprise birthday party for her."

"She didn't say anything about Kristi missing me or..." The man was lovesick, and he didn't know it.

"No." Thor wouldn't lie. "But, hey, if you want to talk to Kristi, send her an email or set up a chat."

"Nah, man. We agreed there would be no strings. I don't want to be the one to break the rules first."

Segal, who was sitting behind them, stuck his unshaven face between their two seats. "Have fun snuggling up with your pride, Jones. I'm sure it keeps you warm at night. What's that old Jewish proverb? Oh, yeah. 'Pride goes before a fall.'"

Thor chuckled. "I saw how broken up Kristi was when we left. What if she's afraid she'll piss you off if she reaches out? You need to be the one to get in touch."

"Why does it have to be me?"

"Who made the 'no strings' rule?"

"We both did—though I guess I'm the one who brought it up first."

Thor had thought so. "In that case, *you* need to be the one to make contact."

"There's really no point." Jones pulled out his phone, started scrolling. "She wants to see the world, so she signed up with some kind of humanitarian healthcare agency. She's going to work for a year as a nurse in Nigeria."

"Nigeria?" That wouldn't be Thor's first choice for a nurse. "Weren't several aid workers abducted and murdered there recently?"

"Yeah." Jones went quiet, his expression troubled.

"Don't paint the devil on the wall. I'm sure they'll keep her safe."

"Don't ... *what*?"

"You don't have that expression in English?"

"Paint the devil on the wall?" Jones arched an eyebrow. "Uh... No."

"It means don't expect the worst—or something like that."

"Crazy Viking." Jones shook his head, went back to his scrolling on his phone.

Thor faced the window again, missing Samantha more than he could say.

Four months later

SAMANTHA WALKED through the airport in Christchurch in search of the gate for her connecting flight, her carry-on in tow. Eight hours of flying behind her. Only twenty-three to go. She wasn't sure there was enough coffee in the airport for that.

It had been a smooth flight, though she'd been acutely aware of the empty seat beside her. Patty ought to have been sitting there. The two of them would have spent those eight hours talking. There would be an empty seat on Samantha's connecting flight to Chicago and in their shared office on campus, too. Patty's parents had flown to Chicago and collected Patty's belongings from the apartment, so there would be empty spaces there, also. So much emptiness.

Patty's death had left gaping holes in Samantha's life—and in her heart.

Returning to the real world wasn't going to be easy this time.

And yet, Samantha had so many reasons to be grateful. She and Thor were alive. Months of hard work had resulted in discoveries that would keep her busy for the rest of her career. She'd overcome her shyness and had friends she'd be in touch with for the rest of her life.

As she walked through the airport, she spotted other winter-overs here and there. Ryan and Kristi in the line at the coffee shop. Jason plugging his phone in to charge. Bai and Kazem walking hand in hand. Lance looking up at the Departures display.

She waved, and they waved back.

She wanted to get to her gate, sit down, and check her email. She hadn't heard from Thor for the past few days. She told herself he was on assignment and that he probably couldn't communicate. Still, she couldn't help but worry.

God, she missed him.

They'd done their best to stay in touch, but seeing his face on the screen and hearing his voice, as wonderful as that was, couldn't replace face-to-face contact.

While she'd been at the South Pole, Thor had been around the world—Afghanistan, Pakistan, South Korea, Egypt, Syria, Kenya. He was never able to say much about his work, though he shared what he could. Malik had emailed her a photo of Thor looking incredible in a suit and tie as part of some businessman's security detail, his face clean-shaven, his hair cut short, his skin tanned. He could have been a movie star.

Her therapist had warned her that her relationship with Thor was heading into new territory. They would both be in the US, at least when Thor wasn't on a mission. That meant setting new parameters for contact and discussing their expectations.

Did he want to be with her as much as she wanted to be with him?

She didn't know. She wasn't even sure when she'd see him again.

Without discussing it with Thor, she'd looked into jobs in Colorado. The University of Colorado in Boulder had a prestigious astrophysics and planetary sciences department, which was attached to JILA—the Joint Institute for Laboratory Astrophysics. They'd had a few positions open. There were other colleges searching for astronomy instructors, too, though she wanted a research position.

Let the future work itself out.

That was easier said than done when her heart was on the line.

She'd walked what felt like ten miles when she found her gate. She sat, tucked her carry-on beneath her seat, and pulled out her phone to check email.

A shadow fell over her.

"I'm sorry, but you're not taking this flight."

At the sound of his voice, she looked up—and Thor was standing right beside her.

For a moment, all she could do was stare, her heart pounding. "Thor?"

"Hey."

With a squeal, she leaped to her feet, his strong arms

enfolding her, his body hard against hers, his scent filling her head.

"*Skat.*" He drew back and claimed her mouth with his in a kiss that was deep, slow, passionate. "I've missed you so much."

"I've missed you, too." Then it hit her. "What are you doing here?"

He rested his hands on her hips in a way that was both casual and sexy. "I was just in Indonesia for a job, and I thought that you might want a few weeks of warm weather before you go home to winter in Chicago."

She stared at him, astonished. "What about my luggage, my flight home?"

"I've got your new ticket home. Someone else can take your seat. We'll just ask them to unload your bags." He kissed her again, slower this time. "I reserved a room for us at a beach resort—and arranged a visit to the Mount John Observatory."

She stared at him, her eyes filling with tears. "You did all of that for me?"

"I want some time alone with you, time away from the rest of the world before work separates us again."

"I would love that." She sniffed, smiling up at him. "Thank you. This is ... *incredible.*"

"I love you, Samantha." He wiped her tears away with his thumbs. "I should have told you before I left the station, but it was all so new. I wasn't even sure what I was feeling. I've never felt this way before. I was a dumbass."

Joy washed through Samantha, bright and iridescent, giving her heart wings. "I thought you'd never say those words."

"I'm not sure I would have if I hadn't met you."

"Get a room!" someone called in a New Zealand accent.

Laughter.

"Good idea!" Thor called back. "Let's get out of here."

They went to the nearest ticket counter and arranged to have her bags unloaded and brought to customs. An hour later, she walked with Thor into the warm sunshine of Christchurch, where a rental car waited for them.

She blinked, squinted. "It's so green!"

He chuckled. "That's because you haven't seen a single growing thing for almost nine months."

"Longer than that. I left Chicago in February the first time, worked as a winter-over, came home in November, and then left again in February. I've been living in winter for two years." Speaking of winter... "I'm going to need to buy some clothes. All I've got with me is cold-weather stuff."

"We can buy whatever you need." Thor smiled down at her, his fingers threading through hers. "But I don't think you're going to have much use for clothes."

Anticipation trilled through her at the thought of what was to come. "I'm so happy to see you. I was so surprised when I heard your voice."

"I thought I told you." He stopped, turned her to face him, his gaze warm. "We're not finished. In fact, we're just getting started."

EPILOGUE

August 15

Thor parked his SUV in the parking garage on campus, grabbed his suit jacket, and strode off toward the auditorium. The debriefing from their most recent mission had gone late, putting him behind, the sun low on the horizon. But this was Samantha's first public lecture at the University of Colorado-Boulder, and he didn't want to arrive late. He wouldn't do anything to ruin this special day for her.

Damn, he was proud of her. She'd worked so hard to reach this moment, applying for a research professorship at CU while keeping up with her research and teaching at the University of Chicago. What she had achieved these past nine months—publishing four peer-reviewed journal articles and landing a prestigious full professorship—would have been a major accomplishment for any young scholar. But she'd done it while coping with the loss of her research partner and best friend.

Thor slipped on his jacket, straightened his tie, and took

the stairs to the auditorium two at a time, people of all ages drifting toward the doors. He made his way into the lecture hall and down the stairs and sat at the end of the second row. Public speaking wasn't Samantha's favorite thing, and he knew it reassured her to see him.

A familiar voice. "Excuse me, but is that seat taken?"

Thor looked up. "Holly?"

Holly Andris stood there with Gabriela Marquez Cruz and Elizabeth Shields. It was the Cobra brain trust—the three former CIA operatives.

Thor raised an eyebrow, stood. "What are you three doing here?"

Holly scooted by him. "I love astronomy."

"Since when?"

"Since it became an excuse to meet Samantha."

Gabriela went next. "You haven't introduced us to her yet, so we had to take matters into our own hands."

Elizabeth scooted by. "You almost died for her, Thor. I have to meet her."

Thor was about to explain that Samantha had been busy moving when she and an older man stepped through the side door below.

She took his breath away, her skirt suit looking sleek and professional, her blond hair done up in a twist. She searched the crowd for him, smiling when she saw him.

He raised a hand, smiled back.

Elizabeth leaned over. "Oh, Thor, she's cute."

"What a sweet face," Holly said. "I was expecting someone older."

Gabriela turned to Holly. "She looks like a ballet dancer, no?"

Then the older man walked up to the microphone, and the lights went down.

"Thank you all for joining us tonight. I'm Dr. Rick Newton, the chair of CU's Department of Astrophysics and Planetary Sciences. It's a tradition for new professors to share their research at a public lecture. The scientist I'm about to introduce comes to us from the University of Chicago. Dr. Park did groundbreaking research on the Cosmic Microwave Background in Antarctica, working with the South Pole Telescope. But I'll let her tell you about it. Please welcome the newest addition to our astrophysics faculty—Dr. Samantha Park."

Thor clapped along with the audience. Beside him, Holly and Gabriela cheered like they were at a rock concert.

"I can't take them anywhere," Elizabeth whispered.

Samantha took a drink of water from a bottle on the podium, then clicked a remote to load her presentation. "Thank you all for the warm welcome. I am Dr. Samantha Park, and I'm happy to be with you tonight."

She shared a little bit about her background and gave the audience a basic explanation of her work in Antarctica. "In scientific terms, the South Pole Telescope measures the faint, lingering emissions from the Cosmic Microwave Background left over from the Big Bang. Variations in these emissions help us understand early matter in the universe and help us find distant objects, like faraway galaxy clusters."

She broke that down for her audience, using examples they could understand. Then she explained how the telescope worked, keeping it simple, showing images of scans and explaining how to read them.

Thor couldn't help but smile, the passion that had captivated him when she'd explained the SPT to him shining on her face, her excitement contagious.

"This is a rare elliptical double-ringed galaxy—our biggest discovery last year. As some of you know, my research partner was murdered early in that research season, and I fought to get the galaxy named after her. In the end, the committee decided to name it after both of us. So, I'm honored to say that this is the Holcomb-Park Object."

Thor applauded with the rest of the audience, love for her filling his chest. He was probably the only one who'd heard the catch in her voice just now. When she'd gotten the news a few months ago, she'd run into his arms and sobbed. They'd booked a weekend flight to Berkeley so she could visit her parents and Patty's and give them the news. They'd all visited Patty's grave together. It had been a hard day, but it seemed to have brought Samantha some closure.

Elizabeth leaned in close. "Damn. That chokes me up."

"Me, too."

~

She'd done it.

Relieved that her first public lecture at CU had gone well, Samantha looked around the auditorium for Thor. She'd spotted him in the audience, looking hot as hell in a suit, and she knew he had to be here somewhere.

"Samantha. Behind you."

She turned and saw him standing about twenty feet away with three beautiful women—one with platinum blond hair and crazy curves, a tall, slender redhead, and one with long dark hair, a beautiful face, and big brown eyes. She'd noticed them sitting beside him, but she hadn't realized they were together. Refusing to feel insecure or jealous, she put a smile on her face.

"Hey, hon. I see you brought friends."

"I didn't bring them." A resigned look on his face, Thor

stepped forward, kissed Samantha on the lips. "They invited themselves."

"We're not his friends, honey," said the gorgeous blonde. "We're family."

The woman with long, dark hair laughed. "A dysfunctional family."

Smiling, the redhead held out her hand. "I'm Elizabeth Shields."

Samantha stared at her, taken aback. "Elizabeth, I'm so happy to meet you at last. Thank you for all you did for Patty —and for me."

"I wish I'd done more."

Samantha knew immediately who the other women must be. She shook each of their hands in turn. "You're Holly Andris."

"I've wanted to meet you for months, but Thor kept you to himself," Holly said. "He told us you were brilliant. He wasn't exaggerating."

"Thank you. That's sweet of you to say. And you're Gabriela Marquez Cruz."

Gabriela took her hand. "Thanks for the lecture. I learned so much."

"You're welcome. I'm glad you came. I've wanted to meet all of you, too. Thor has told me about the three of you."

Holly gave Thor a playful jab with her elbow. "Really? What did he say?"

Samantha lowered her voice. "I don't think we can talk about that here."

They laughed as if she'd said something funny.

"It's okay, Samantha," Holly said. "Yes, we all worked for the Agency."

Samantha had to say it. "He's right. You don't look like spies."

That made them laugh again.

Holly leaned closer. "You don't look like a badass astro-physicist who once stabbed a murdering bastard in the face."

It shouldn't have made Samantha laugh, but it did, something about the way Holly said it making her feel like part of their kick-butt sisterhood. "Thank you."

Thor put his arm around Samantha's shoulders. "Samantha needs to get to the reception. Are you three coming?"

"Is there food and alcohol?" Elizabeth asked.

Samantha nodded. "Appetizers and a cash bar."

"We're in," Holly said.

Samantha led them up the stairs to a reception hall, where one of the campus kitchens had catered refresh-ments. "That looks so good."

She'd been too nervous to eat before the lecture, so she was starving.

Hors d'oeuvres. Cheese. Pastries. A cake.

"Do you want a glass of wine?" Thor asked.

"That would be wonderful. Chardonnay, if they have it."

Thor walked to the bar, Elizabeth, Holly, and Gabriela behind him.

Samantha made her way to the buffet, picked up a paper plate, tried to decide between the bruschetta with olive tape-nade and mushrooms, the crab and avocado toast, or the smoked salmon crisps. Hungry, she took one of each.

"So, they gave *you* the job."

Samantha turned, the voice somehow familiar. "Nathan."

Her pulse skipped. She hadn't known he worked here. *Damn.*

He stood there, a sneer on his face, a beer in hand. "I've

worked here as an instructor for a year, and they gave the job to *you*. Did you sleep with the entire hiring committee or just Professor Newton?"

Taken aback by the ugliness of his words, she stared. "Why are you so bitter?"

"Bitter?" Nathan snorted. "I'm not bitter. I'm *pissed*. I've worked hard, too, just as hard as you. But they hired you because you're a *woman*. They're all on a crusade to hire women in the sciences."

Heat rushed into her face, his words like a blow. "My getting this job has *nothing* to do with my sex. I've worked hard to get here. Maybe if you'd quit blaming other people for your shortcomings, you'd get farther. The common denominator in all of your failures is *you*."

An ugly grimace on his face, Nathan took an aggressive step toward her—then looked up and backed off.

Thor was there, a glass of wine in one hand, a beer in the other. "*Er alt i orden, skat?*" *Is everything okay, sweetheart?*

He'd been teaching her conversational Danish in preparation for their visit to his parents this Christmas.

"*Ja, tak.*" *Yes, thanks.* She took the wine, slid her fingers through Thor's. "Thor, this is Nathan Collins. Nathan, this is my partner, Thor Isaksen. He's a veteran of Danish special forces and works in security."

She probably hadn't needed to add that last part, but she'd enjoyed it.

Nathan took another step backward, his gaze still on Thor. "Your partner? Isn't that egalitarian? What's it like being married to a computer?"

Thor smiled, but Samantha could sense his anger. "It's great. I admire Samantha's intelligence and her passion for science—and life."

They weren't married, of course, but neither Samantha nor Thor corrected him.

Prof. Newton hurried over, outrage on his face. "Dr. Collins, I need you to leave. You are out of line. What you said to Dr. Park is unacceptable. Report to my office—"

"I quit. I worked for you for a year, busted my ass, and didn't even get benefits. And you hired *her* over me and gave her a full professorship. This is bullshit. I'm done."

And for the second time, Nathan walked out of Samantha's life.

Dr. Newton looked imploringly at Samantha. "I'm so sorry, Dr. Park. We don't tolerate sexual harassment in this department. Please accept our apologies. I hope this won't change your mind about joining the faculty."

Samantha tried to reassure him. "I don't blame you or the department. Thank you for addressing it so quickly. I know Nathan from grad school. He felt like I got ahead because of my sex."

Dr. Newton shook his head. "Then he's an idiot."

But how had Prof. Newton known?

Samantha looked over her shoulder and saw Holly smiling, a martini in her hand.

Holly winked and bit the olive off the end of a toothpick, Gabriela and Elizabeth standing beside her, knowing smiles on their faces.

THOR SAT BACK in the hot tub, lazily fondling Samantha's breast, Samantha resting against his chest, nothing above them but the night sky. They'd made love the moment they'd stepped through the door, his desire for her as strong as it had been when they'd first become lovers in Antarctica. "I've been thinking."

"Yeah?"

"We should buy a studio apartment near campus so you don't have to drive up and down the canyon when I'm away on assignment." He'd find a building with a security entrance, a place where she would be safe while he was away. "The canyon isn't the easiest drive in snow. I don't want anything to happen to you."

"If you think it's a good idea, I'm for it." She took a sip of her wine. "I suppose you could stay there before or after missions. It's a lot closer to Denver and the airport. When you have early flights, you'd be able to sleep longer."

"Yeah, that, too."

"I love it up here, Thor. I love this house. I love living with you."

"Good." He loved sharing his life with her, too.

From its perch in a nearby pine, a great horned owl hooted, and another answered.

Who-who-who. Whooo-whooo.

Thor kissed the top of her head. "You made a great impression on Elizabeth, Holly, and Gabriela tonight."

"I like them a lot, but it's hard to imagine them as spies."

Thor chuckled in part because it was true. "I'm not sure they would have called themselves spies. Holly's job was to date foreign visitors—people who posed a danger to national security—and set them up for surveillance."

"You mean she bugged them or something?"

"Yes, or put a GPS tag on their vehicle."

"Wow."

"Gabriela worked undercover for eighteen months as a nun. She was taken hostage by a drug cartel, and we came to rescue her. That's how she met Cruz."

"You're not the only Cobra guy to hook up with someone you rescued?"

That made Thor laugh. "Oh, hell, no."

It was a hazard of the job.

"What about Elizabeth?"

"She was a counter-terrorism analyst and interrogator. She's also a top-notch hacker and communications person —an all-around genius and good judge of people. I think the two of you would get along."

"She still feels bad about not uncovering Delaney's identity sooner."

"That's the thing about our jobs. When you screw up, you lose data or make an instrument malfunction. When we screw up, people die."

"That's a lot of pressure."

"Yeah." There was no denying that.

"I think Holly tipped off Dr. Newton about Nathan. When I looked back at her, she winked at me."

"We all overheard him. When I came over to you, she went for Dr. Newton. In her own way, she's more dangerous than any of us men."

"I believe you."

But Thor hadn't been able to put what that bastard had said to Samantha out of his mind. "I'm sorry about tonight. I should have ripped his fucking head off or made him eat his own balls. What a son of a bitch."

"You did exactly what I needed you to do."

"Yeah? And what was that—stand there looking big and scary?"

Samantha turned to face him, wine glass in hand. "You made me feel *safe*."

Okay, he liked that. "I'm glad I did something."

From somewhere in the distance came a long, drawn-out cry.

Samantha's eyes went wide. "What was that?"

"Probably a mountain lion. We have a lot of them up here. One jumped up on the deck once and looked through the window. I've seen bears on the property, too."

Samantha gaped at him. "An apartment in Boulder is a great idea. I'm not sure I'd want to come home in the dark if you're not here."

Thor couldn't help but smile. "Does the city girl find the wild animals scary?"

She leaned in, kissed him. "Not when you're with me."

Thor drew in a breath and decided to come right out with it. "There is something that bastard said that I can't let go."

"What's that?"

"Remember when he asked me what it's like being married to a computer?"

"You said, 'It's great.' You didn't correct him and tell him we aren't married."

"Why would I do that?" Thor lifted a strand of wet hair off her cheek. "It's none of his shitting business, and, to be honest, I *like* the idea."

"You liked the idea of being married to a computer?"

He laughed. "Of being married to *you*."

Samantha stared at him through wide eyes. "You want to … to marry me?"

Thor was as surprised as she was. "I do."

"I didn't think you believed in marriage."

"Neither did I—but then I've never been in love before either." He sat up, caught her face between his palms, needing her to understand. "The day before I left for Antarctica, I sat on that bench over there, thinking how the one thing missing from my life was a woman who loved me despite my lack of appreciation for expensive shoes and my ridiculous job. Then I met you."

He chuckled. "You had a pencil in your hair, and I don't think you wanted us there. But you blew me away with your intelligence, your courage, your sweet face—and that was before we ended up in bed. I don't have an engagement ring —yet—but I can't imagine a future without you. I love you, Samantha."

Then because only Danish expressed what he wanted to say, he switched. "*Du er ikke bare min kæreste, Samantha. Du er blodet i mine årer. Du er mit hjertes slag. Du er åndedrag i lungerne. Du er alt for mig.*"

Tears filled her eyes as she tried to work through his words, her face lighting up with a wobbly smile. "I didn't understand that—something about a heart?"

Thor did his best to translate, though it didn't sound as good in English. "You aren't just my girlfriend. You're the blood in my veins. You're the beating of my heart. You're the breath in my lungs. You're everything to me."

"Oh, Thor. I don't need a ring. I just want you. *Jeg elsker dig.*"

I love you.

"Is that a *yes*?"

Tears spilled down her cheeks. "*Ja. Jeg siger ja.*"

Yes. I say yes.

Heart full, Thor kissed her, the stars glittering overhead.

THANK YOU

Thanks for reading *Hard Line*. I hope you enjoyed this Cobra Elite story. Follow me on Facebook or on Twitter @Pamela_Clare. Join my romantic suspense reader's group on Facebook to be a part of a never-ending conversation with other Cobra fans and get inside information on the series and on life in Colorado's mountains. You can also sign up to my mailing list at my website to keep current with all my releases and to be a part of special newsletter giveaways.

ALSO BY PAMELA CLARE

ABOUT THE AUTHOR

USA Today best-selling author Pamela Clare began her writing career as a columnist and investigative reporter and eventually became the first woman editor-in-chief of two different newspapers. Along the way, she and her team won numerous state and national honors, including the National Journalism Award for Public Service. In 2011, Clare was awarded the Keeper of the Flame Lifetime Achievement Award for her body of work. A single mother with two sons, she writes historical romance and contemporary romantic suspense at the foot of the beautiful Rocky Mountains. Visit her website and join her mailing list to never miss a new release!

www.pamelaclare.com

www.ingramcontent.com/pod-product-compliance
Lightning Source LLC
Chambersburg PA
CBHW030421180626
46812CB00005B/2111